The Toll Gate

The Toll Gate

Gordon Donnell

Writers Club Press
San Jose New York Lincoln Shanghai

The Toll Gate

Writers Club Press
an imprint of iUniverse.com, Inc.

For information address:
iUniverse.com, Inc.
5220 S 16th, Ste. 200
Lincoln, NE 68512
www.iuniverse.com

ISBN: 0-595-17169-9

Printed in the United States of America

CHAPTER I

"I guess you know they killed the fellow before you," the Telegrapher said, eyeing Edwin McIntyre dubiously.

Quietly dressed and compulsively neat, McIntyre was neither tall nor robust. Wire-rimmed spectacles emphasized the sensitive cast of his features.

"Shot him dead," the Telegrapher said. "That's what they did."

"Who did?"

"Nobody knows. But he's dead all the same. We put his casket on this morning's train. Helped load it myself. Sorta plain, it was."

Outside a hiss of venting steam issued from the locomotive that had drawn McIntyre on the last leg of his thousand mile journey; the panting of an iron leviathan anxious for another victim to carry away.

"Where can I find the Section Superintendent," McIntyre asked.

"Mr. Knowlton's upstairs. Name's on his door. Leave your bag here, if you want. No sense lugging it up just to fetch it down again."

McIntyre carried his suitcase across the Spartan waiting room, excusing himself past other recent arrivals who had taken refuge in the stale warmth. A scruffy boy hawked newspapers. The headline screamed *Anniversary of the Armistice*. November 11, 1919. A year since the Great War ended. Next to the stairs a forgotten Liberty Bond poster still reminded travelers that saving the world for democracy was costly. McIntyre climbed to the second floor.

An orderly clerical area had been vacated temporarily so the staff could attend to the train and its passengers. The Superintendent's door was closed. When McIntyre's polite knock went unheard he let himself into Knowlton's office.

A woman stood up startled from the corner of the desk. Composure returned immediately to luminous green eyes that held a dignity not common in isolated mining centers. She needed only a smile to serve notice that she expected to be treated as a lady.

At thirty, G. Robert Knowlton was five years her junior. Framed varsity boxing photographs decorated the wall behind his chair. Overseeing a section notorious for rugged terrain and primitive facilities required a man ready to use his fists to back up his college-bred arrogance.

"Sir, this is a private office. If you need assistance, kindly inquire downstairs in the depot."

"I apologize for the interruption, Mr. Knowlton."

A glance at McIntyre's business card brought the Superintendent to his feet. "Of course. Division wired you would be coming."

To McIntyre a handshake was just one of the rituals that made the business world predictable and comfortable. To Knowlton it was an opportunity to make an impression. He combined a strong grip with a hearty smile.

"May I present Evelyn White?"

McIntyre removed his hat.

"Evelyn, this is Mr. McIntyre. The Railroad sent him out from Chicago to look into the trouble here."

She offered her hand. Warmth was palpable through a leather glove that wear had reduced from stylish to serviceable. Her ankle length coat had seen more than one winter, and had begun to mold itself to the curves beneath.

"I was stunned to hear about Mr. Floyd." Probing eyes unsettled McIntyre as much as unaccustomed feminine closeness. "Were you friends?"

"We never met. Christopher Floyd worked for the Audit and Investigations Department of the Controller's Office."

Knowlton found no title on McIntyre's card. "Are you not an investigator?"

"I work for the Treasurer's Office."

The Superintendent drew himself erect. "May I ask if your visit concerns my tenure with the Railroad?"

"No," McIntyre assured him. "It doesn't."

Evelyn seated herself in one of two chairs facing the desk; a simple act that served to remind Knowlton of normal business courtesy.

He offered McIntyre the other chair and re-established himself behind the desk. "Frankly, with three Railroad employees murdered and an express car looted of one hundred twelve thousand dollars, I wonder if I shouldn't resign now, rather than wait to be humiliated by a discharge."

"Do local trains usually carry that much currency?" McIntyre asked.

"This was a special shipment. Aaron Crowder, the city's leading mine owner, was transferring his entire cash reserve from Denver to fight the Bolsheviks agitating for a strike."

"Do you have that directly from Crowder?"

"In no uncertain terms," Knowlton said, as much in response to McIntyre's skepticism as to his question. "As the senior Railroad representative in the city, I was obliged to suffer his outrage following the robbery."

"Floyd's reports mentioned labor agitators in connection with a depot robbery last week," McIntyre recalled.

"He was in the city to investigate that incident. That's how he happened to be on hand when the express car robbery was discovered."

"Floyd thought a Bolshevik leader named Hennessey was behind the depot robbery."

"Floyd was found murdered near the miners' shanty town," Knowlton said significantly. "Hennessey makes his headquarters there."

"What can you tell me about Hennessey?"

"Very little, I'm afraid. I've seen him only once. He's an exceptionally tall fellow. Gaunt. Physically imposing. Floyd told me he was mixed up in the labor riots in Seattle."

"Do you know where Floyd was staying?"

"The Paragon Hotel. I had to retrieve his belongings."

"How can I find the Paragon?"

"The Comstock jitney will take you to the door."

Evelyn stood up smiling, as if she had been listening for her cue. "I can walk you to Comstock Street."

Compulsive politeness brought McIntyre to his feet. "I don't want to be a nuisance…if you could give me directions?"

"Oh, it's on my way. I just need a minute to find my daughter. She's probably sold everything and looking for mischief to get into right now."

Knowlton stood and explained, "Evelyn is the widow of the former Superintendent. I've arranged a small concession for her to meet incoming trains and sell baked goods."

She favored him with a grateful smile.

"Unfortunately," Knowlton said, "both Evelyn and her daughter were on the platform when the local arrived and we found the express car crew murdered."

A shiver tensed the small muscles of her face. "I was going to take Anne—my daughter—away as soon as I could sell our house," she told McIntyre. "Now I'm ready to abandon the property. This city is no place to raise an impressionable girl."

He nodded politely to acknowledge her decision and lifted his suitcase.

She extended a hand to Knowlton and bid him goodbye. The staircase was not wide, but she went down beside McIntyre rather than go ahead as he offered.

"I'm worried about Robert," she confided. "Resigning a good position during an economic recession is such a drastic step. But he's afraid a discharge might haunt him for years. Particularly if the circumstances became known."

At the bottom of the stairs Evelyn called to a girl. The girl left a woman whose baby she had been admiring and came with teenage petulance, carrying an empty wicker tray and a folded checkerboard cloth under her arm. Evelyn picked a stray hair from the girl's coat sleeve.

"Anne, this is Mr. McIntyre. He's with the Railroad. We're going to walk him to the jitney stop."

"What do you do in the Railroad, Mr. McIntyre?" Anne asked as they left the depot. She had her mother's green eyes, but the effervescent curiosity of youth filled them with innocence.

"Mr. McIntyre is a financial person," Evelyn said before robbery or murder could find its way into the conversation.

"Do you understand logarithms, Mr. McIntyre?"

"School subject," Evelyn explained.

"I don't see why we have to learn them," the girl complained. "What good are they, anyway?"

"Engineers used them to calculate every curve and grade in the railroad," McIntyre said. "All the way across the country."

Anne lost her buoyancy and hung for an instant on the verge of tears. "I wish they hadn't. My dad would still be here."

Evelyn put a comforting arm around her daughter's shoulders. "My husband—Anne's father—was lost in a railroad accident," she told McIntyre.

"I'm sorry."

They crossed a sturdy footbridge. The creek beneath was deep, and swift enough to be dangerous. Evelyn stopped on the far side, where a paved street began.

"You can catch the jitney here."

"Thank you. You're very kind."

She took his free hand in both of hers. "I hope you'll be in the city long enough to have dinner with us. I'm simply starved for news from civilization."

"I don't know." He retreated from the invitation with an apologetic shrug.

Evelyn released his hand with a hopeful smile. She and her daughter walked on, leaving no hint why an attractive woman had lavished attention on an obvious and ordinary introvert. He set down his suitcase and turned his overcoat collar against the razor-edged wind.

The nearest building was an abandoned commercial outlet, boarded shut against nocturnal access by tramps. Across the street stood a similarly boarded warehouse. Blackberry vines encroached on wagon ruts that paralleled the disused loading dock.

From there the city spread up the gradual lower slope of a mountain toward a distant evergreen forest held at bay by massive reefs of mine tailings. Run hard to stoke the engines of war, it lay now in the malaise of peace, festering under the arsenic-laced smoke from a towering smelter stack.

An open Ford came wheezing down Comstock and lurched to a stop where McIntyre waited. The driver wore a faded plaid coat and a sweat-stained hat. He needed a shave.

"Paragon Hotel," McIntyre said, eyeing the man's seedy appearance with ill-concealed contempt as he climbed into the back seat beside a middle-aged woman.

She was not favorably impressed when the driver needed two tries to get the Ford turned. "Soon there'll be no more of your drinking, Mr. O'Haney. The law changes on the sixteenth of January next. Prohibition, 'tis called. There'll be no more spirits to be wasting good money on."

"Drink is God's gift to the working man, Missus Doolin. No government will ever take it away."

She sniffed indignantly. "Blaspheming. And before a visitor to our city."

"A bookkeeper by the look of him."

"There's no shame in the keeping of books, Mr. O'Haney. 'Tis the honest work of sober men who live long and contented."

"The sober don't live no longer. It just seems longer to them."

Mrs. Doolin turned her attention to McIntyre. She had a frugal woman's eye for clothing, and McIntyre's was to her liking. He had spent what money he had on material and workmanship, not style.

"Is it work you've come seeking here, Mister?" she asked.

"I work for the Railroad, Ma'am."

"Used to be work hereabouts," O'Haney put in. "Before old man Crowder closed the factories because the War ended and they wasn't making him rich off honest men's sweat no more."

"Don't speak low of the Quality," Mrs. Doolin said.

O'Haney hawked and spat out over the running board. "I suppose the government's investigating his war profits for the fun of it?"

"Don't go believing everything you read in them Denver papers."

"Like folk hereabouts don't know the truth of the Crowders. A greedy old man and a daughter that's the devil's own child."

"Geneva Crowder is just young. She'll be a fine lady when she gets her growth."

A signal gong brought the Ford to a stop and left it vibrating at a syncopated idle. Beyond the intersection masonry buildings rose four and five stories along Comstock Street. Stylish shops lined the sidewalk. An ornate theater marquee advertised Eric von Stroheim in the film *Blind Husbands*.

The cross street was less cosmopolitan. Lower wooden frontages prevailed, pushcarts were visible and an A-board in front of a small cinema house offered Lillian Gish in *Broken Blossoms*.

Six massive Clydesdale horses drew a ponderous Hercules compressor across the intersection. Riding on its own thin, hard tires, it was meant to be trailered by motor transport and lacked any provision for a driver or swamper to ride. Two teamsters walked with the lead animals, hands firmly on the halters.

A powerful Winton touring car idled protectively behind. The canvas top was up, but the side curtains were out, probably to clear a field of fire for the man in back. He held a .351 Winchester rifle across his lap.

"Mine Police," O'Haney said sourly. "The thugs of your Quality, Missus Doolin. That's Luther Grimes himself, in front beside the driver."

Grimes sat tall in the car seat; the habitual erectness of an experienced horseman. His hip-length woolen coat and flat brimmed campaign hat belonged to an outdoorsman. A grizzled mustache drooped over the corners of his mouth. He drew smoke from a straight-stem pipe and took in the jitney with eyes primed for trouble but too wise to jump at shadows.

"Who is Luther Grimes?" McIntyre asked.

"Head of the Mine Police, that's who," the jitney driver said. "Them as know such things say he rode with the Wild Bunch in the younger days. Maybe he's the one robbed your bosses' train. They done that, y'know. The Wild Bunch. They robbed trains."

"No," McIntyre said. "I didn't know."

"Well, he's come down some now," O'Haney said, "taking bread from the mouths of poor little children."

"Beer from the gullets of their good-for-nothing fathers," Mrs. Doolin shot back. "The mines pay a living wage, but only when it's give over to a good woman to see to the spending of it and make sure none is wasted."

"John Hennessey will see to the changing of the miners' lot," O'Haney declared. "You mark my words, the both of you."

Mrs. Doolin limited herself to a skeptical, "Humph!"

"When does Hennessey plan to take the miners out on strike?" McIntyre asked.

"The high and mighty owners would pay a pretty penny to know that," O'Haney said.

"What's he waiting for?"

"He's waiting," Mrs. Doolin said for O'Haney's benefit, "because their womenfolk would lay a cast iron skillet across the fool head of any man who didn't bring home no bacon to be cooking."

The signal changed and the Ford moved forward with an indignant lurch. O'Haney drove half a dozen blocks in pointed silence. They passed through the city center then turned from Comstock onto a more crudely paved street less free of horse droppings. O'Haney stopped in front of a three story wooden building; solid looking but wanting fresh paint.

"Paragon Hotel," he announced. "Not where the Quality stays, but better than the likes of me will ever sleep in."

A girl in her late teens stood behind the registration desk. A baggy sweater pushed back over skeletal forearms made her seem even scrawnier that she was. Her hair was a shade of red perilously close to orange. Acne scarred her thin face. If that were not misery enough, she also had buck teeth.

She primped a bit, more from habit than hope. "You'll be wanting a single, sir?"

"You had a Railroad man here. Christopher Floyd."

"Oh, Mr. Floyd, he died, sir," she said in a hushed voice that worried about the effect her words might have.

"I'd like the room he had, if it hasn't been rented yet."

The scrawny girl recoiled and crossed herself. "No, no, Mister. You won't be wanting that room. Me father would be hiding me for telling you, but Mr. Floyd, he was chasing the haints, and they took away his life."

"Haints?" McIntyre asked.

"Them as died with mortal sins against their souls and can never sleep in consecrated ground."

"Do you mean haunts? Ghosts?"

"They robbed the Railroad. Killed two men dead in an express car and took all the money."

"Did Mr. Floyd tell you that?"

"They lock them express cars out of one station—lock them on the inside—and they don't open up 'til the next stop. This one was still locked when it got here and both men dead inside and all the money gone and no one on the train the wiser. None but the haints could do such a thing."

"Did you tell Mr. Floyd that?"

"I told him he couldn't catch the haints." Round eyes implored McIntyre to understand that she done her duty. "But he was bound and determined to be going after them."

"Were you and Mr. Floyd friends?"

Her cheeks colored. "Oh, I know I ain't no beauty, and him so handsome and all, I knowed he was just teasing me around, always stopping to talk to me like he thought I was pretty, but I liked him anyway. I told him he couldn't catch the haints."

McIntyre dipped the desk pen into the inkwell. "If he couldn't catch them, why did they bother to take his life?"

She caught her throat and stared fearfully at him. "Mister, are you crazy?"

"Yes. I am."

It was a solemn statement from a man resigned to inescapable fate. His eyes, when he raised them from signing his name, were sad and honest.

She held out a key at arm's length.

The room was on the third floor, high enough to minimize the risk of a ladder being used to reach the single window and far enough from the fire escape to leave only the door to be defended.

McIntyre took a hard rubber wedge from his suitcase and pushed it under. He hung his overcoat carefully on a wall rack, likewise his suit coat. After recording the nickel he had spent on the jitney ride in a small ledger, he counted the currency in his wallet then inventoried his pocket change to satisfy himself the resulting balance was correct. The remaining contents of his pockets he laid on top of the dresser; a watch, handkerchief and a sturdy folding knife, arranging everything square to the front edge with ritual precision. He sat on the bed and removed his shoes. Those he set precisely square to the footboard. Only then did he lie back on the mattress.

Fatigue sapped the tension from his body, but he could not banish from his mind the 3:00 AM telephone call that had started him on what threatened to be his final journey.

Chapter 2

McIntyre had trudged alone through the early morning desolation of Chicago's financial district. Gusty wind off Lake Michigan whipped stray leaves under the street lamps and drove sleet between his upturned collar and his hat. He was shivering when he reached the Railroad headquarters building.

Typewriter noise echoed in the dim hallway of the executive floor. It told him what to expect when he opened the only door with light behind its marbled glass.

"Good morning, Violet."

Violet Sprague, whose desk dominated the anteroom and guarded all beyond, was a fixture. She had raised three sons in widowhood on a Railroad salary and found them work with the company when post-war recession left them competing with legions of idle veterans. Her loyalty was absolute. Near-freezing indoor temperature was no excuse for violating the strict economy rule that forbade turning on the steam radiators before the business day began.

"Good morning, Mr. McIntyre. You're to go straight in."

McIntyre hung up his overcoat and hat, knocked respectfully on an inner door and went from the cold antechamber into the Treasurer's warm, spacious office.

"Good morning, Mr. Jason."

Mortimer Jason returned the greeting in a silken whisper that demanded the listener's full attention to be heard. His three hundred pounds of self-indulgence were expertly tailored into the finest woolen suiting and ensconced in a high backed leather swivel chair behind a baronial desk.

"I trust this appointment is not an imposition?"

"No, sir."

Jason tugged delicately on a gold chain to retrieve an engraved watch from a vest pocket. "I believe I telephoned you one full hour ago, did I not?"

"Yes, sir."

"Earlier this morning I was summoned to a conference at the Chairman's estate. The subject was sufficiently urgent that I telephoned from there. I departed expecting to find you here when I arrived."

Jason replaced the watch and waited for an explanation. False dawn had not yet begun to color the window behind him. Beyond the silhouettes of intervening skyscrapers, McIntyre could make out the distant aura of the South Side, where the Railroad's money was actually made amid the stench of the stockyards and the cacophony of freight transfer.

"I can't change the off-hours street car schedule," he said. "Nor shorten the walk from Michigan Avenue."

Jason used a manicured finger to wave him to a wing chair before the desk; no more of a gesture than a Mandarin might expend on a supplicant peasant.

"These are dangerous times. Those of us charged with stewardship of a national asset—and we are a national asset, this Railroad—must be prepared to react upon the most minimal notice to any threat."

McIntyre seated himself carefully, centering the creases in his trouser legs, and waited for the Treasurer to elaborate.

"Labor radicals have murdered a railroad investigator."

McIntyre blinked in astonishment.

"In Rocky Mountain Division," Jason went on with no effort to conceal his disgust. "In one of those mining centers that is too rich in population to be called a town and too poor in culture to properly qualify as a city."

"How did it happen?"

"The Controller's information is sketchy. Early reports led Audits and Investigations to believe their man had been killed pursuing bandits who robbed an express car. That has been disproved."

"Disproved how?"

It was a sharp question from a man to whom logic meant more than obedience. Jason chose to ignore the slight to his authority.

"You recall what befell the Railroad during the War?"

"A few misguided souls in Washington thought the rail transport system would better serve the national effort if it were placed under direct Government control."

"Inept bureaucrats," Mortimer Jason corrected with as much passion as he ever mustered. "Capital assets were run beyond their maintenance limits. Sound operating procedures were ignored as not germane to war requirements. Labor unions were even permitted to organize. Did you know, Mr. McIntyre, that common laborers now talk directly to the Chairman? Not that I mean to minimize the contribution of loyal workers. The Chairman himself takes every opportunity to visit the operating units to encourage them. But for them to impose upon his time to negotiate their own wages—it turns every known management theory on its ear."

"The investigator?" McIntyre reminded him.

"During the war hysteria, all express car safe combinations were restricted to the responsible messengers. The policy is trivial, so it hasn't come up for review yet. Since the looted safe was opened by combination and the messenger murdered, Audits and Investigations is convinced the messenger betrayed his trust and was then betrayed himself. For once, their reasoning appears sound."

"What about their facts? Was the combination actually changed in that express car? As I recall, the Government was long on directives and short on follow-up supervision."

Mortimer Jason smiled approval and put his fat hands together in silent applause. "Excellent, Mr. McIntyre. The Chairman asked that very question."

"Did he get an answer?"

"The only other person who would have had the combination before the War was the previous Section Superintendent. He was killed in an accident during Nationalization. The express messenger was based in Denver and had no connection with the city where the investigator was killed. Physical evidence found subsequent to the discovery of the investigator's body proved the bandits left the train before it reached the city."

"Is there any direct evidence he was killed by labor radicals?"

"You know as well as I that the Bolsheviks care nothing for the lot of a few grubby miners. They showed their true colors during the general strike in Seattle last February. Their goal is nothing less than a nation-wide economic shutdown. In that remote area, the only possible target is the Railroad. You are to eliminate them before they can make any more mischief."

McIntyre's soft voice fell until it was barely audible. "Even if it means raising demons from the Id?"

Mortimer Jason put the tips of his fingers together and leaned back. "Demons from the Id," he repeated, and contemplated the neatly dressed man before him. "Freudian psychology, is it not?"

"Psychiatry," McIntyre corrected.

"The Id being the part of the unconscious mind that harbors impulses?"

"Yes."

"Did your course of treatment include insights into the methods of psychiatric analysis?"

"My doctor used it to explain why it was important for me to tell him everything about my childhood and my dreams."

"Childhood. Dreams. I have never asked before, Mr. McIntyre, but I have always been curious. How did they treat your condition?"

McIntyre sat perfectly still. The office was soundproof; a vault to hold the Railroad's deepest secrets. Its absolute silence would magnify any word he uttered.

Jason leaned forward so as not to miss a syllable. "What is the cure for homicidal insanity?"

"I'm not a monster."

"But you did kill a man."

"Witnesses at the preliminary inquiry said he might have hit his head when he fell."

"Surely you know whether or not you struck him."

McIntyre shook his head. It was little more than a shiver.

"You have no memory of what happened?"

"Witnesses said the man was drunk. He pushed me and demanded money."

"If you were simply defending yourself, why did the police arrest you?"

"They said I was incoherent. Mumbling to myself. They said I wouldn't stop straightening my clothes."

"Straightening your clothes?"

"The only thing that makes me different is an obsessive need for order. My mind fixates on having everything in its proper place and my blood is too full of adrenaline to let me rest until it is."

"Then when you are inserted into labor unrest, your hormone level rises in proportion to the disorder you encounter. When it grows intolerable, you react. Like the safety valve on a steam boiler."

"That's the theory," McIntyre conceded.

Jason's fat face was bright and still with rapture. "I must confess, I never fully appreciated the Chairman's brilliance in selecting you."

"More likely it was the Chief Psychiatrist at the asylum who recommended me."

"Indeed?"

"I'm sure he was well paid to testify that I was ready to assume a responsible position with my former employer. I expect other payments also had to be made. I had been committed only a year earlier, with no prospect of ever being released."

"I doubt the Chairman would condone such action," Jason said indulgently, and waited for McIntyre to recant.

"I remember his lecture to me verbatim." McIntyre rendered his best imitation:

"When I was a lad, I saw life in its simplest terms, as a primal struggle between good and evil. As I grew older, I came to discern shades of gray, areas of compromise. In the hubris that comes with the middle years of maturity, I saw this as the viewpoint most appropriate to a responsible adult. I know now that I was quite wrong. I was right as a child, short only two facts. The first is that the forces of evil will always vanquish the forces of good. The second is that the forces of evil are disparate and quarrelsome, and that they will always fall out and rout themselves from their chosen objective.

"You, Mr. McIntyre, embody evil in its purest form. Murderous rage that not even you, its author, can predict or control. It shall be your place to go among selected inferior evils and by your actions and example hasten their downfall. That contribution to the greater good of society is all that dignifies the petty corruption that released you from your just and responsible confinement. Should you ever shrink from it, your freedom will be swiftly and irrevocably terminated."

Mortimer Jason's whisper filled with awe. "Eloquent. Masterful."

"Silly," McIntyre said. "I haven't thrown any fits in the twenty months since I was released."

"How do you know?"

McIntyre stared blankly.

"If you have no memory of your episodes, how do you know they haven't recurred? For that matter was the man you killed the first, or merely the first time you were caught?"

"I'm not a walking time bomb," McIntyre insisted.

"The medical authorities obviously thought otherwise."

"They were wrong."

"What would they have done with you had the Chairman not intervened?"

"The examining psychiatrist testified at my competency hearing that I should be surgically altered."

"Lobotomy?"

McIntyre's eyes darted from one corner of the room to another, as if he expected to see the hounds of hell tensing to leap for his throat.

Mortimer Jason reconsidered his line of inquiry. "Have you any questions regarding your current assignment?"

"May I read Floyd's daily reports?"

"Mrs. Sprague is typing a summary of radical activity extracted from my notes taken at the Chairman's estate."

"The actual dailies might still be useful."

"I do not intend to ask for them. The Controller is an ambitious fellow. He believes the Treasurer's Office could function more effectively under his supervision. You will remove the Bolshevik threat without any action that might buttress his case, even something as trivial as a request for reports. That man will seize upon anything. Particularly in a matter like this, where he knows the Chairman's eye is on him."

McIntyre unhooked his spectacles and began to clean them with his handkerchief. It was an act of compulsion, and the worried thoughts behind it were evident in his voice.

"I don't mean to be difficult, Mr. Jason, but the probability that a Railroad investigator was murdered by labor radicals is too small to consider. Logical or not, he caught up with the express car bandits and they killed him."

"Would you prefer to resume your course of treatment?"

McIntyre replaced his spectacles. "Did you know, Mr. Jason, that you can actually taste certain electrical shocks?"

"I am not an unfeeling man, Mr. McIntyre. I could not in my blackest nightmares conjure up an understanding of what your life has been to this point, or a prediction of what lies ahead. But, in fact, your lot is no harder than that of men who toil daily with machines capable of swallowing them whole, or who ingest noxious dusts and vapors for hours on end, or who endure the myriad other unpleasantness necessary to the uninterrupted functioning of an industrial society. I think it is not too much to ask you to do your part."

"What is my part?" McIntyre asked. "Am I supposed to resolve this situation? Or am I just being thrown into it, like a grenade?"

"No one is asking you to employ violence. If you can remove the Bolshevik threat by reason, or by subterfuge, or even by some limited payment of money, so much the better."

"What are my limits, Mr. Jason? What am I permitted to do and what am I not?"

The Railroad's three hundred pound Treasurer smiled benevolently. "As always, your written reports will be unobtrusive. Your expense vouchers will be nominal. Telegraphic contact will be minimal, fully encrypted and addressed to Mrs. Sprague. Telephone calls will be made from secure facilities only, and only in the most extreme emergency."

"Mr. Jason, you're sending me a long way on short information. To a city where the authorities may not be as pliable as they are in Chicago."

"You have considerable intellect upon which to rely, and your appearance and manner are sufficiently innocuous to put off suspicion."

"Newspapers are full of innocuous men who turned out to be anything but."

"You fail to understand the press, Mr. McIntyre. They exist to pander, not to inform. They emphasize the lack of obvious difference between the sane and the insane only because that touches a primal fear in all people. Who among us has not wondered whether he has a touch of madness in his own soul?"

"I don't have to wonder. I'm only a few surgical incisions from drooling lethargy."

Worry narrowed Jason's eyes. "Do you harbor any notion of rebellion?"

"My only immediate notion is to go home and make arrangements for my cat. The westbound transcontinental leaves in three hours."

CHAPTER 3

McIntyre rose shivering from his hotel bed. A clammy undergarment of perspiration pasted his clothing to his skin. He collected his toilet kit and found a shower at the end of the hall. Icy water bothered him less than the worry that he might leave some speck of travel dirt. Back in his room he dressed meticulously in fresh clothing and loaded the smaller of his two automatic pistols, a .25 Colt. His watch pocket smothered the tiny weapon with no telltale bulge.

A proprietary man of fifty had replaced the talkative girl at the reception desk. He promised McIntyre's travel clothing back cleaned the next day.

"Is there trouble?" he asked in an oily Irish burr when McIntyre requested directions to police headquarters.

"No. I just need information."

The City Administration Building was three stories of dun colored masonry with massive terra cotta cornices. Homebound workers trickled out into the deepening dusk. Lights inside a ground floor fire station reflected in the gleaming red paint and shiny brass of a pumper truck and a hook and ladder. Illuminated globes flanked the entrance to the police department.

McIntyre went in and handed the desk officer a business card. "I'd like to see the Chief, please."

The officer's smile spoke volumes. Here was another earnest citizen who thought his business was important enough to take the Chief's time.

He glanced at the card and his smile vanished. "Chief'll want to see you, right enough."

He led McIntyre back to a private office.

The Police Chief stood with the hulking agility of a bear and thrust a paw across a paper-strewn desk. "Virgil Tulley," he rumbled cordially during a brief, powerful handclasp.

Tulley was past sixty. Sloped shoulders and a barrel torso kept his suit coat from fitting well. A full head of gray hair managed to look shaggy even with a fresh trim. He offered McIntyre his choice of two padded chairs drawn up in front of the desk then put his bulk back into his own swivel and hooked a pair of spectacles over his ears.

"I can see just fine if something is a little ways off, but I don't read so good no more without these here cheaters."

He was not a man who was quick or comfortable with written words. The photographs that crowded his walls were mementos of an outdoor life; men in and out of uniform posed self-consciously against back-drops of dirt streets, wooden buildings and primitive motorcars. Formalities like business cards would always be difficult for him.

"Don't say here what exactly you do for the Railroad, Mr. McIntyre."

"I'm with the Treasurer's office."

"I sent the insurance company investigator packing off to see the County Sheriff. Express car robbery happened outside the city limits. Ain't my jurisdiction."

McIntyre's only reaction was a bland smile. "Have you eaten supper, Chief?"

"I was just about to." A policeman's suspicion came readily to Tulley's rumbling voice and drew his bushy gray eyebrows together.

"I wouldn't expect to buy anything," McIntyre assured him quickly, "beyond a little good will."

"That's free to anyone who deals straight with me. But I reckon it won't hurt none to take you up on your meal."

The Police Chief heaved himself up from his chair and unlocked a closet. He pulled out an overcoat and a Stetson and locked up again, taking care to test the door before he put on his outdoor clothing.

A seven-foot tall Packard sedan waited under a bare electric bulb in a small yard behind the building, resplendent in emerald green paint and gold pin striping. The passenger door was so perfectly balanced that the frailest millionaire could open it easily. It closed McIntyre in with a firm click.

The springs barely noticed when Tulley settled his considerable weight behind the wheel. He retarded the spark, cracked the hand throttle and switched the ignition coil into the circuit. The car had a self-starter unit combined with the generator, so he didn't need to go out and use the crank. The engine ran with uncanny smoothness and near silence.

"I wouldn't want you to get no wrong ideas about this here vehicle," Tulley said. "Some folks see a gent with a police salary and a twelve cylinder motorcar, they figure he can't be none too honest."

McIntyre mumbled an incoherent apology.

"This car is City property—impounded legal and correct," Tulley said as he backed out to the street. "Belonged to a dude that come here from Portland a couple of years back to go partners with a gent name of Crowder."

"Aaron Crowder?"

"He's the closest thing we got to a Rockefeller hereabouts. He put up a pot of money, then found out the War Bonds he got for collateral was counterfeit. Dude wasn't nowhere to be found. Caught a train, I reckon."

McIntyre traced a finger along finely figured hardwood trim varnished to the smoothness of glass. "And left an expensive car like this behind?"

"First off I figured he stole it someplace, but his title checked out legal. He must have figured he couldn't disappear so easy driving this here carriage. I got in front of the City Council and told 'em how they could save the cost of a squadrol if they voted to give it to the Department instead of auctioning it to recover the impound and storage costs."

"That makes sense." Practicality appealed to McIntyre.

"Might have, if old man Crowder hadn't been trying to finagle the car for liquidated damages. Good sense ain't always good politics."

Tulley turned onto a boulevard where skeletal deciduous trees lent a threadbare elegance to the forecourt of a rococo hotel. A few cars were privileged to park on the curving access drive. Tulley led McIntyre under a terra cotta awning and into a lobby paneled in lustrous walnut. They rode the elevator with a middle-aged man who squired a younger woman. The woman recognized Tulley. She tried not to show it.

Subdued light and white linen filled the top floor restaurant. The overflow crowd idled at a mahogany bar or took advantage of a parquet dance floor and a demure foxtrot played by an unobtrusive orchestra. The upper crust seemed to be weathering the economic downturn in style.

The maitre'd knew Tulley and seated them at once. A waiter arrived promptly. He knew what Tulley wanted to eat.

The Police Chief waited patiently until McIntyre selected a light dinner from an elaborate menu. "I don't reckon we'd be eating this high if you didn't have something you wanted to chew over."

"Christopher Floyd," McIntyre said. "I understand he was murdered in your jurisdiction."

"Anything in that file is restricted police information."

"Can you tell me if you recovered his revolver?"

Tulley's face darkened. "Neither Floyd nor any other private citizen carries a revolver in this city. Way I see it, nobody but a sworn law officer needs a gun, and most of them won't never shoot theirs."

"Floyd was issued a .32 Colt."

The Police Chief took a closer look at McIntyre's clothing. "You ain't carrying no gun. Unless I'm missing something."

"I'll get the serial number of Floyd's. Where it turns up might tell you something about his murder."

"If it turns up."

"Did Floyd ever mention anyone he was afraid of?"

Tulley snorted in amusement. "Never met the man, did you?"

"No. I never did."

"He was a right big gent, and strong in the bargain. Had him a real knack for making friends, too. If he couldn't charm your socks off, he could likely knock your block off. I don't feature him being afraid of no one."

"He made friends with the girl at the Paragon. It wasn't romance, and she was uniquely placed to warn him if anyone came to the Hotel asking for him."

"More likely he wanted gossip," Tulley said. "Molly's got sharp eyes, and a tongue to go with them. She's told it on a few gents in town, them as was fool enough to use her dad's hotel for their fun."

The waiter brought garlic bread for the table and a glass of beer for Tulley. Tulley tucked a napkin into the vee of his vest and slathered warm butter across a fat slice.

Rather than watch the Chief eat, McIntyre let his attention wander to a broad window. Street lamps made patterns across the rolling slope of the city, a huddle of illumination with endless gloom pressing in on all sides. Isolated pinpricks of light marked the mine workings above town.

"Had any trouble with labor agitators?"

"Nothing but." The subject put an edge on Tulley's voice.

"Any sabotage?"

"Some talk. Ain't come to nothing, but I put extra watch on the water works and electric generating plant. That ain't so much the problem, though."

"What is?"

"This ain't no company town—never has been—but Old Man Crowder figures he owns it anyway. Figures he owns me and the police along with it, and we should be putting anyone in jail he don't like." A long, gurgling draught of beer only made the Chief sullen. "Wouldn't be so bad if the Mayor and the City Council wasn't cozying up to him for campaign money."

"I thought the mines had their own police force."

"Bunch of damn thugs. Crowder hit the ceiling when I wouldn't deputize them. Had the council vote them an exemption on the gun ordinance."

"What about the miners?" McIntyre asked. "Are they ready to strike?"

"Crowder figures to shut down shaft four at the Jade Elephant for the winter. That ought to shift the balance. Be more men out of work than there are in the mines."

"Christopher Floyd mentioned labor radicals in his reports. He thought they robbed the depot here."

"Floyd found him some witnesses—but none as would go to court and say to a jury what they told him." Tulley's eyes narrowed shrewdly. "I figured you was here about the big robbery."

"Are you sure the depot robbery wasn't just a warm-up for the express car?"

"Like I told Floyd, I'll look at most anything you bring in, so long as it's got evidence to back it up."

"Would I bring it to you?" McIntyre asked. "Or the County Sheriff?"

"Anything in my city, you bring it to me. I'll do the deciding where it goes from there."

The waiter brought dinner. Perfunctory service suggested that generous tippers were waiting for tables. Tulley ate with gusto, paying no heed to the decorative presentation of the meal, washing it down with draughts of beer. McIntyre ate with polite restraint, cutting his food carefully into bite-sized pieces and ignoring anything that did not precisely suit his taste. He was not quite done when the waiter returned with a note for Tulley.

The Chief read it and scowled. "You'd better eat up," he advised McIntyre. "Old Man Crowder heard you're in town. He wants to see you."

Boulevard electroliers made highlights in the hood of the Packard as it climbed to the heights of the city. Tulley turned along a darker street flanked by large houses set to command the best views. The street ended at a decorative brick wall. Tulley brought the Packard to a stop with its headlamps shining on an iron gate and lowered his window.

A ruffian swaggered to the car with a hand on the butt of a holstered revolver. "Get out and check your hardware, gents. No vehicles or guns past here."

Tulley thrust out a paw, caught the man by his coat collar and pulled him close to the window. "You're Mine Police. Mine Police watch their mouths in my city."

The man released a sodden plug of tobacco onto the running board. "You won't be pushing people around much longer. Not from what I hear."

"Get that damned gate open."

Tulley shoved the man backward, sent him stumbling. The ruffian moved crabwise toward the gate, eyeing Tulley resentfully.

The Police Chief's voice grew bitter. "Forty years a lawman. That's a heap of time. Small towns to bigger ones, small responsibilities to bigger ones. You'd think a man would have more to show than just a city ready to throw him out on his ear, for no better reason than he done his job the way it was meant to be done, and not according to some convenience of politics."

McIntyre said nothing.

Tulley eased the Packard through the gate. Manicured shrubbery made mysterious patterns in the headlights then gave way to the gothic mass of a gabled and gloomy mansion. Tulley parked behind a stately Pierce Arrow town car that dwarfed his big sedan.

"Come on," the Chief said. "I'll give you an introduction."

A uniformed maid let them into the warmth of a high-ceilinged entry. She took their coats and hats. Her movements were unhurried. In this house, things went at a certain pace, and no faster.

"You will wait here, please."

"Sure," Tulley muttered when she had passed through a door. "We wouldn't want to mess up no doilies on no fancy sofas."

Piano music drifted from the depths of the mansion, a haunting melody that stopped in mid-phrase. A door opened under an ornate staircase. A young woman emerged, injecting an unexpected flash of life into the drab hallway. Blonde hair cut short and waved in the latest fashion caught highlights from the chandelier. Finishing school carriage gave an air of refinement to lithe, uncorsetted movements that brought her along the noiseless run of carpet to confront McIntyre.

She looked him up and down with eyes that danced like sunlight reflected in the blue depths of ice. The disbelieving laugh she emitted was wild and musical.

"Is this it?" she asked Tulley.

"This here's Mr. McIntyre, Miss Geneva." The Police Chief sounded almost bashful when he spoke to her. "Railroad investigator here to see your father."

"Not exactly Doug Fairbanks, is he?"

Never comfortable at the center of feminine attention, McIntyre was startled near panic by the abrupt and direct encounter. He hid his terror behind a nervous smile and quick words.

"Doug wanted to come, but Mary Pickford wouldn't let him out of the house."

Merriment vanished from Geneva Crowder's eyes and left her flawless features still with dread. "Are you really everything they say about you?"

McIntyre's smile flickered out in a gust of guilt from the secret he harbored. "I don't know what anyone might have said about me, Miss Crowder."

"My name is Geneva."

"I'm sorry. Geneva."

"I had a lot of pictures in my head of what you would look like. You're worse than all of them put together." She shivered suddenly and put her arms around her shoulders.

Tulley didn't know what to make of her behavior. "You feelin' all right, Miss Geneva?"

She didn't hear him. She seized McIntyre by both arms. Her hands drew intense strength from the sudden desperation that possessed her eyes.

"I'm Satan's daughter, McIntyre. Don't believe anything you hear tonight. It will all be a lie. Every word."

Another door opened. She released McIntyre and retraced her steps without a word, without a glance at the man who watched from the doorway. Her departure, graceful and serene, made her distress of an instant previous seem simply an error of perception.

Aaron Crowder dominated the doorway where he stood, filling it from side to side and nearly from top to bottom. His coat was black and lusterless, cut to the swallow-tailed fashion of the last century. A wing collar pinched his neck like the discipline of the righteous. His black bow tie called to mind a less profligate time, but hard, hot eyes made his presence as immediate as the next second.

His voice was deep and measured, notice to the world that everything he said would be profoundly significant. "Thank you for bringing Mr. McIntyre, Chief. I won't detain you any longer."

Tulley opened his mouth, but closed it without speaking. The maid was moving to retrieve his hat and coat. Aaron Crowder had already forgotten he existed.

"Come into my study, McIntyre."

It was a cavernous room where a crosshatch of logs burned in a fireplace large enough for a man to walk into; spreading a flickering aura over gilt-framed oils and long shelves of leather bound volumes. Crowder waved McIntyre into a wing chair. He enthroned himself behind a massive desk. Firelight put a demonic glow into his probing eyes.

"Investigator," he said, dismissing the idea with a disgusted snort. "Is that the tale you told that miserable excuse for a Police Chief?"

"He drew his own conclusions," McIntyre said. "I thought it best not to argue."

"I prefer to be blunt. The business I am in is a very simple one. Do you know the price of gold?"

"Thirty two dollars an ounce. It's fixed by law."

"And do you know what happens when the cost of production rises above thirty two dollars an ounce?"

"Are we talking about shaft four at the Jade Elephant?"

"Specifically about water infiltration," Crowder said. "Shaft four is the deepest of the six. Winter seepage there is so bad that the cost of pumping and lost work time between December and March make the shaft uneconomic."

"The local Bolsheviks know that," McIntyre supplied, "and have been using the shaft closing to whip up strike fever."

"I am on the horns of a dilemma. On the one hand I confront the iron laws of economics. If I give in to my charitable nature and continue to operate shaft four for the benefit of the thirty odd men who work there, I risk bankrupting the mine and turning out every soul on the payroll. On the other hand I face heathen Bolsheviks. Godless predators who see my misfortune, and that of the miners, as their key to power."

"Hunker down and ride out the storm," McIntyre advised. "You're better financed than the miners. You can outlast them."

"Assuming," Crowder said pointedly, "that the Bolsheviks didn't loot your express car of my money."

"I'm curious, Mr. Crowder. Why did you ship currency? Why not arrange a bank transfer?"

"That's a damned bookkeeping entry. The kind of men I need to fight a strike want cash. Hard dollars to spend in saloons and whore houses. Now, I'm a Christian, McIntyre, and I don't condone such behavior. There isn't a drop of intoxicating spirits in this house, and everyone under its roof lives by the Word of God. But I'll do whatever is necessary to win this fight."

"Any bank would make up a payroll in cash on request." It was an unreconciled fact, as disquieting to McIntyre as dust or disarray, and it left his eyes bright with adrenaline.

Blood pressure rose in Crowder's face. "Currency is strength. The more I brought in, the stronger I would have looked."

"Whom did you tell it was arriving?"

"You were not sent here to question me!" Mounting rage brought Crowder towering to his feet. He slammed huge, hard fists down on the desk and leaned over them to glare down at McIntyre. "You were sent because Bolshevism is not an economically sound proposition. Do you grasp the importance of that fact?"

McIntyre straightened his suit coat unnecessarily and brushed a bit of imaginary lint from the lapel. "Mr. Crowder, I'm just trying to under-stand—"

"It means that not even King Solomon's Mines would keep it afloat, let alone the pathetic bit of ore we scrape out of this God forsaken mountain. When the Bolsheviks learn that, survival instinct will send them forth as a plague of locusts across the land; primitive, parasitic organisms devouring anything in their path. The Railroad, Mr. McIntyre, is in their path. And that is why you have been sent to wipe them out."

"I'm not arguing, Mr. Crowder."

The Industrialist subsided into his chair, his fury spent and exasperation leaking out in his voice. "What was your Chairman thinking?

Sending one man into a situation that calls for the National Guard. And not a very impressive man, at that."

"I don't speak for the Chairman, Mr. Crowder. I just follow his orders."

"And how do you expect to succeed where the toughest men in Colorado have failed?"

"Luther Grimes has the wrong incentive. The longer the strike threat persists, the longer he gets paid to ride around in an expensive Winton."

"Incentive or no, you will keep him advised of what you are up to."

"I'm sorry, Mr. Crowder. Those are not my instructions."

"Your instructions have been amended. I've spent considerable money, and lost considerably more, fighting this strike. I will not abide interference with my efforts."

"Sir, I—"

"I have told your Chairman as much," Crowder said, and waved a hand at the telephone on the desk. "You may call him if you have any doubts."

McIntyre fell silent under a pall of resignation.

Crowder used a pull cord behind his desk.

The door opened and a loose-jointed ruffian sauntered in. The man wore a laborer's jacket and a hat that had fallen a long way from its beginnings in a fashionable haberdashery. The lopsided grin he gave Crowder suggested that he thought the best way to get through life was not to take it too seriously.

"Yeah, Boss?"

"Rufus, take Mr. McIntyre to Grimes."

"Sure thing, Mr. Crowder."

The ruffian was no more impressed with McIntyre than Crowder, though in a good-natured, unconcerned way. He held the door.

McIntyre didn't move. "Give the miners their strike, Mr. Crowder. Let them walk off their frustrations on the picket line. When they get tired and hungry, they'll come back knowing they can never beat you."

"Are you afraid of a fight, McIntyre?"

"If you whip men into submission, they'll just lick their wounds and wait for another opportunity."

"And the agitators? The Bolsheviks?"

"Discredit them. Don't martyr them."

"I know the miners, McIntyre. I make it my business to know them. They're my people. It's my duty to keep them safe from immoral ideas and heathen influences. A duty I will not shirk."

McIntyre stood to go.

"One more thing," Crowder said. "I wouldn't say or do anything to upset Luther Grimes. I hired him because he was the most ruthless and capable killer I could find."

CHAPTER 4

Icy November wind brought the vegetation outside the Crowder mansion to life, filling it with the whispers of madmen and sending shadows twitching and crawling. McIntyre climbed into a battered Maxwell touring car and sank deeper into his overcoat. Rufus cranked the cold engine to a semblance of life.

While they waited for a ragged idle to settle down a uniformed chauffeur came out and started the stately Pierce Arrow. The massive town car drew silently past and turned toward an open carriage house. The headlights reflected in the finish of a low-slung yellow roadster parked inside.

"Austro Daimler," Rufus said reverently. "That's the motor for me."

"Does Crowder let you drive it?" McIntyre asked.

"Ain't been in town long, have you?"

"What would I know if I had been?"

"None but Geneva Crowder drives that motor, and none but Lucifer hisself would ride with her when she's got it on an open road."

"What's troubling her?"

"Her maw died young. I guess the women hired to raise her up done what they could. But in the end there wasn't nobody to stand between her and an old man with a Bible thumper's peculiar way of thinking wrong was right, so long as nobody done it but him."

Rufus set off down the drive. He tooted the asthmatic horn to let the gatekeeper know they were coming and exchanged amiable profanities with the man as they passed through.

"You some kind of bookkeeper?" he asked McIntyre. "Old man Crowder hire you to make sure nobody picks his pocket while he's busy picking everyone else's?"

"I work for the Railroad."

"You here about that express car push?"

McIntyre made a noncommittal noise in his throat. "What were you doing before you joined the mine police?"

"Five years in Walla Walla." Rufus had a good laugh over the irony. "Nothing so big as that train job, mind you. Three of us figured easy pickings pushing in a road house outside Seattle. Place called Shadow Lake. Goddamn King County Sheriff must've owned a piece of it, the way he come after us."

"How many bad boys are in town these days?" McIntyre asked.

"Well, there's bad and there's bad."

"I don't understand."

"I told you my story and I'm down at the bottom. Mean dogs rule, and you can guess what's above me."

McIntyre fell silent.

Exclusive homes had given way to frame houses on city lots. Those gave way to bungalows packed shoulder to shoulder, and those in turn to shut up commercial frontages, huddled and dark between electric lamps at the intersections. The street turned to hard-packed dirt. The buildings became narrow and old.

Curtained and dark, Luther Grimes' Winton stood at the wooden sidewalk where a vague glow showed behind a painted-out window.

"Dantini's, it's called," Rufus said as he brought the Maxwell to a stop.

"Thank you." McIntyre's door was sprung, and he couldn't open it. "Is there a trick to this?"

Rufus reached across, lifted the door lightly and let it swing open. "You ain't muscle," the ruffian observed, "and you don't ask questions like a dick. I guess that makes you a shooter."

"If a mine strike heats up into shooting, do you plan to stick?"

"I guess I do at that."

"How many others have that attitude?"

"Ain't so much an attitude. It's just I already wrote my maw, told her how I was a mine cop here. Now she's all proud."

"And the others?"

"I guess they'll have reasons, too."

McIntyre climbed down, shut the door and watched the Maxwell chug away. Tinny ragtime music filtered out into the night, an annoying staccato that honed his nerves to a razor edge. An unmarked door let him into the place called Dantini's.

Beneath a low ceiling smoke eddied slowly around bare electric bulbs. Roughly dressed men stood with their backs to the door, lining a bar that stretched into the depths of the room. A dice game went on in back, under a hooded fixture. A sassy young woman played a phonograph with a huge speaker horn. She wasn't having any luck persuading customers to dance with her. Serious drinking and sullen conversation prevailed.

McIntyre moved to the bar.

The bartender thought he saw a big tipper and flashed a smile with a prominent gold tooth. "What'll it be, friend?"

"I don't see Luther Grimes."

The bar man looked around, lazily. "Me neither. What'll it be?"

"Aaron Crowder sent me to see him."

Silence fell over the bar as far as McIntyre's words carried. Hostile eyes measured him.

The bartender hit a brass spittoon. "Hey, Walt!"

A man detached himself from the bar and came quickly. An oversized flannel shirt made him look even smaller than he was. Jittery eyes wondered what the bartender wanted.

"Go on up and tell your boss he's got a visitor. A real important visitor. Straight from old man Crowder."

The little man scurried up a flight of stairs. The bartender moved away and left McIntyre looking at a framed oil painting of a voluptuous nude. A voyeur's guilt flushed his face. He averted his eyes and occupied himself removing his gloves and unbuttoning his overcoat. Strong perfume made his nostrils twitch.

"Buy a lady a drink?"

It was the woman who had been playing the phonograph. Her eyes were older than her twenty years, her skin pale against a peach colored dress. Her pose tantalized and her smile taunted.

Rather than add questions of his virility to an already sour impression, McIntyre forced a crooked leer. "Give me a rain check, sweetheart. I've got to see a man."

"You'd rather see a man?" She rolled her hips, toying with him.

Coarse laughter rippled along the bar.

A sudden charge of adrenaline left McIntyre's eyes bright and scary. "Why don't you forget the drink and come up with me? We can have a little party after."

"You better talk to Ruby." She shot a nervous glance at a hefty woman who smiled from a nearby table. "I got a social condition. I can't work upstairs for a while."

The man named Walt reappeared at McIntyre's elbow. "Fresh bottle," he called.

The bartender handed over an unopened fifth of rye. Walt jerked his head for McIntyre to follow. The stairs took them up to a dim hallway. One door they passed stood ajar. At the sound of feminine moaning McIntyre reached automatically to pull it shut. He caught a glimpse of a woman propped on a brass bed in her underwear, reading a magazine and exercising her throat. A sturdily built man sat fully clothed on a wooden chair, anxiously wringing his powerful hands while his reputation was upheld. McIntyre left the door as it was and followed Walt through another into an office.

Behind the big old desk sat a broad man with an olive complexion and handsome Mediterranean features. His supper was spread before him. His shirt, behind the napkin tucked in at his throat, was silk. Two carats of diamond glittered on the hand he used to roll spaghetti onto a fork. A black pencil mustache made his teeth seem even whiter when he opened his mouth to eat. He was gaudy enough to make Luther Grimes look dignified by comparison.

Grimes, sitting erect in a thinly padded wooden chair beside the desk, half-turned from his own supper with the stiffness of fifty years. The coat and campaign hat McIntyre had seen earlier hung on a wall peg. Grimes wore a faded flannel shirt buttoned to his neck and a string tie with a small silver clasp.

"You come on the jitney today," he recalled in a voice as coarse as trail dust.

"My name is Edwin McIntyre. I work for the Railroad."

"You ain't exactly what I pictured when old man Crowder told me they was sending a strike breaker."

The gaudy man finished chewing his spaghetti. Resilient muscles brought him to his feet. He put a strong hand across the desk.

"Frank Dantini's my name. If it weren't for the dry laws and the Temperance Union, I'd hang it out front."

"Why bother?" McIntyre asked. "How many more men could you cram in downstairs?"

Dantini laughed heartily. "Pull up a chair. How about a little supper?"

"I just ate, thank you." McIntyre angled the room's one remaining chair to keep both Grimes and Dantini in front of him.

Dantini sat back down to his supper. "Name your poison, then," he said and laughed again. "Before the Volstead Act hangs us all out to dry."

"Nothing for me, thank you."

"Come on. This is an occasion. You just met a man who's going to pay you ten dollars for five hours work."

"Two dollars an hour is generous money." McIntyre's voice had more questions than gratitude.

"Seen the posters around town?" Dantini waved a forkful of spaghetti at the wall behind him, where hung an advertisement for a prize fight. Tiger Stevens was a boyish pug with a devil-may-care expression. Gentleman Jack Harding was older; austere and formally posed. "The Tiger fought his way out of the mines."

"And if this were Pittsburgh," McIntyre said, "he would've been a stoker in the foundry, or whatever else it took to get two wagers of every three down on him."

"Four of five," Dantini corrected. "Jack got in yesterday. He's been hamming it up good, telling how anyone who didn't go to Princeton is a bum."

"What round does Stevens take the dive?"

"As long as the action holds up, so do Jack and the Tiger."

"Twelve rounds is a long time to fool a savvy crowd."

"There won't be much fooling. Maybe none, if the crowd gets the wind up. Jack's the better fighter. He can out-point the Tiger in a legitimate match."

"It's still a pretty tired game."

Dantini used the napkin to wipe spaghetti sauce from his teeth. "It's been a whole month since the Chicago Black Sox threw the World Series. The suckers are begging for more. Especially in a burg like this, where they roll up the sidewalks at sundown."

"What would I do to earn your ten dollars?" McIntyre asked warily.

"A money fight will draw every leather lifter in the county. I need sharp eyes to make sure I have a chance at my pigeons."

"That's a little out of my line."

Dantini flashed a wide, skeptical grin. "You're no strike breaker. Hell, there's no strike to break. You're here shopping for that express car bundle."

McIntyre removed his spectacles and began to clean the lenses with his handkerchief. Grimes considered the Railroad man carefully while he used a piece of bread to soak up the last sauce from a plate of beans. He washed down the bread with a jolt of rye.

Dantini glanced at the empty plate. "Say, listen, Luther, are you sure that's all you want to eat? I can send out if you don't like Italian food. No hard feelings."

"Too many years on trail biscuits and beans," Grimes said. "Them fancy vittles you ate in St. Louis would likely queer my gut."

Dantini shrugged and winked at McIntyre. "Don't worry about any rough stuff. Luther's boys will provide the muscle. And you'll be there anyway, won't you? To see if any express car money turns up?"

"How would I know express car money from any other?"

"I guess you've got your ways." Dantini spread his arms in an expansive gesture of innocence. "Me, I'm a simple promoter. My life's dream is to visit the old country someday and hear Pagliacci the way it was meant to be heard."

"When is your prize fight?"

"Tomorrow night. The old Pendleton Street lumber yard. Be there by seven. All right?"

McIntyre replaced his spectacles.

Grimes began filling his pipe. He worked with the patience of a man who had learned to divide his attention between trivial tasks and constant alertness.

"You ain't mentioned yet what you wanted to see me about," he said, not looking at McIntyre but listening intently to catch every nuance of his reply.

Dantini laughed to take the edge off the situation. "I can vouch for Luther. He hasn't robbed a train in years. Have you, Luther?"

"At my age you tend to forget."

Grimes struck a match on a thumbnail and lit the pipe, holding the flame to the bowl until he could draw smoke then shaking it out. McIntyre watched the dead match fall to join others on the floor. He curtailed an impulse to pick it up.

"I'd appreciate any information you could give me on the Bolshevik leader. His name is Hennessey, isn't it?"

"I wouldn't bet on any of them skunks giving their right name. Or using the same wrong one more than once."

"Where does he hole up when he's not rabble rousing?"

"At the bottom of shanty town, down by the creek. Only place with a wood roof. His idea of class, I reckon." Grimes exhaled a long streamer of smoke and watched thoughtfully as it broke apart and curled away in the room currents. "You could likely search the place tonight, if you've a mind. He's supposed to be holding one of his big revival meetings."

"How would I get there?"

"Shanty town is built in a wash east of the city. Only two ways in. By footpath down from the workings, or along Hatcher Street."

"How about the creek bed?"

"Good way to drown yourself. You can ford it in places, but the woods run right down to the water on the other side. Steep slope and heavy undergrowth."

"It sounds like you've scouted the ground," McIntyre said. "Could a rifleman get close enough to Hennessey's shanty to be sure of his shot?"

"If one did," Grimes said, pouring himself another jolt of rye, "the working stiffs wouldn't have anyone to make noise for them." He put down the fiery liquid in a single swallow and held McIntyre's eyes hard with his own. "Old man Crowder could push me out of a soft spot and save himself a little money."

Dantini laughed at the idea and found an extra glass for McIntyre. He poured Chianti from his dinner bottle and raised his own glass.

"Well, here's to the working stiffs. May they live long and lose with a smile."

McIntyre drank sparingly.

"Want a quick flop before you leave?" Dantini asked. "Ruby's got a couple of lookers she keeps for the money crowd. She'll comp you in if I say so."

"No thanks." One corner of McIntyre's eye twitched at the suggestion.

"Clean stuff. Checked once a week. The doctor who does the checking knows his business. He has over two hundred abortions to his credit."

McIntyre shook his head and stood, straightening his overcoat.

Dantini came to his feet saying, "seven tomorrow night, then," and they shook hands solemnly.

Grimes just smiled, showing teeth yellow from years of tobacco. "Go easy on Hennessey. He's a good living. I'd hate to lose him."

The little man named Walt opened the door. McIntyre went quickly along the hall and down the stairs, out of the saloon and on his way. Urban instinct gave him his directions. No one could have known where or when to wait for him, but he watched each doorway and alley he passed against ambush. The eyes behind his spectacles were bright and darting and not discernibly rational.

Moonlight danced on the swift creek when he crossed the footbridge below Comstock. It shimmered along the railroad tracks as he approached the depot. Voices came muffled over the quiet rush of water. McIntyre gained the platform with the silence of an intruder. He moved in the shadows as if he were one of them, peering in through the windows he passed. The waiting area was empty, the lights dimmed, the ticket and baggage windows closed.

A hooded bulb lit the telegrapher's station. Young Anne White stood at the counter, bundled in an outdoor coat, with the pinch of night air still in her cheeks, engaged in an animated conversation with the boy on duty.

The noise of the door brought her head around. "Mr. McIntyre!"

"Hello, Anne. How are you?"

"Jimmy said you came all the way from Chicago to find out who robbed the express car."

A year or two short of twenty, Jimmy licked two fingers and nervously plastered down a stray lock of hair as McIntyre crossed to the counter.

"Pleased to meet you, sir." He seemed uncertain whether he should offer to shake hands.

McIntyre pushed through the swing gate. "I'll need your key for a few minutes."

The young telegrapher opened his mouth to protest, but closed it immediately, spooked by the unnatural brilliance of McIntyre's eyes.

The girl was too excited to notice. "Jimmy knows how the robbers locked the express car from inside after they got out," she informed McIntyre in a voice that dared him to guess.

McIntyre sat down and tugged off his gloves.

"They did it with doubled over twine," she revealed. "They thought they fooled everybody."

"The only person you ever fool," McIntyre responded, "is yourself."

A guilty flush warmed her face. She collected school books that had probably served as an excuse to leave the house, waved good-bye to Jimmy and hurried out the door.

McIntyre had nothing written in the way of a message. His fist was quick, edgy. The youth listened to him secure a repeater circuit through to Chicago but seemed unable to follow beyond that.

"That wasn't the operational cipher," he said when McIntyre finished.

"I've no idea what Operations uses."

"Do you carry the same kind of gun the express guards do?"

"It's not legal to carry firearms in this city."

"But after Mr. Floyd got killed…?"

"Floyd was killed confronting someone he had no authority to arrest for stealing money that had no reason to be in an express car that should-n't have been found locked. Do you have any idea how that happened?"

The youth blanched in surprise. "N-no sir."

"Floyd never sent any messages? Or used the key himself?"

"Not the night key. No sir. Maybe on the day shift."

McIntyre thanked him and went out, pausing on the platform to pull on his gloves. Street lights across the creek showed the distant figure of Anne White. She had not crossed at Comstock, but was making her way toward a footbridge farther down. Movement on the other side of the creek caught McIntyre's eye. A man lurched unsteadily beneath a street light, paralleling the girl's path. The purposeful lean of his posture suggested he meant to intercept her when she crossed.

Built at the edge of the city where the sound and smoke of rail commerce would intrude as little as possible on daily life, the depot stood only a hundred yards from virgin forest. A mountain cat screamed in the distance. The night became a place of primal urges.

McIntyre slipped the sturdy folding knife from his pocket. Rather than open it, he rolled his fingers around it tightly and deliberately, so the brassbound ends protruded half an inch from either side of a clenched fist. Crossing the Comstock footbridge, he paralleled the creek on the same side as the man ahead, pursuing out of his quarry's range of vision. His pace was swift and utterly silent, his concentration absolute.

The man stumbled to a stop near the end of the footbridge and waited there for Anne to cross. His attention was riveted on the girl. He had no inkling that lethal violence was closing fast from behind.

He lurched from the shadows and seized her. There was a scream of surprise and liquor slurred words.

"C'mere, cutie. Le's have li'l fun."

The man began to drag the struggling girl. Rather than slowing to balance himself for a confrontation, McIntyre accelerated in the final burst of a panther making its kill.

CHAPTER 5

McIntyre found himself standing under a street lamp on an unfamiliar corner. His ragged breathing suggested recent exertion, but offered no clue to why he had come. He was startled to see a shabbily dressed man at his feet, face down in a blackberry thicket at the edge of a vacant lot. A shapeless hat had fallen from the man's head. Blood seeped into the shaggy hair in back, mute testimony to a savage blow. McIntyre became aware of the closed knife clenched in his hand. He slipped it into his overcoat pocket and glanced around.

Anne White stood beside him. She held her school books protectively across her chest. Her eyes were fixed on the fallen man.

"What happened?" McIntyre asked.

"That man grabbed me." Quick words punctuated by a sudden shiver.

"Your coat is dirty." He compulsively plucked a weed from her sleeve.

"I fell when you knocked him down."

"Did he hurt you?"

"Oh, I'm okay."

An automobile started in the distance and she stifled a cry. The irregular chug of its cold engine carried on a perfect stillness. She drew back from the brink of hysteria.

McIntyre scanned their surroundings. Nearby buildings were dark, either closed for the night or abandoned. No pedestrians were abroad. Except for Anne, his encounter with the tramp had attracted no attention.

"We'd better go," he told the girl.

"What about that man?"

"We'd better talk to your mother. She may not want you involved in a police report."

A small gasp tightened her throat. "You can't tell my mom."

"She's bound to notice your coat."

"I'll say I tripped. She knows I'm kind of clumsy. You don't have to tell her. Really, you don't."

"She'll hear about it quickly enough when you've told a few school friends."

"Oh, we never tattle on each other."

Her buoyant confidence was returning. She and McIntyre set off along the sidewalk. He was the adult, and she seemed willing to accept his implied assurance that nothing need be done about the fallen tramp. Once the man was out of sight, the short attention span of the teen years had her off on a subject nearer her heart.

"Mom treats me like such a baby. She never even told me you were here to catch those robbers. She's probably afraid I'll start bawling about Mr. Floyd."

"Did you see him at the depot that afternoon?"

"I was kind of busy," she replied with the gravity of a youth suddenly drawn into mature conversation. "I had to bring the baking and meet Mom there."

"Don't you walk to the depot together?"

"Mom had some appointment that day."

"Did you notice anything unusual at the depot?"

She shook her head and sounded disappointed. "Mom took me home as soon as the police would let us leave."

They came to a block of quiet homes behind picket fences. Curtained windows glowed softly and muted piano music infused the night with tranquility.

The girl stopped at a gate and glanced anxiously at the house. "Thanks for walking me home, Mr.—"

The front door opened. Interior light silhouetted Evelyn White and cast her shadow outward, where the porch steps twisted her willowy curves into a dark, angular presence.

"Anne, Honey? Is that you?"

"Yes, Mother," the girl said timidly.

"Who is that with you?"

"Mr. McIntyre."

"Invite him in, Dear."

"Remember," the girl said under her breath, "you promised not to tell on me."

Courtesy left McIntyre no choice. He followed the girl up the steps and into a warm entry stripped of furniture. Cheerful wallpaper was spotted with darker rectangles where pictures had hung recently. In the flanking parlor and dining room, packing cartons stood open on bare hardwood.

Evelyn shut the door, smiling apologetically. "I'm afraid we're a bit upside down here." Her glance at her daughter was automatic. "Anne! Your coat is filthy!"

"I just tripped, Mom. I didn't hurt myself."

"Oh, Honey! I shouldn't have let you out after dark."

"Last week I tripped on the way to my music lesson," the girl reminded her.

"We'll talk about it later, Honey. Don't you have homework to do?"

"Yes, Mom." Delighted to escape so easily, the girl disappeared upstairs and left McIntyre alone with her mother.

Evelyn smoothed her apron. "Where did you find her? At the depot?"

An uneasy smile spared him the need to elaborate.

"I'm sorry you were put out on such a cold night. The least I can offer is some coffee to warm you up."

McIntyre peeled off his gloves, surrendered his hat and coat. He followed her to a spotless kitchen where the aroma of baking lingered.

Evelyn seated him at a brightly covered table and slipped off her apron. A coffee pot warmed on an iron stove trimmed in white enamel. She brought steaming cups to the table, moving with a ballroom glide that emphasized the fluid swing of her hips.

To McIntyre's discomfort, their knees touched briefly when she sat down. He reached quickly for his coffee. The cup rattled and liquid coffee spilled over onto the saucer.

"You're shivering."

Evelyn took one of his hands in both of hers and began to rub it. McIntyre was trapped between the embarrassment of contact and impoliteness if he pulled away. Words failed him.

"The Railroad must have great confidence in you to send you to deal with the express car robbery alone." Her voice fell to a worried hush. "Particularly after Mr. Floyd was killed."

McIntyre was glad to turn the conversation to an impersonal topic. "Did you happen to see Floyd at the depot the afternoon of the robbery?"

Her contrite smile was little more than a flicker. "I was pretty badly shaken. All I could think of was to get Anne away from there. Now I just want to get her out of this wretched city."

"I'm surprised you've stayed this long."

She took McIntyre's other hand. "Oh, I had dreams of outlasting the recession, selling the house, recovering the equity. But my late husband's insurance and what little savings we had are gone. There is only so much I can bring in baking. The house will be taken in foreclosure in a few—"

Tentative footsteps brought Evelyn's head around. She released McIntyre. Anne appeared in the doorway with a school book held open across her chest.

"Can I ask Mr. McIntyre a question?"

"Honey, Mr. McIntyre isn't here to do your homework for you. I'll help you later."

"But Mom, you don't understand this interpolation stuff any better than I do." Frustration swept her to the verge of tears.

Her mother relented with a hopeful smile at McIntyre.

He took the girl's book and pored over a convoluted paragraph that explained how to use tables of logarithms.

Anne studied his perplexed expression with worried eyes. "Do you understand it?"

"I know how interpolation works."

Anne put a sheet of story problems in front of him. Her smile was as fetching as she could make it.

McIntyre handed them back. "You can do these."

"I don't know how."

"Think about a train ride. Let's say it lasts sixty minutes and goes thirty miles and the train keeps a constant speed. If the conductor says you've been riding thirty minutes, how far have you gone?"

"Um—fifteen miles?"

"How did you know that?"

"If you've used half the time, you've gone half the distance."

"That's what interpolation is."

"Like if the express car robbers were hiding on the train and couldn't see out, they could know where they were by looking at their watches?"

"Anne!" her mother scolded.

"Well, I bet they could."

"Why don't you thank Mr. McIntyre and go work your problems now?"

Evelyn watched her daughter out of the room. "Sometimes I don't know what she could be thinking. I feel so lost."

"Speaking of lost, I wonder if I could impose on you for some directions?"

"Where do you want to go?"

"I need to find Hatcher Street."

Alarm filled her eyes. "That's where Mr. Floyd was killed."

He shrugged.

"You're not going tonight?"

"Something unexpected happened. I'll have to move faster than I planned."

"You seem like such a cautious man."

"I thought I knew what kind of man I was." He steadied his cup in both hands, but ripples of trembling still disturbed the liquid. "Maybe I've just been denying the truth about myself."

She put a comforting hand on his sleeve. "I don't want to pry, but I am a good listener."

McIntyre declined with a quick shake of his head. "If you could just tell me how to get to Hatcher Street."

He followed her directions on foot. Few pedestrians were abroad and none paid him any attention. Automobile traffic was sparse. The city was hunkering down against the deepening chill of night.

Hatcher began where a sturdy timber bridge crossed the creek from the rail yards, and from the mountain of coal that fed both the smelter and the city's electric generating plant. Crudely paved, it lacked both sidewalks and street lamps. Low buildings hung back in the darkness on either side. Windows were few and small, and shone dully with the malignant glitter of reflected security bulbs. Not even the icy Colorado wind had been able to scour out the poisonous smell of industry; exhaust fumes and sulfur accented by the lingering smoke of lubricants and cutting oils. McIntyre walked alone in a desolate world.

The street turned to hard packed earth under his shoes. A faint noise stopped him. Several blocks back an electric torch stabbed the darkness. A patrol officer used a police call box. A drunken Irish ditty piped up from a side street between McIntyre and the police patrol. McIntyre stepped back into the blackness between two buildings. Tiny feet scampered away from him. The stink of decaying rubbish grew strong. He let the drunk weave past and fell in behind at a discreet distance.

They passed the last of the buildings. The ground sloped away. Fragments of moonlight through thickening clouds reflected faintly in a jumble of tin roofed shanties that seemed to cascade down the hillside. Darkness and silence were mute testimony to a lack of electricity and an early work day tomorrow.

The drunk found a path down the slope. Dogs set up a furious yipping. He was too engrossed in trying to pronounce 'cockles and mussels, alive, alive-o' to notice. No one woke up to complain. The drunk wandered off among the shanties, losing himself in a mist scented with the residue of boiled cabbage. McIntyre kept to the path.

Far down amid the vague shimmer of tin lay a dark patch that might be a wood roof. Barking abated and the rush of the creek asserted itself. Wind made mysterious noises in a forest that grew dark and close on the other side. A wide log, flat on top, lay across the stream as a makeshift bridge; a quick escape into the trees for anyone pursued. This area of shanty town would be a natural refuge for labor radicals.

Slightly more elaborate than the haphazard structures flanking it, the wood-roofed shanty had a small porch. The whole building creaked as McIntyre climbed up. He held his breath. Nothing. He fumbled with a crude latch. The door squeaked on its hinges. He stood as far to one side as the little porch allowed and pushed the door to swing it inward.

Three nearly simultaneous flashes lit the interior of the shanty. Shotgun blasts shook the night. Lead charges ripped through the door, slamming it shut. A startled leap launched McIntyre off the porch. Rough ground sent him stumbling on impact. Darkness and erratic movement saved him from pistol fire originating in and around the shanties on either side. McIntyre sprinted for the log bridge.

He hit the slippery surface at a dead run. Momentum carried him most of the way across before he lost his footing. He fell only a few feet, scrambled up the far bank and plunged into the blackness of the forest.

Bushes snatched at the skirts of his coat. Branches whipped into his face. Gunfire probed the night, urging him up the thickly overgrown hill. A fallen tree caught him at shin level and sent him sprawling. He lay on the ground, gasping for air.

Angry voices erupted behind him, only to be drowned by a thundering orator's bass. "Get after the bastard! Twenty to the man who brings him back."

McIntyre pulled himself up to peer over the log that had tripped him. He had to straighten his spectacles. Lanterns appeared on the far side of the creek and made shifting, scary patterns in the intervening undergrowth. A file of men moved across the makeshift bridge. They spread into a ragged line along the bank of the creek and moved forward to search up into the forest.

McIntyre had no time to free his pistol. He slipped down behind the fallen tree. There was just enough clearance to squirm partway under its lower curve. Bathed in sweat and beginning to chill, he lay on his back in the darkness and tried to control his wheezing breath. The ground beneath him was rough, home to thorns and knobby roots.

Nearby undergrowth began to rustle and crackle. Lantern light showed in the branches of trees. Profanity marked the progress of his pursuers.

"This way! He come this way!"

The log that concealed McIntyre groaned under the weight of hastening men. Lantern light trickled down through vegetation. A boot heel hit the ground a foot from his face. Voices were all around, calling angrily for some sign of his trail. A pistol discharged a few yards away.

"Who's shooting?"

"I seen him! He went up there!"

A great thrashing arose. The boot moved away from McIntyre's face. The lantern light went with it. Darkness closed in again, deeper than before. The thrashing and cursing receded up the hill.

McIntyre squirmed carefully out from under the log and froze. A warning aroma of Bay Rum mingled with the natural scent of the forest. He found a loose fragment of fallen branch and tossed it as far as he could in his original direction of travel. It hit with a small noise in the undergrowth.

Soft, satisfied words came out of the dark. "Faith, and the little people are good to Michael Corrigan this night."

Slits of light from a shaded lantern outlined a man as he climbed over the log. McIntyre rolled the closed knife into his fist. He gathered his legs under him, rising silently and striking in the same movement. The man went down with a rustle of brush and no sound from his throat.

McIntyre was over the log in an instant, retracing his steps to the creek and escape. He reached the log bridge and stopped short. Light leaked through the open door of the wood-roofed shanty into the mist and outlined two men. One was a giant in height and width, but seemed to lack depth. The other was the little man called Walt, from Dantini's saloon.

"I come across for you, didn't I?" Walt whined. "That Railroad dick come here, didn't he? Just like I told you he would."

"You'll get your twenty." It was the orator's bass that had sent the searchers thrashing into the forest above, the voice of a man who lived to project his will.

"Pleased to make your acquaintance, John Hennessey," McIntyre said to himself.

A third figure came out into the light and handed Hennessey a pouch. Hennessey opened it and gave something to Little Walt. Walt scampered away into the darkness.

Hennessey handed the pouch back to the other man. "That Railroad scum knew this was here. Someone's ratted us out. Get it hidden where he won't find it again."

Impatient strides carried Hennessey back into his shanty. The other man started up the path skirting shanty town. He would pass close to the log bridge.

McIntyre moved quickly down the embankment and plunged ahead into the creek. Swift, icy water reached his thighs. He had to give ground against the current. His feet slipped on wet stones, threatening to spill him. Once across he clambered up out of the creek bed and reached the path ahead of Hennessey's man.

Unable to avoid being seen, McIntyre broke into song. He was no singer under the best of circumstances. Shivering and short of breath, his off key rendition of a half-remembered *Kathleen Mavourneen* was enough to get him arrested for public intoxication on its own strength. Legs wobbly from fear and exertion made a drunken weave easy to imitate. When the unsuspecting man drew abreast, McIntyre stumbled against him.

"Hey!" The man was neither large nor strong enough to shake off McIntyre's grip on his collar. "Get off me. You're all wet. You fell in the damned creek, you drunken—"

McIntyre put the point of his knife to the man's throat. "Move or make noise and I'll kill you where you stand."

The man believed the desperate rasp of McIntyre's voice. McIntyre snatched the pouch and stuffed it into his overcoat pocket. He made a quick check for weapons and pocketed what felt like a small revolver. The epileptic wail of a police siren started dogs howling.

McIntyre seized the man's collar again. "We're moving now. Don't cry out and don't dawdle."

They started up the path.

The man offered no physical resistance, but resentment boiled under his voice. "You're that damned Railroad dick."

"Just keep moving."

They stumbled up into the unpaved section of Hatcher. At the crest of the hill was an aura of oncoming lights. McIntyre herded his prisoner into the middle of the street to wait.

The man shrugged himself to a defiant erectness. "We knowed you was coming."

McIntyre threw a worried glance back down into shanty town. Lights showed at random down the slope. Hostile voices demanded to know who had broken the peace. McIntyre's prisoner listened to them and his own voice grew bolder.

"Not just tonight. Even before you left Chicago. We know all about you. You come to break the strike."

"Is that why you thought Christopher Floyd was here?"

"He's dead and you're all alone," the man taunted. "You're dead if you keep after us."

"There's a higher price to pay if I don't."

CHAPTER 6

Two police vehicles crested the rise in Hatcher Street. McIntyre raised an arm to shield his eyes as from the onrushing headlights. His prisoner covered his ears against the scream of the sirens. Tulley's Packard slid to a stop only yards from where they stood.

The Police Chief climbed down and lumbered into the glare to confront McIntyre. "Was that you doing the shooting?"

"I w-was the t-target."

"Who's this?"

McIntyre's prisoner spat into Tulley's face. The Chief cuffed him hard, sent him sprawling. A uniformed officer seized his collar and hauled him up. The prisoner flailed with both arms. The officer caught one arm and twisted it into a compliance hold. Pain contorted the prisoner's features. He was young, sallow. The struggle left a snap brim cap sitting at a foolish angle on his head.

Tulley turned his displeasure on McIntyre. "All right, Railroad Man, what's this all about?"

McIntyre's answer was lost in a spasm of shivering. He handed over the pouch. Tulley opened it impatiently. He pulled out a sheaf of bills fastened by elastic and read a handwritten summation bundled with the currency.

"Money from the depot robbery," he realized.

"This man g-got it from H-Hennessey," McIntyre stammered.

"What's the matter with you? Can't you talk? Christ, look at you. You're half soaked."

"I h-had to c-cross the c-creek."

"You're damned lucky you didn't drown yourself. You wouldn't of been the first."

"He h-had this too."

McIntyre handed over the revolver.

"Damn Saturday night special," Tulley growled. "Was you hoping it was Floyd's?"

"I c-couldn't tell in the d-dark." McIntyre's teeth began to chatter.

"You better get in the car," the Chief said, "before you catch your death of cold."

Tulley had two uniformed officers with him, one apparently the rounds officer for Hatcher Street. "If there's any more trouble," the Chief told him, "get to the nearest call box and report it. Don't try to do nothing on your own."

Tulley instructed the other officer to follow with the prisoner. He climbed into the Packard and ground the transmission into gear. The heavy car bumped along Hatcher until it found paving again. Tulley turned onto a lighted arterial. This time it was the tires that protested his angry handling.

"You don't remember so good," he told McIntyre. "I said anything you come across in my town, you bring to me."

"I just handed it to you." Protected from the wind, McIntyre had stopped shivering.

"You should have told me you knowed where the depot money was. Instead of going after it yourself and starting a shooting match."

"I didn't know Hennessey had the money."

"Was you trying to prove Floyd's killing on Hennessey?"

"I heard Hennessey was holding a rally tonight. I thought it would be safe to go into shanty town for a quiet look."

"Who told you that?"

"Luther Grimes."

"You damn fool! Grimes sent you into shanty town to get yourself killed so's I'd have to arrest Hennessey and bust up this here strike for him."

"It looks like he'll get his wish," McIntyre said.

"You ain't killed."

"No, but Hennessey tried. And he was in possession of stolen property."

"Hennessey was clean across town playing Chinese Checkers. Leastwise, that'll be his story. And he'll have five or six jaspers to back him up."

Tulley drove to the City Administration Building and they went into his office. The Chief unlocked the closet to put away his overcoat and Stetson. McIntyre took advantage of a clothes tree to hang his sodden overcoat. He reached to take off his hat. It was gone. Fleeting irritation at its loss was replaced by embarrassment. He had not been properly dressed.

He edged close to a steam radiator to dry his trousers and shoes. "I'm sorry if I broke up your evening."

"You wasn't the night's first trouble." Tulley locked his closet and rattled the knob to be sure it was secure.

"Anything serious?"

"Patrol found a gent stretched out in the weeds down near the tracks."

McIntyre turned his face to the wall and made a production of warming his hands over the radiator. "What did he have to say for himself?"

"He was DOA at City Hospital. Doc said his skull had been cracked like an eggshell. From the smell of liquor on him, he may not have knowed what hit him."

"Any witnesses?" McIntyre held his breath.

"We'll have us a roust at first light tomorrow. Pick up some of them tramps that hole up down there. Night's full of eyes, if you know where to look for them."

McIntyre kept the panic in his own eyes out of his voice. "What about this fellow I caught with the money? Do you know anything about him?"

"That one—he's a beaut. What you brought me there is John Hennessey's sweetie. His very own little cupcake."

McIntyre turned from the radiator. "Are you sure? Or is that just talk?"

"They call him Peaches. Him and Hennessey don't seem to be no secret."

"May I sit in on the interrogation?"

"The rules say I keep you two separated. Take statements from you and him and compare them."

McIntyre shrugged to lighten his disappointment.

"Oh, hell," Tulley rumbled. "Come on."

He led McIntyre to a small room. There were no windows. The light fixture was protected by a metal screen. Peaches slouched in a chair at a wooden table. He spat a harsh profanity when McIntyre took one of the two chairs across from him.

Tulley closed the door. "That ain't no way to talk, son. We got all we need to send you up for a good stretch. And I'm talkin' about a place you won't be picking your roommates, and them you get won't take 'no' for an answer."

Peaches repeated himself. Tulley leaned across the table and cuffed his face, hard enough to make the chair squeak sideways.

Peaches glared defiantly. "John Hennessey'll get you bastards. He'll get the both of you."

Tulley sat down across from him. "You figure he'll use the same jaspers he used to stick up the railroad depot?"

"He's got plenty of guys that can do the big job. And I don't know nothing about no depot stick up. Except maybe you cops got tired of living on your salaries and done it yourselves."

Tulley drew his fist back, but caught a warning look from McIntyre. "What's the matter?"

"I think he likes it."

"What?"

"He's needling you because he likes to be hit," McIntyre said. "Probably the same thrill Hennessey gets hitting him."

Tulley subsided in his chair. He looked at his hand, as if he expected to find visible corruption on the skin.

He turned narrow eyes on the sullen youth. "We got a pretty good idea who done the actual stick up."

Peaches made a coarse suggestion.

"We ain't pulled 'em in because we got no witnesses. But if we was to pull them in tonight and cut you loose come morning, what would your friends think?"

Panic jerked Peaches erect in his chair. "I ain't no rat," he shrilled. "They know I ain't no rat."

"If you was to tell me how things really was," Tulley offered, "I could hold you in jail like you wasn't cooperating and let on like I had other witnesses."

"I ain't telling it on John Hennessey. You won't never prove nothing on him."

McIntyre stifled a yawn. "It's probably not worth the effort," he told Tulley. "All we'd get for our trouble is another cheap crook behind bars."

Peaches bristled. "John Hennessey ain't no crook. He only takes from the bosses. They're the real crooks."

"I'll bet he was steamed that someone else got the bundle from the express car."

"Wouldn't you like to know."

Tulley eyed the smirking youth closely. "You saying Hennessey robbed that train and done them killings?"

Peaches slouched triumphantly. "John Hennessey's going to wreck this stinking town. And the Railroad along with it. He's going to have the whole country before he's done. The workers are with him."

"Were you with Hennessey in Seattle?" McIntyre asked.

"That's for me to know and you bums to find out."

Tulley nodded. "The story around town is that Hennessey picked him up there. The police run the both of them off after the big dust-up last February."

"The general strike," Peaches boasted. "We shut the city down for five days. The five greatest days there ever was."

McIntyre's expression soured. "You terrorized innocent people and made yourselves a lot of enemies."

"The workers have been terrorized for years. Now we're giving some back."

"That's fine for an angry young punk," McIntyre said. "But what does it do for decent men who need a steady income to feed a family?"

"You're the punk," Peaches shot back. "You'll find out we got the power. Then you'll be sorry. All you lackeys will be sorry."

McIntyre pushed his chair back. "I've heard this nonsense before, Chief. Do you mind if I get some sleep and give you my statement in the morning?"

"Just so you're here first thing."

Bone chilling wind had emptied the sidewalks of pedestrians. Hanging signs squeaked on metal straps. McIntyre walked rapidly, keeping to the shadows and watching to be sure the few passing automobiles posed no threat. He was shivering again when he reached his hotel.

On the way up the stairs he pried the .25 Colt from his watch pocket. Keying his door open, he stepped in quickly, put his back to the wall and pushed the light button. An empty room mocked his precautions.

From his suitcase he retrieved the heavier of his two pistols, a compact .38 Colt automatic, which he concealed in his clothing when he went down the hall to the shower. He washed with exacting care, rubbed liniment onto the nastier welts on his legs then returned to his room and wedged himself in. The butt of the clasp knife where he had hit the tramp was clean and shiny but to McIntyre sin was a visible presence. He buffed and polished until fatigue overwhelmed him, then collapsed into bed.

The next day began before dawn. Noise and movement in the hotel roused McIntyre and sent him on his obsessive morning ritual of washing and shaving. His overcoat had dried. He was able to brush away most of the dirt caked among its fibers. The stains he could not remove made him visibly nervous when he left his room. Partway down the stairs he stopped and climbed back up to make sure he had locked his door.

The scrawny red haired girl was on duty downstairs. Her acne scars were less obvious when her thin face lit with excitement.

"Mr. McIntyre! You caught the man who robbed the depot last week."

"Where did you hear that, Molly?"

"'Tis in the morning newspaper. On the very first page. You're famous."

McIntyre glanced around swiftly, as if he expected to catch the curious eyes of strangers fixed on him. No one was looking.

He handed over a bundle of clothing. "It was your friend Mr. Floyd who traced the money."

Painful memories welled up in her eyes. She stepped quickly into a small alcove to bag and tag McIntyre's laundry and drop it into a bin.

When she stepped back to the desk, her voice was low, haunted. "He traced the money from the express car, too, didn't he? That's how come he's dead, isn't it?"

"Did he ever talk to you about the express car?"

Her eyes would not meet his. The flush that hung in the hollows of her cheeks might have been guilty knowledge, or just embarrassment at some fleeting, forbidden emotion. He had no chance to pursue the matter. People were waiting behind him.

"Is there a reasonably priced restaurant close to here?" he asked. "One where they know a small breakfast with some flavor is better than a big one where all you can taste is grease?"

Her directions took him to a narrow frontage on Comstock. The interior was plain and clean, the breakfast crowd quiet, dressed with threadbare respectability. A small table stood empty in one corner.

McIntyre bought a newspaper and sat down. The day's banner screamed: 'Legionnaires Murdered'. The article beneath had come from the wire service.

> The tiny lumber town of Centralia, Washington has witnessed the most outrageous act of Bolshevik terror yet visited upon this nation. Three stalwart members of the American Legion, parading to celebrate the anniversary of the Armistice that ended the Great War, were shot to death in the street before the eyes of horrified onlookers. A fourth died bravely in the nearby Skookumchuk River apprehending one of the perpetrators of the atrocity. The authorities have moved swiftly to quell the red uprising. The total of Bolshevik arrests, including those in the nearby cities of Seattle and Tacoma, is said to have surpassed one hundred.

The article went on in that vein for the remainder of the column. The theme was picked up in a locally written editorial, which concluded that a mine strike would have the city's virgins deflowered and its buildings in flames within hours of beginning. Aaron Crowder was not listed on the masthead, but his influence was unmistakable.

A garbled version of Peaches' apprehension also appeared on page one. McIntyre read far enough to verify that he had been credited by name with an arrest. His eyes shifted to the window. It was a reflexive act of paranoia. He was surprised to actually see a man lounging outside.

The fellow was roughly dressed and did a poor job of pretending to read a newspaper posted in a sidewalk kiosk. A decrepit Willys-Overland wheezed to a stop at the curb where he stood. The loiterer jerked his head. A big, deliberate ruffian climbed down from the car and headed off in a direction that would take him around to the back of the restaurant. Two other men got out, leaving the driver with the motor chugging raggedly.

The first was squat and muscular, his face notable for a daring smile and a bandage over one eye. He pushed into the restaurant and tossed a nickel on the counter for coffee.

Following him was a giant who ducked instinctively coming through the seven-foot doorway. A plaid woolen coat hung to his hips from wide bony shoulders. Shapeless khaki trousers bagged around slat legs. His black hair was thick and tousled, untrimmed in several weeks. His face was narrow and rawboned, his jaw sharp and strong and his eyes bright with coiled menace.

He strode to McIntyre's table and flung a flattened, filthy hat down on the checkered cloth. "You ought to be more careful," he said in the orator's bass that had sent men scouring the forest for McIntyre the previous night, "leaving your fancy clothes all over the place."

He reversed the chair across from McIntyre and sat down. The quiet of the restaurant fell to a frightened silence. Customers ate without a word. The slightest utterance could draw attention to them. They did not look away from their meals. Any glance might be misinterpreted. Across the room a woman began chirping mindless gossip in a pointless show of feminine bravado.

McIntyre picked up his hat and tried to straighten it, but its original shape eluded and frustrated him. He brushed compulsively at it with a napkin.

John Hennessey wasn't used to being ignored. "You really are crazy, aren't you?"

McIntyre looked up and blinked in surprise, as if he had forgotten the man's arrival.

"That's what Chicago wired about you," Hennessey recalled, as if he were beginning to put some stock in the idea. "They said the Railroad had turned a lunatic loose on the Movement."

McIntyre set his hat on the newspaper, where no dirt would fall on the table cloth. "What do you expect to gain from this strike, Mr. Hennessey?"

"Justice."

"How much would it cost to persuade you to look for it elsewhere?"

A cynical laugh rattled in Hennessey's throat. "Buying me out of town won't get your bosses anywhere. Not long now they'll face a general strike all across the country."

"You people tried that in Seattle," McIntyre reminded him. "It fizzled in five days."

"Seattle was just the beginning. We're building one big union. The Industrial Workers of the World. No more divide and conquer. No more playing one craft against another. One union big enough to shut down the country until the bosses agree just terms of peace."

"If you shut down the country, you shut down the food distribution system."

"The workers will run what they need and shut down the rest," Hennessey said.

"We're all cogs in the same big machine. No part of it will operate properly for very long unless the other parts are functioning as well."

"Then we'll starve, if need be."

"You and a few zealots, maybe. The police will break your heads soon enough."

"The cops themselves struck in Boston, just two months ago."

"The Mayor called out the National Guard and hired new police."

Hennessey ran out of patience and produced a gray Luger. He ignored a gasp from a nearby table to point the .30 caliber muzzle at McIntyre's face.

"Are you committed enough to die in a grimy little mining town?"

McIntyre moistened his lips. "Are you suddenly rich enough to turn down money without asking how much?"

"You can forget framing me for that express car heist. Or that Railroad dick that got burned."

"Was Floyd murdered in Hatcher Street? Or was his body just dumped there."

"How would I know?"

"You have Hatcher Street watched night and day. It's the only road access into shanty town. When Luther Grimes comes for you, that's the way he'll come."

Hennessey laughed harshly and slipped the Luger away under his coat. "Grimes is a broken down outlaw. He's getting fat on the bosses' salary."

"If somebody did dump Floyd's body, they needed a car or a wagon to carry it."

"So?"

"A vehicle can be traced, if there's a description."

Hennessey shrugged. "The driver came in fast with no running lights. The kid wasn't close enough to see much. He didn't think anything of it until the cop came along and found the body."

McIntyre muttered a frustrated, "Thank you."

"I came here wondering if maybe you amounted to something," Hennessey said derisively.

"I amount to the same thing you do," McIntyre said. "Somebody's quick, violent solution to a situation that can't be resolved either quickly or by violence."

"You're a four-eyed nothing," Hennessey snarled. "A little man hiding behind a gun. Got a gun, little man?"

"Maybe I should use it," McIntyre said. "Maybe reasonable people can settle this when you and I are gone."

"Reason be damned!" Hennessey hit McIntyre's face a savage backhand. He stood up, looming over him. "Now, I want Peaches out of jail, and I want you on the first rattler out of town."

He turned on his heel and strode from the restaurant. The ruffian at the counter drifted out after him. Silence evaporated into nervous chatter.

A middle-aged waitress scuttled to McIntyre's table. "Mister, do you know who that was?"

McIntyre dabbed at the corner of his mouth. Blood came away where the skin had split. He looked at it oddly, still stunned by the force and surprise of the blow. When he spoke, his voice was detached and serene.

"May I have an order of French Toast and a glass of grapefruit juice, please?"

"That was John Hennessey. He's the worst of those red monsters that's trying to have a strike here."

"Is he usually this bold? Brandishing a pistol in public?"

"Never that I've heard. He's a creature of the night, so says the talk."

"Then maybe he really has graduated from robbing depots to express cars."

CHAPTER 7

McIntyre cut his French toast into small square bites, chewing each with obsessive thoroughness and using the last few to soak up the remaining syrup, moving each in the same ritual pattern until his plate was clean. He noted the twenty five cent check in his pocket ledger and left the restaurant. Shop windows reflected the morning bustle on the street. He watched as he walked, making sure he wasn't followed. Finding a haberdashery, he left his battered hat to be cleaned and blocked. The best bargain in a temporary replacement was a snap brim cap. He wrote its eighty cent price into his ledger then set off again.

A police van chugged past as he neared the City Administration Building. It turned into the lot behind the station, listing precariously. Muffled curses leaked from the windowless confines.

The desk officer remembered McIntyre from the previous evening. "Watch the switchboard, will you? Black Mariah's in with a new load."

The officer hefted a night stick and disappeared down the hall that led to the rear door, leaving McIntyre to confront a bewildering PBX array. Numbered jacks probably corresponded to call boxes spread throughout the city. Above each glowed a ruby bulb to warn against circuit faults that could isolate patrol officers and blind the department during the first critical minutes of developing trouble. A log book lay open. McIntyre flipped back through until he found the call on the tramp he had killed.

The time notation told him he had escaped detection by mere minutes. There was no telling how many unseen eyes had witnessed the encounter. He could hear reluctant men being herded into the rear of the station, shuffling and grumbling. If any were brought forward there would be no place for him to hide.

"Move 'em downstairs to the holding cells," came Tulley's rumble. The Chief lumbered out to where McIntyre stood and slapped down a tightly rolled newspaper. "Didn't waste no time puttin' yourself on the front page, did you?"

McIntyre made a disgusted face. "Do you seriously think I'd paint a target on my back?"

"Then how'd they know?"

"Whom did you report the arrest to?"

"Just the Prosecutor." An idea flickered through the hostility in Tulley's eyes and his shoulders sagged under a load of resignation. "I reckon he found some re-election money up to old man Crowder's place."

"Why would Crowder undercut you in the newspaper? That will only make the strike organizers bolder."

"Old man Crowder has more on his mind than a strike. Government bookkeepers are looking at his war business, seeing if maybe he made some money he shouldn't have."

"How would a Federal investigation turn him against you?"

"He wants his own man in as Chief. To make sure the bookkeepers don't get no cooperation."

"If he's moving that aggressively, the Government must be getting close to something."

"I got enough headaches on my own beat," Tulley said.

"I can give my statement later, if this isn't a good time."

Tulley handed him a printed form and pointed to a table in the waiting area. "Write up everything just the way it happened. Don't leave out nothing. Wait while the desk man types it up and sign all the copies original. Don't forget to initial any changes you make."

"Will you need a formal interview?"

"Maybe later. I'll look over what you wrote when I get done listening to what a bad fellow I am on account of I'm always pushing working men around when they get down on their luck." Tulley glanced at a loud complaint from the holding cells. "Bum luck ain't hard to spot. It's blowed its nose on both its sleeves."

O'Haney blew his nose into a large red handkerchief and capped the radiator of the idling jitney. "Well, if it ain't the Railroad man I thought was a bookkeeper."

"I'd like to go to the depot." McIntyre climbed into the rear seat and shut the small door.

O'Haney strapped the water can back on the running board. He got behind the wheel, took a pint bottle out from under the seat and fortified himself with a stiff swallow.

"Snatching working folks out of their homes to frame for robbery. Ought not to ride you anywhere."

"Are you running a jitney, or a crusade?"

O'Haney put the bottle away and got the Ford moving with an angry lurch. "Tain't my fight. The workers will settle you. I'll leave it to them."

"The Wobblies weren't so generous in Seattle last February. Anyone who ignored the strike to earn a little drinking money had his head broken."

"I'll not be turned against the workers." O'Haney's sharp retort was followed by an uneasy silence that suggested he was giving his first serious thought to the impact of a strike on his own life. The jolt to his comfortable notions put an edge on his voice. "Not by the likes of you."

"Save it for Mrs. Doolin."

"Don't talk down widow Doolin. There's just things women don't understand."

"If you like her, why pick fights with her?"

"Wouldn't do me no good to shine up to her. Widow woman, she'll have expectations of a man."

"You could start by sobering up and taking a shave."

"What then? Supposing she took a liking to me? I got nothing to offer. I got no experience satisfying a woman, except what you buy at four bits a try. I got no property."

"I thought jitney drivers owned their own cars."

"Used to be that way. Last year the city passed an ordinance you had to have a taxicab license. Protect the public they claimed. Only give out one license. Old man Crowder owns the company that got it. You sold your hack to him cheap and drove it at his wages afterward. Still call them jitneys so passengers will think they're giving their money to an honest man."

"Clean yourself up and tell your story to widow Doolin," McIntyre suggested.

"Wouldn't be right," O'Haney said solemnly.

"What wouldn't? Sobering up? Or courting the widow?"

O'Haney hawked and spat out over the running board. The smoke of a departing train rose above the low skyline. New arrivals were waiting for the jitney at the base of Comstock.

McIntyre paid his fare and crossed the footbridge. More arrivals were milling in the depot, collecting luggage and meeting friends. He saw G. Robert Knowlton out on the boarding platform, engaged in an earnest and unheard conversation with a young woman.

The young woman's coat was fashionable and expensive. Dull brown hair peeked coyly from under a stylish cloche hat. Powder and rouge did what they could with a healthy set of freckles. Her eyes made no secret of admiring Knowlton; ruggedly handsome in whipcord trousers and a leather jacket open at the neck to show a supervisor's starched collar and the knot of a tie. They flashed angrily when he saw McIntyre come out of the depot and excused himself.

The Superintendent crossed the platform with a congratulatory smile and put out a hand. "I see by the newspaper that you caught one of the Bolsheviks who robbed us."

"I'm sorry to interrupt your conversation with your lady friend," McIntyre said.

"That's her idea. Not mine." Knowlton scowled back along the platform. "You were a varsity man, weren't you?"

McIntyre shook his head. "My father died when I was young. There was no money for school. I took a bookkeeping course and graduated at the Post Office."

"I fought forest fires in the summer to pay my books and tuition," Knowlton said, "and waited tables the rest of the year to cover my living expenses. It was naive, I suppose, to think that hard work and good marks counted for as much as the proper pedigree and a gentleman's 'C', but it still annoys me when I'm told I can only better my prospects by marrying well."

"You're fairly young as Section Superintendents go. Your prospects should be excellent."

"Perhaps in a less troubled posting."

"The express car robbery will blow over."

"The robbery is part of a pattern. Belligerent tramps. Trespass. Vandalism. It's only going to get worse, in spite of your success in catching that fellow last night."

"Why so?"

"When the War ended, the Government turned more than a million soldiers loose to find their living in a shrinking economy. Until they can be absorbed, there'll be a struggle between the haves and the have-nots. And wherever you find a man like this Hennessey, you'll find a flash point."

"Is there any way Hennessey could have known in advance about the money being shipped in the express car?"

Knowlton nodded, his face grim. "The Railroad's hourly workers are all unionists. They have been since Nationalization."

"When were you notified of the shipment?"

"I wasn't."

McIntyre blinked in surprise. "That sounds pretty irresponsible. Sending that much cash without notifying you to have proper security in place to receive it."

"The money was manifested directly to Aaron Crowder. If he hadn't been here to take delivery, it would have stayed on the express car."

"That isn't the correct procedure. Will calls are always processed through the destination depot."

"Mr. Crowder is a large shipper. I presume he was able to negotiate a waiver."

"Why would he want to?"

"He didn't confide in me."

The violation troubled McIntyre visibly. He unhooked his spectacles, realized the handkerchief he needed to clean the lenses was buttoned away inside his overcoat and put them back on.

"May I use your inspection buggy?"

"For what purpose?"

"I'd like to look over the route the train was on when it was robbed."

"The Eastbound local just went through," Knowlton said. "We'll have three and a half hours of clear track. Give me a few minutes to re-arrange my schedule."

"You needn't waste your time. I can operate a standard buggy."

"Inspection buggies are local procurement items in this Division. The only thing standard is the gauge of the wheels."

Knowlton's was a primitive ironbound platform of four by four planks. Crudely riveted sheet metal protected a small gasoline engine. Knowlton set the spark, switched in the ignition coil and put his strength into the crank. The engine had been dormant too many hours to make even a pretense of starting. It took Knowlton two more pulls to get enough gas through the carburetor to make it sputter, and another two to coax a ragged idle out of it.

"See what I mean?" he asked McIntyre, puffing a little.

"Mr. Knowlton, if word got back to Chicago that you were drawing a management salary to chauffeur me, we could both find ourselves out of work."

Knowlton drew breath to argue, but let it out in a frustrated sigh. "I suppose you're right."

A maintenance worker helped them switch the buggy onto the main line. He smiled at McIntyre's efforts to master the controls; a unionist's perverse pleasure in the spectacle of white collar struggles.

McIntyre got the buggy under way. Factory buildings and warehouses meandered past at the yard limit of five miles per hour. Soot from the smelter chimney and from the shorter stacks of the electric generating plant had dirtied everything within wind drift.

Shanty town came into view, hidden away like a secret shame in a wash below and largely out of sight of the city. The shacks were flimsier in daylight, thrown together out of scrap lumber and clinging precariously to the hillside. Wisps of smoke curled from stove chimneys. Women hung laundry that would never be cleaner than dingy, but at least had the stink of hard labor washed out.

Ragged children played by the creek. One boy saw McIntyre and threw a rock. The missile fell short of the right of way. The boy picked up another and tried to interest his friends, but they just pointed and giggled at the man chugging past on the funny little railroad car.

The right of way passed through a notch with granite walls serrated by blasting powder then the rails curved around the side of the mountain however the engineers had been able to reach a compromise with nature. Tall evergreens came down almost close enough to touch on one side. A deep gorge fell away steeply on the other, where an unseen river had cut through millions of years of geological history.

The downgrade grew steeper. McIntyre had to experiment with the throttle and spark settings until engine compression moderated the buggy's speed. He managed to reduce the spitting and popping to a mild sputter punctuated by an occasional cough. Miles passed. A tunnel appeared and swallowed him. Pitch blackness dilated his eyes without allowing him to see anything. Morning sun at the far end forced him to squint, even through a heavy overcast.

McIntyre stopped, set the brake and left the inspection buggy idling. The ground had been heavily trodden in an extensive police search. Investigators had taken pains to avoid a narrow maintenance path that led from the tracks up to the top of the brick-faced tunnel entrance. The path had been used since the last rain. One person had come down, quickly and sure-footed, in a large size of city shoes. Two people had gone back up, a smaller person struggling ahead and the larger climbing protectively behind. Their tracks were deeply cut in the herringbone pattern common to skiers carrying loaded packs up slope. A second path, wider and winding and less steep, had taken them up through the woods.

McIntyre followed that and found a dirt road that skirted the mountain parallel to and above the tracks, making use of the same pass but screened from view by the intervening forest. There was no nearby habitation that might contain witnesses. Frequent traffic kept the surface packed as hard as concrete.

McIntyre watched a Franklin sedan go by at speed then he went back down and got the inspection buggy going again. The next stop was a small crossroads town.

"I guess you want to know if that express car was locked when it pulled out," the Station Master said after he had inspected McIntyre's business card. A lined face and spade whiskers gave him the gravity of a church elder.

"That's not why I stopped," McIntyre said.

"Locked tight. Checked it myself. Always do. Them cars carry the United States Mail. Federal crime to tamper with 'em. Always make sure nobody can."

"That's a Railway Post Office car you're thinking of. Those carry loose mail for sorting. An express car carries mail sorted and bagged. The Postal authorities don't care what happens in them, as long as the mail isn't disturbed."

"Wasn't strictly an express car, you know. Carried baggage too. A combine. That's what they're called."

"I know," McIntyre said. "I work for the Railroad."

"Had to open up the baggage section. Put some suitcases in. Fellow checked 'em through to his sister. Went off to get married, she did. Phoned up for him to send along her goods and chattels. Right nice gent, he was. Offered to help me load 'em on. What do you think of that?"

"I'm not really interested in—"

"Against the rules. Railroad personnel only in the baggage section. Tried to trip me up there, didn't you? But I did my job. Did it proper and locked up afterward. Always do. Them express cars carry the U.S. Mail. Federal crime to tamper with 'em."

"Do you have any gasoline here? I'd like to refill the inspection buggy."

"Have to lug the can yourself. I'm a busy man. Can't be taking time for other folks' chores. Don't matter how important they think they are."

"Fair enough."

He led McIntyre to a shed behind the small depot and unfastened a padlock. "Used to be you didn't have to lock nothing around here. Times have changed. Can't trust nobody these days."

McIntyre lifted a heavy can by its wire bales and wrestled it out. The Station Master locked up.

"I'll have to go with you. Watch you pour it. See how much you use. Got to account for everything. Nobody trusts nobody no more. Always somebody checking up."

McIntyre struggled with the unwieldy can, doing his best to minimize spillage. He was breathing noticeably when he capped the can and lowered it to the ground.

"Thanks," he said to the unhelpful Station Master.

"Ain't finished yet, are you?"

McIntyre capped the gasoline tank. "This ought to do it."

"You got to put the can back in the shed. Wouldn't be right to leave a job half done."

"You'll have to unlock the shed anyway," McIntyre said in a fair imitation of the man's clipped speech. "No sense both of us going. Waste of Railroad resources. Got to be efficient, you know. Specially in hard times like these."

The man scowled. "Ain't going to answer no more questions if you don't."

"My only question was whether you had gasoline."

"What about the express car?"

"What about it?"

"Ain't you supposed to find out who robbed it?"

"Do you know?"

"I might know something that helps you find out."

"Then you'd better tell the County Sheriff," McIntyre said. "It's a crime to withhold information about a crime."

He set the throttle and chugged off, leaving the Station Master staring after him. The return trip was upgrade. He struggled for a time with the cranky controls and finally settled for something about the pace of a fast walk, which seemed to produce the most comfortable level of vibration through the plank floor of the buggy. The effect was hypnotic. He lounged against the warm engine housing and filled his lungs with clean, cold mountain air. Birds floated in lazy circles and squirrels scolded his noise from the safety of tall pines. A deer paused its grazing long enough to watch with placid brown eyes as he chugged past.

The crack of a passing bullet shattered the idyll.

McIntyre was flat on his stomach almost before the thunder of the rifle rolled down out of the trees above. A second bullet clanked through the engine housing. Sheet metal mushroomed a foot above him, followed by another rifle report.

He was helpless. To jump and sprint for the cover of the forest would expose him fully to the rifleman. If he were lucky enough to make it, he would be lost as soon as he was out of sight of the right of way; at the mercy of an unseen sniper who certainly knew the terrain.

A third bullet cut off a branch in the intervening forest and cracked harmlessly overhead. A fourth clipped the platform.

Then there was only the chug of the engine. Minutes crept by on cat feet. McIntyre sat up slowly when he was sure he was out of range.

Ahead lay several miles and another hour on the exposed platform of the slow moving buggy. He tugged off his gloves and unbuttoned his coat to clear the way to his .38. His hands trembled.

Knowlton was on the platform when he reached the depot. The Superintendent hopped down onto the buggy. His face was bright with important news.

"You had a telephone call. From Mortimer Jason."

Surprise left McIntyre momentarily wordless. "What did he want?"

"He wouldn't say. I told him you'd have to return before the after-noon local came through. He said he'd call back then."

McIntyre stopped the inspection buggy at its siding.

Knowlton hopped down to throw the switch, and noticed the dam-age to the housing. "That looks like a bullet hole."

"Do you have much random sniping in this section?"

"Only one incident in all the time I've been here. The National Guard was turned out to catch the fellow."

"The National Guard?"

"This was during the War. What the Government thought was a German fifth column turned out to be a feeble-minded fellow in his seventies. Something about his grandfather losing a farm. His quarrel, assuming he actually had one, appeared to be with the Chesapeake and Ohio."

Knowlton hopped back on and ran the buggy onto its siding. His boots and clothing had picked up some dirt since McIntyre had seen him last. His morning's exertion had left an impatient edge on his voice.

"I hardly think this was random."

"Perhaps not," McIntyre conceded.

"While you're here, I'm responsible for your safety. I don't mean to be overbearing, but if there are any more inspection runs, I'll have to insist on going along."

"I've seen all I need to."

"What are your plans?"

"Nothing very dangerous."

"Now look here, McIntyre, Christopher Floyd went off without telling anyone where he was going. Five hours later, he turned up dead. Last night you went into shanty town and very nearly met the same fate. And now another incident."

"If I survive lunch, I'll be back to meet the afternoon local. You can keep an eye on me while you tell me about the express car robbery."

CHAPTER 8

Wary of establishing a pattern, McIntyre ate lunch in a coffee shop some distance from his hotel and set off for the depot on foot. Passing an abandoned storefront, he noticed a stray cat lazing in a transient patch of sunlight. He stopped and removed one glove. The animal sniffed his fingers and purred quietly when he stroked its fur. The distant note of a steam whistle called him back to reality. He scratched the cat's ears and went on.

Evelyn White stood alone on the boarding platform, gazing away along the tracks. Perfect stillness and patrician bearing made her a portrait in elegance against a backdrop of faded paint and smoky sky. The air had grown colder as the day wore on and her breath condensed in a trance-like cadence.

"Oh, hello," she blurted when she saw McIntyre.

"I'm sorry. I didn't mean to interrupt your thoughts."

An embarrassed flush warmed her cheeks. "I'm not in the habit of moping around train stations. It's just that I had to sign a deed in lieu of foreclosure on our home this morning. I can't afford to have a court action following me when I leave, and I do so want to be away from here, but to give up something I've struggled so long to keep, to admit defeat with the stroke of a pen…" Her voice trailed off hopelessly.

"Where will you go?"

"Somewhere I can make a decent life for Anne."

"Do you have some place in mind?"

She gave her head a tense, tiny shake. "I've been putting off any decision. With Anne's future at stake, I'm so worried about making a mistake."

"You're right, it's none of my business."

She smiled a quick apology. "I'm really not being evasive. And I hope I didn't sound too silly last night. Warning you to stay away from shanty town."

"No. You were right about that, too." McIntyre caught himself touching the corner of his mouth where Hennessey had hit him.

"Thank you for trying to spare my feelings, but I did read in the newspaper that you caught the man who robbed the depot. You obviously knew exactly what you were doing."

The soft light of admiration in her eyes heightened the discomfort in his. "I was groping for one answer and found another," he confessed. "I'm not sure I haven't spent my life groping for the wrong answer."

"I know something is troubling you," she said quietly. "Something very personal. I saw it when we first met."

"I didn't mean to be obvious."

"Troubled souls have an affinity for each other. You couldn't hide yours from me any more than I could hide mine from you."

McIntyre managed a nervous smile.

"Is it hard for you to talk about it?"

"I'm not sure I understand it any more. I thought I'd come to terms with who I am...with what I am. I thought I had my life under control. Now I just don't know."

She stepped close, not touching him physically but caressing him with her warmth and with the fragrance of gardenia. "Would you be more comfortable talking in private?"

Panic tightened the small muscles of his face. A sharp, sustained whistle startled Evelyn and spared him the need to reply.

A locomotive drew the local up through the yards, blowing thin, hot smoke skyward and releasing condensing clouds of steam as it passed grimy factories and warehouses. Doors opened in the depot. Passengers drifted reluctantly out of the heated waiting area.

Anne White came out with her covered tray and moved close to her mother. "Hello, Mr. McIntyre. I got all my problems right, except one."

"Congratulations."

"My teacher said I multiplied wrong, but I don't think so."

"Sometimes," McIntyre said, "you have to look at a situation more than once before you see it clearly."

The locomotive drew in, putting the platform in shadow and radiating the heat of hard running. Brake shoes squealed, dragging the great iron wheels to a stop and adding their stench to the smoke of lubricating oil. Sibilant valves and the hammer of steam pressure inside piping made Anne visibly nervous. Evelyn was accustomed to the scale and cacophony of railroad machinery. She bid McIntyre a demure good-bye and took her daughter to canvass the arriving passengers.

McIntyre consulted his watch. "Exactly on time," he remarked when G. Robert Knowlton appeared at his side.

"The afternoon schedule is pretty tight. We have the Transcontinental coming through."

"Then the bandits knew exactly how much time they had to work with."

The wooden express car door slid partway open in iron runners. A middle-aged blond man stepped into a gap barely wide enough to accommodate his bulk and traded canvas mail sacks with the baggage clerk. Knowlton introduced him to McIntyre.

"I got to see authority to let anyone inside," the man apologized with a heavy accent of puritanical Swedish upbringing. "I got to have something in writing."

Knowlton slid the door back. "I'll take responsibility."

The big Swede's eyes darted around, like a housewife letting unexpected neighbor women into a kitchen she hadn't had time to tidy up.

Built in the last century, the express car had a raised clerestory that ran the length of its roof, lined on either side with narrow windows. Dirty glass filtered the afternoon sun. Distorted rectangles of light lay across sacks of mail tagged and neatly hung along one wall. The other wall held a bank of pigeon holes and beneath them a work table where a steaming coffee cup stood among orderly stacks of paper. A wooden bulkhead divided the car. McIntyre retracted an iron bolt and opened a door.

The baggage clerk was working on the other side, exchanging arriving luggage for that of departing passengers, sweating in the chilly air. McIntyre closed up.

"Is the door bolted from this side during runs?"

"Regulations," the Swede said. "Mightn't be safe in here otherwise. Baggage can shift if the engineer has to make an emergency stop."

Knowlton nodded confirmation. "It was bolted when I forced my way into the car."

"Did you discover the crime?" McIntyre asked.

"When there was no response from the men in the car, I went to the forward platform for a look."

McIntyre's eyes followed Knowlton's to the platform door. It was strongly bolted, its window protected by iron grille work. One of the panes was new, the putty around it fresh.

"Was the door locked from the inside?"

"When I saw the men on the floor, I thought there had been an accident so I broke the glass. In the urgency of the moment I managed to push my hand through the bars and slip the bolt. I found the men dead and the safe open."

The safe was a hulking presence under the work table. McIntyre tried the handle to be sure it wasn't left unlatched as a matter of convenience. A compulsive twist of the number wheel established that the lock was precision built and properly lubricated; not subject to manipulation.

"When was the combination last changed?" McIntyre asked the agent.

The Swede maintained a stern silence.

"It's quite all right," Knowlton said. "Mr. McIntyre is a Railroad official."

"I ain't so sure it is, Mr. Knowlton, sir. When I signed for them numbers at Division, they said I wasn't to say nothing about them. Not even if the Division Super himself asked me."

"I don't understand your attitude," Knowlton said. "Two men were murdered in this car. Mr. McIntyre is trying to learn who was responsible."

"Trying to put the blame on the dead express agent," the Swede said. "That's the truth of it, sir."

"Nonsense."

"They questioned his poor widow. Drove her to tears."

"Don't repeat idle gossip," Knowlton ordered.

"It was in the Denver newspaper for all to see," the Swede said, with a glance that defied McIntyre to deny it.

"If someone tried to rob you," McIntyre said, "what could you do about it?"

"Keep the door locked and don't let nobody in." He shot a glance at Knowlton. "Like I'm supposed to."

"Only guards are issued weapons," the Superintendent explained. "And they are only assigned to ride with certain high value shipments. Although the dead express messenger was found to have a small personal pistol in his pocket."

"Had either man tried to defend himself?"

"Not that I could see."

"Were any windows broken?"

Knowlton was momentarily blank. "I do remember it was quite warm inside the car. It would have cooled quickly with a window broken and no one to stoke the stove."

The Swede glanced nervously at the old iron pot belly tucked into the corner, as if he feared he might catch a phantom stirring the charcoal glowing inside.

McIntyre opened the door Knowlton had used to gain entrance to the car and stepped out. The end platform was narrow. With the roof extended overhead and the black mass of the engine tender a scant two feet away, no one standing where he stood could be seen by anyone on the train. Stairs descended close to ground level from either side, but even with great strength and skill, dismount from a moving train could easily be fatal. McIntyre stepped to the depot platform with Knowlton in his wake.

"What did you do after you discovered the robbery?"

"I instructed the baggage clerk to call the police and find Christopher Floyd."

"How soon did they arrive?"

"Floyd within a minute of my alarm. The police shortly after that."

"By the police, do you mean the County Sheriff?"

"The Sheriff has no personnel in the city," Knowlton said. "His investigators were at least an hour behind the city police."

"The city police conducted the investigation?"

"Yes."

"Who was in charge?"

"The Chief. A man named Tulley."

"What did the Sheriff's investigators think of that?"

"They were satisfied enough with his work to release the train only half an hour after they arrived."

"What exactly did Tulley do?"

"First he had the train shunted onto a siding so it could be held for investigation. Then he assigned several officers to interview the passengers and surviving crew. I understand the results were negative."

"What was Tulley doing while the interviews were going on?"

"He put an officer to work spreading powder on the express safe to find latent finger marks. He also opened a crate in the baggage section. The only one big enough to conceal a person."

"What did he find?"

"Spittoons."

"Shipped as baggage?" McIntyre asked skeptically.

"This is a sparsely settled division. It's not economical to make freight stops at every depot. Local odd lots are usually sent with passenger baggage."

"And this was a legitimate shipment?"

"Yes. Manifested to a local saloon owner."

"Do you remember the name?"

"Dantini."

"Right tidy fellow," the big Swede remarked. He had come out from the car and grown restless waiting for McIntyre to notice him. "Got a schedule to keep, sir. Mail to be delivered. They're talking about using airplanes to deliver it, you know. Army bomber planes. Saying trains aren't fast enough. If you're through, sir, I'd like to lock up and be ready when the engineer is."

McIntyre hesitated on the brink of an affirmative nod. "What did you mean by 'right tidy fellow'?"

"Second load of spittoons he got in recently. The other come from Spokane on the freight. I handled freight manifests, before I got promoted to express agent."

"Thank you," McIntyre said. "I've seen all I need to."

The Swede responded with an economical nod. Returning to the express car, he passed Evelyn White and acknowledged her by name. His regard for propriety didn't prevent him from eyeing her surreptitiously while he closed the door.

McIntyre returned to his conversation with Knowlton. "Where was Floyd when Tulley opened the crate?"

"Watching."

"What did he say?"

"Nothing."

"When did he leave the depot?"

"I don't recall seeing him go. I first became aware he was gone when Aaron Crowder demanded to see the him."

"What time did Crowder arrive?"

"He met the train with several armed mine police to claim his shipment. When he learned the express car safe had been looted, he was beside himself."

"The shipment was insured."

"So I tried to explain," Knowlton said. "But Crowder just stormed into the depot. I had to get the train shunted onto the siding, so I didn't hear what went on, but apparently he spent half an hour haranguing the telegrapher until he verified his money had indeed been shipped. I next saw him when he returned to the platform. He excoriated Tulley and demanded to speak to whoever was investigating on behalf of the Railroad. I was unable to locate Floyd. At first I thought he had beaten a cowardly retreat, but—"

"Mr. Knowlton!"

The day telegrapher called out from the depot that Mortimer Jason was on the telephone. He wanted to speak with McIntyre immediately.

"Hold the call for transfer to my office," Knowlton instructed. He walked into the depot with McIntyre, and when they were alone at the top of the stairs, stopped him. "My status may come up in your conversation with Mr. Jason. If I tell you something, may I have your promise to keep it confidential?"

"I'll do what I can." McIntyre's voice was cagey, but his eyes were curious.

"I've sent my two weeks' notice to the Division Superintendent," Knowlton revealed.

"Have you another position?"

"No, I haven't. As you can imagine, I feel like a traitor resigning at a time like this, but I believe it is the only reasonable course for me under the circumstances. I just wanted you to know my situation, and to offer whatever help I can in your investigation."

"Thank you."

"The express car robbery happened on my watch, and I feel personally responsible, regardless of the fact that I am now a lame duck."

A telephone rang insistently.

McIntyre excused himself with a polite smile. He shut himself into the Superintendent's office, sat in Knowlton's swivel chair and lifted the earpiece, pausing a moment to compose himself before he spoke.

"Good afternoon, Mr. Jason."

"Mr. McIntyre, I am in receipt of your telegram of last night," came the silken whisper. "May I inquire precisely what the serial number of the revolver issued to Christopher Floyd has to do with the Bolsheviks? Mrs. Sprague's decryption of your transmission was correct, was it not? You did request the number?"

"Floyd's revolver is missing," McIntyre explained. "If your theory that he was murdered by the Bolsheviks proves correct, possession might send one or more of them to the gallows."

"I see." Jason read six digits slowly enough for McIntyre to copy into his pocket ledger. "You also inquired about a man named Dantini?"

"A local saloon owner who is going out of his way to cozy up to the head of the mine police. He may be a Bolshevik spy."

"Do you know his background?"

"Not beyond the casual mention of St. Louis referenced in my telegram."

"You were not aware that he is a member of the Black Hand?"

"No."

"He was personally administered the blood oath of the Mafia by Ignazio Saieta."

"Who?"

"Lupo the Wolf. The most powerful member of Sicilian criminal society in the country at the time."

McIntyre located a sheet of foolscap in the center drawer of Knowlton's desk and made notes in a precise hand. "Is Dantini currently involved in Black Hand activities?"

"Saieta's successor, a man called Joe 'the Boss' Masseria, has reportedly provided him with immigrant Sicilian thugs on occasion."

"Do any of these people have Bolshevik leanings?"

"There is nothing remotely Bolshevik in Dantini's background. He came to this country with a circus troupe in 1905, as part of an aerial act. The troupe folded in New York, where Dantini was initiated into the Mafia in 1911 or 1912. Some time later police scrutiny prompted him to move to the Midwest. He fled St. Louis suspected of murdering an accomplice in a counterfeit War Bond scheme. That crime, not coincidentally, involved a .22 caliber semi-automatic pistol, probably fitted with a silencing tube."

"Not coincidentally?"

"You were not aware that both the express messenger and guard were killed with a .22 caliber weapon?"

"I thought I was to concentrate on the Bolsheviks."

"Well, obviously a silencing tube would have been necessary to commit the murders on an occupied train," came the testy whisper. Neither loud nor harsh, the words were still a rare show of temper from a man who prized equanimity.

"Mr. Jason, I don't think you've risked a direct telephone call just to pass on information you could have sent far more safely in a coded third party telegram. What is bothering you?"

"By some horrendous fluke you seem to have blundered into one of the express car bandits. Worse, the Controller is aware of the evidence. He wants to send investigators."

The irritation in McIntyre's face was magnified in his voice. "What happened to his theory about the dead express messenger?"

"Not only did his investigators eliminate the man as a suspect, but they didn't use tact in doing so. The widow complained to the Denver newspaper and the Railroad was vilified in this morning's edition. The Controller is smarting, and he needs a victory."

"Can you keep him away?"

"It will help if you can show results."

"I'm moving as quickly as I can, Mr. Jason."

"Are you now, Mr. McIntyre?" The Treasurer's whisper became cold and delicate. "I have word from the Section Superintendent that you apprehended a suspect in connection with a local depot robbery last week. He seemed quite impressed. Needless to say, I am not."

"The depot robbery was committed by the Bolsheviks," McIntyre said. "The man in jail is the sweetheart of the Bolshevik leader."

"The Bolshevik leader is a woman?"

"No, a man named Hennessey."

Mortimer Jason's, "My God!" came across the line as a drawn out wheeze. "Faggots as well as Bolsheviks."

McIntyre said nothing.

"Perhaps you think me naive for being surprised?"

"I've never concerned myself with what people did behind their pulled shades," McIntyre said impatiently. "Is there anything that can be done to deny the fellow bail?"

"I shall look into the possibility," Jason promised. "Meantime, a summary of your progress to date and your overall plan to deal with the Bolshevik menace will help me press our case in upcoming discussions with the Chairman."

"I haven't anything to report, Mr. Jason. I've been here only one day."

"What are your immediate intentions?"

"I'm going to a prize fight. I've been promised ten dollars to check the crowd for pickpockets."

"This is hardly the time for moonlighting, Mr. McIntyre. Certainly not at a trivial sporting event."

"The event is neither trivial nor sporting."

"Mr. McIntyre, you are not trained for routine security work. You wouldn't notice someone picking your own pocket."

"The head of security at the fight is also head of the mine police," McIntyre said while he folded his notes. "He is a potential ally against the Bolsheviks."

"Then you do have a plan." Jason's whisper hovered at the verge of vicarious ecstasy.

Closing the desk drawer, McIntyre noticed two shiny cartridges half-buried in the pencil drawer. Both were .30-30's, and both had tiny scratches on the extraction rims, as if they had been worked through the action of a rifle to clear the weapon.

"What I have, Mr. Jason, is a gnawing feeling that I am following Christopher Floyd into the Valley of the Shadow."

"Are you being melodramatic? Or are you in immediate danger?"

"I have no way to be sure whether that feeling is my subconscious mind screaming the truth of my situation at me, or simply the paranoia of a pathetic lunatic."

CHAPTER 9

"Just follow the crowd," Molly said when McIntyre asked at the hotel desk for directions to the Pendleton Street lumber yard.

Men moved in close packed knots on the sidewalk outside. Night had brought with its darkness a penetrating cold. Voices condensed into plumes of fog beneath street lamps. Reverent talk of boxing was punctuated by crude jokes. Raucous laughter set McIntyre's nerves on edge.

The crowd thickened on Comstock, filling the sidewalks and overflowing into the street to impede the progress of the few cars there. Ticket collection created a bottleneck on Pendleton and trapped McIntyre in a milling mob. Something hard touched his arm and startled him. He looked to find the big, loose-jointed thug named Rufus who had driven him to Dantini's the previous night.

Rufus tapped a billy club against a white rag tied around his sleeve. "They got me doing real cop stuff," he said with a foolish grin. "Can you feature that?"

"What would your friends in Walla Walla think?"

"They'd croak theirselves off laughing." Rufus guffawed and leaned closed enough for McIntyre to smell beer on his breath. "The main gate's for the suckers. You come along with me."

The ruffian used a combination of bulk and easy-going manner to make way through the dense, electric crowd.

"Dantini has a big turnout," McIntyre remarked.

"He's an operator, all right. I wouldn't mind getting next to him for a while. Just to see how he pulls it off."

"If this mob learns what he's up to, things could get ugly."

They reached a building flanking the street and Rufus pulled McIntyre to the privacy of a doorway. "There ain't going to be gun trouble tonight, is there?"

"I hope not. I didn't bring my .38."

"I figured guns was your stock in trade."

"I was trained as a bookkeeper."

"Only training I ever had was altar boy. You can see where that got me." Rufus laughed heartily and pushed ahead.

They passed a side street that flanked the lumber yard, separated from it by a high fence. Slivers of brilliant light leaked between the fence boards and showed two men in white arm bands parking a red touring car half a block down.

Rufus and McIntyre climbed two wooden stairs from Pendleton. Rufus rapped on a door and gave McIntyre's name to the thug who peered out.

Frank Dantini's voice came from inside. "Better let him in. He's liable to put us all in the same cell as Hennessey's boy, Peaches."

Snide laughter greeted McIntyre as he stepped into a plank-floored room. It had been a sales in office better days, and the hollow return of McIntyre's footfalls indicated a cutting room below. Light from the yard outside infiltrated chinks in the walls and sent daggers of illumination slicing across the shadows that haunted empty shelves and a barren counter. Half a dozen men sat on crates. Dantini stood in the center under a single incandescent bulb dangling at the end of a waxed wire.

"Mr. McIntyre is a Railroad investigator here from Chicago to find the gang that cleaned out that express car," he told the assembled group. "He's going to make sure we have a few less pockets picked tonight."

One of the men stood, naked in the bone chilling air except for knee-length purple tights and canvas shoes. His powerful chest was bare of the red hair that covered his head with stubborn unruliness. Midway through his thirties, with the exuberance of youth gone from a face that had been hit hard and often, he was barely recognizable from poster pictures of Tiger Stevens. He came forward cautiously and put out a tightly taped hand.

"McIntyre is it? That's your name?"

"Yes." McIntyre shook hands with the man.

"Been waiting more'n a year to learn what it was. Knew I'd see you again. Felt it in my gut."

"I'm sorry. I don't recall meeting you."

"You was pointed up to me," Stevens said. "In the Chicago yards."

"What were you doing there?"

"I won a fight I wasn't supposed to win and I had to leave town on the fly. Just me and this old geezer in a boxcar. He seen you through a crack where the door didn't quite close. I never seen a man go as white as he did. Like he didn't have no blood in him at all. He pointed you up. 'See that one? You can cross any man you want, but don't never cross that one.' That's what the old guy said."

The room fell silent. Every eye was on McIntyre. A nervous smile flickered across his face.

"Are they still drinking stove alcohol in the hobo camps?"

"That wasn't it," Stevens said. "Never seen a man so blind scared. Wouldn't even say your name. I seen your face sometimes, when the bad dreams wouldn't let me wake up. Maybe it'll let me be, now I finally met you."

A second man stood. He wore a paisley dressing robe. His features were square and patrician, and his smooth black hair was shiny with Stacomb. He stepped forward and offered a manicured hand, also tightly taped.

"Jack Harding, McIntyre. I travel first class, and I've never heard of you, but it's always a pleasure to meet anyone who gives the working slobs nightmares."

A third man stepped from the shadows. He was as large as either fighter, but soft and corpulent, wearing an overcoat against the chill.

He tugged off a glove. "Burton Underhill. Insurance investigator." His hand was warm and damp. He made too much of his grip, and held it too long. "Did you get any more than I did from those dim-witted Sheriff's dicks?"

"I didn't get anything."

"You made good time down and back," Underhill said. "That Knowlton fellow told me you took his inspection buggy this morning."

McIntyre said nothing.

"Hired a car myself," Underhill said. "The trip was three hours, travel time alone. Paced the local train on the way back. We could have beaten it, with a more powerful motor."

"You are very thorough, Mr. Underhill." McIntyre's eyes darted around to see who else was present.

Four other men sat on crates, two with Harding and two with Stevens, obvious seconds. The men with Harding shared his composure, if not his aristocratic bearing. The two with Stevens were surly, restive. One saw a rat scurry in the shadows and flicked a boot knife at it. The knife clattered against a wall. He went to retrieve it.

Dantini snapped his fingers and held his hand out for the knife. He gripped it by the blade, watched the shadows. His silence and stillness were contagious. The musty smell of time and neglect began to assert itself.

Tiny feet scurried.

Dantini whipped the knife forward past his ear in a fluid motion. It missed the scampering rodent by less than an inch. The blade buried itself in the plank wall. The haft shivered from the impact, humming briefly like a tuning fork.

"Nice throw," McIntyre said. "Did you pick that up in the circus?"

"As a matter of fact I did." A thin, dangerous smile formed beneath Dantini's black satin mustache.

The street door opened to admit another man. A bowler hat and a soup strainer mustache gave him the look of a prosperous immigrant. He might have come into an empty room for all the notice he took of anyone. Shuffling to the disused counter, he set down a heavy black comptometer, dusted off a spot next to it and set his hat there. He seemed to be settling in for a long stay.

Dantini consulted a gold pocket watch. "You're running a little late here, Otto."

"Yah."

Underhill had to move so Otto could bring a high stool over to the counter. "Not very social, is he?" the insurance investigator asked Dantini.

"Otto handles my business. The less he says, the better I like him."

A door opened back in the shadows and light poured in from the lumber yard, silhouetting Luther Grimes. "We'll need axle grease to get any more people in."

Dantini slapped his hands together and grinned at the two heavy-weights. "Well, Gents, if the house is full and the bean counter is here, I guess we'd better have a fight."

Tiger Stevens bounced to his feet and threw a couple of imaginary punches before he settled down to allow his seconds to lace on the gloves. Gentleman Jack Harding was the picture of serenity as he was prepared.

Dantini turned to McIntyre and Underhill. "You two better work your way into the crowd. There'll be plenty of light fingers out there by now."

The door Grimes had used let the two men out onto a plank landing that commanded a view of the yard. The ground below lay in the rough configuration of an amphitheater, with the cutting room under the sales office at the bottom so that a gentle slope would always be available to move lumber down for processing. The slope was standing room only. Men were packed tightly into the fenced confines, waiting for something to happen in the canvas-floored ring under the glare of electric lights that were fastened beneath the landing and the stairs that led down to the yard.

Underhill caught McIntyre's elbow before he could descend. "You didn't talk to the Sheriff's people. You didn't have time."

"Then you've stolen a march on me."

"There's only one reason you wouldn't want the Sheriff's information," Underhill insisted. "You already know who knocked over the express car."

"You said the Sheriff didn't have any information."

"That Railroad dick, Floyd. He caught up with the bandits and they killed him. He left something behind that put you on the track."

"The trick in breaking the express car robbery isn't learning what Christopher Floyd knew. It's learning what he didn't know."

"Well, we'd better learn it fast," Underhill said. "I guess you heard the express messenger idea was a bust?"

"Yes."

"So far this burg has been a side-show. Now it'll be the main event. If we don't hustle, someone else will move in and grab the credit."

"This city is a dangerous place to be in a hurry."

"That's why you need to work with somebody who's ready for trouble." Underhill patted a bulge beneath his arm.

"The local police chief doesn't like anyone but his people carrying guns."

"Jesus Christ! You mean you're walking around with no heat? After you pinched a Red for that depot heist?"

"You might want to give me a little room," McIntyre suggested. "The last gang of Bolsheviks that came after me couldn't shoot very straight."

"Hey, we've got to work together." Frustration throbbed beneath Underhill's words. "I've never drawn a blank like this. I talked to Blue Blood Bascomb in Tacoma before I came here. He worked this burg in the War, when it was booming. He gave me a list—every grifter in town. Nobody knows scratch."

"You've talked to all of them?" McIntyre asked skeptically.

"All I could find. My dogs are killing me. I've been drinking like a B-girl since before lunch."

Inspiration sharpened McIntyre's voice. "Can you chat up the seconds after the fight starts? Find out when they were notified about this trip?"

"What am I looking for?"

"Are you familiar with a stereopticon?"

"You mean one of those parlor gadgets where you look at two pictures that don't quite match and the image jumps out at you?"

"Exactly."

"And if we find two stories that don't quite match, what do you think will jump out at us?"

"Don't you wonder what an operator like Dantini is doing in a tank town like this?"

"I already checked him. He was mixed up in counterfeit War Bonds. Somebody who knew about it came down with a sudden case of dead. The St. Louis cops want to ask him some questions he doesn't want to answer."

"When was the last time you heard of anyone ducking the police by promoting prize fights?"

"Okay, so it don't exactly listen. That doesn't put Dantini in the picture on the express car job."

"Suit yourself." McIntyre started down the steps.

Underhill trotted down with him. "By the way, Lily told me to say hello."

"Lily?"

"From Dantini's. Come on, McIntyre. We're grown men."

Bright light at the bottom showed the tiny muscles of McIntyre's face tense with disapproval.

Underhill's expression was as loose and licentious as his voice. "I wish I could make the girls remember me like she remembered you. You really dynamited that little twist."

"See a doctor and get some sulfa," McIntyre advised.

He passed a mine police guard at the base of the stairs. Confronting him was the forward phalanx of spectators; forbidding rows of strangers standing shoulder to shoulder to deny him passage. He steeled himself against a visceral abhorrence of crowds and excused his way into the mass of men.

The assignment Dantini had given him was pointless. Every man worth robbing was encased neck to knees in a heavy overcoat against a chill that permeated even the densely packed audience. Wallets and money clips were all but inaccessible to their owners, let alone a shivering sneak thief. McIntyre settled among the waiting spectators where no vantage offered a shot at his back.

The wait was short.

"Your kind attention, Gentlemen!"

Dantini stood at the center of the ring, bellowing through a megaphone. He kept repeating himself until he had enforced a hush of anticipation over the crowd.

"For your entertainment and pleasure, Gentlemen, a twelve round contest of heavyweight pugilism. Welcome, from a triumphant tour of the Midwest, unbeaten in his last twenty three fights, the one, the only, Gentleman Jack Harding!"

Most of the limited applause came from McIntyre's vicinity, from the men who could afford the better positions. Boos and catcalls greeted Harding from the back of the crowd as he slipped between ropes held obligingly by his seconds. He stood aloof in his corner, taunting the crowd with his arrogance.

"Challenging tonight," Dantini bellowed, "bringing to the ring the boundless confidence of his youth and an indomitable courage born in the stygian depths of the mines, Tiger Stevens!"

Stevens came easily through the ropes and bounced on the balls of his feet, shadow boxing to acknowledge his wild applause. The stage was set. The champion of the common man would do battle with the Paladin of the powerful. Impossibly complex social issues would, for this one night, be reduced to juvenile simplicity. The endless tug of inconclusive reality would be suspended. There would be a decision. A winner and a loser. A moment of satisfaction. Or of despair. McIntyre turned his collar against the chill.

Gentleman Jack Harding was agile for an aging heavyweight. His footwork was flawless and smoothly executed. Tiger Stevens made up the difference with a quickness that might or might not last out the match. Both men hit with intensity and professional skill. The crowd sensed the concentration and controlled fury of the two fighters and came alive, urging their favorites on and groaning at hard strikes by the opponent.

A man slid in front of McIntyre. "Give you Stevens, even money."

McIntyre shook his head, and the man moved on, slipping through the crowd like oil through the gears of some ponderous machine, stuffing the wager money he collected into an envelope and scribbling names and numbers on the outside. McIntyre watched until he saw the envelope transferred to a man with a white arm band. Lost to McIntyre's sight for a moment, the collector reappeared going up the stairs to the sales office.

The bell rang to end the round. A nudge told McIntyre Burton Underhill had returned.

"That was a pretty good guess, telling me to talk up the seconds," the insurance investigator remarked in a voice that doubted McIntyre had used only intuition.

"What did they have to say?"

"The fight was moved up two weeks. Stevens' guys said Harding had a schedule problem. Only, when I got to Harding's guys, they said it was Stevens who had the conflict."

"When were they told about the switch?"

"Eight days before the express car push," Underhill said significantly. "Old man Crowder didn't tell anyone he was moving the money until three days before he actually did it."

"According to Crowder?" McIntyre asked.

"Are you saying Crowder was behind the heist? That he's trying to fleece the insurance company?"

"What does the insurance company think?"

Underhill shook his head. "Insurance swindles don't happen that way. They're low profile jobs. Somebody might get sapped out or tied up, but nobody risks capital murder. They don't have to. The swindlers control the assets. They can fake the loss any way they want to."

The bell rang to signal a new round. A roar went up from the crowd. Conversation would, for the next three minutes, be an exercise in lip reading. McIntyre was content to watch the fighters, discovering how they maneuvered to create openings, when they counter-punched and when they retreated, how they rested and evaded punishment when it was the other's turn to win a few points.

By the time the bell rang to end the round, Underhill's patience was gone. "Look, I'm breaking the rules just talking to you. You know that? I was told to stay strictly the hell away from you."

"I won't mention this," McIntyre promised.

Underhill would not be put off. "Dantini wasn't the only one I checked up on. Maybe the local cops would like to hear about a guy named Dinty Colbeck, and how he caught that bullet in the Chicago yards."

"Is that a threat?"

"I just want a little cooperation, McIntyre. I'll do my share of the leg-work."

"You don't need me, Mr. Underhill. You're a capable investigator. You can clear up the express car robbery by yourself. Just don't move too quickly and wind up like Christopher Floyd."

"Take it slow and let you beat me out? Thanks, McIntyre. For nothing." Underhill shouldered his way off into the crowd.

When the bell rang to end the next round, Luther Grimes appeared at McIntyre's elbow. Grimes took out his pipe and tamped in a wad of tobacco.

"I hear you had a hot time down in shanty town last night." His coarse voice was cagey.

"Hennessey's rally must have broken up early," McIntyre said with uncharacteristic lightness.

"Maybe I had the wrong night. Sometimes I get confused."

"No harm done. I got in, got lucky and got out with a whole skin."

Grimes struck a match. It flared in the semi-darkness, giving the age lines in his face a satanic aura that was reinforced by the smell of sulfur. He took his time lighting the pipe, making sure it was drawing properly before he spoke.

"Which route did you take?"

"North, along Hatcher."

"How far did you get?"

"All the way down to Hennessey's shack." McIntyre's tone suggested that it could be done again.

Grimes exhaled a cloud of smoke. "Are you still of a mind to put me out of a soft job by breaking this strike?"

"How long do you think Crowder will pay you to ride around in a fancy touring car?"

"I had my heart set on finding that out for myself."

"Crowder seems to think we ought to work together. Do you want to give him the bad news?"

"Speaking of news, Dantini wants to see you."

"Has something happened?"

"You better talk to Frank."

Grimes drifted off as the bell rang for the next round, leaving in his wake the aftertaste of harsh tobacco and a residue of cunning.

Chapter 10

Frank Dantini waited at the base of the plank stairs, just out of the glare that bathed the ring. A white silk muffler added a dashing touch to his Chesterfield topcoat and pearl gray fedora. He smiled with the contentment of a Broadway impresario basking in the marquee glow of a sold out opening night.

"Well, McIntyre, how do you like my little prize fight now?" Concentrated crowd noise all but drowned his words. Cold air turned them to vapor.

McIntyre shivered inside his overcoat. "You needn't worry about pickpockets. Every wallet in the yard is buttoned away out of reach."

Dantini's smile vanished. He took McIntyre's arm and led him under the stairs. They stood next to the boarded up door to the cutting room under the sales office and waited until the round ended and the noise abated.

Dantini kept his voice low. "I had to give you that pickpocket story for Luther's benefit. There's a big haul up in the office. Enough to retire on. Luther isn't getting any younger, and his boys have Otto outnumbered two to one. I need you up there to protect my interests."

"Is that my easy ten dollars?"

"I'll make it fifty."

"No thanks." Quick words edged with suspicion.

"Not even to earn a week's worth of silk shirt wages?"

"No."

"Last night you were the hero. Tonight you've lost your nerve?"

"Last night I was a sucker."

Dantini released McIntyre's arm with a good-natured laugh. "All right, tell me how much this is going to cost me."

McIntyre rubbed his coat sleeve compulsively, smoothing away any wrinkles Dantini's grip may have left. "Talk to Underhill. He might quote you a price."

Disgust hardened Dantini's voice. "Underhill is a back slapping bluff artist. I invited him for window dressing. So Luther wouldn't get wise to why I brought you."

"At least he's armed."

"Aren't you?"

"You told me Luther's boys would handle the rough stuff."

Dantini laughed at the consequences of his own duplicity. "Look, do me a favor. Just go up and look over the layout. If there's anything you don't like, keep going."

McIntyre's eyes darted to the crowd. Men were packed shoulder to shoulder. There were no aisles making way to an exit. Whatever trouble Dantini's proposition threatened, the sales office offered the quickest escape.

"All right."

"I'll find you a gun," Dantini promised. "I'll bring it up myself."

His nod let McIntyre past the Mine Police guard at the base of the stairs. McIntyre climbed quickly to the dim landing. Below him the bell rang for another round. The two fighters moved away from their corners. They closed fast, moving expertly and hitting hard. Crowd noise welled up. For the next three minutes, nothing that happened outside the ring would draw the least notice. McIntyre tugged off his gloves and unbuttoned his overcoat. He checked his watch pocket. The miniature Colt was cold to his touch. He stood to one side and rapped on the door.

"Yeah?" The voice was arrogant, with an undercurrent of taut nerves.

"Dantini sent me up."

The door opened a careful few inches. The face that appeared in the crack was handsome, heavy-jowled, oily. Small, wise eyes took in McIntyre with a scornful glance.

"You the Railroad dick?" A stale aftertaste of cigar smoke came with the question.

"I work for the Railroad."

The man let McIntyre in. A crude white arm band marked him as Mine Police, but he moved with the quickness of a schemer rather than the sullen measure of a thug. He threw a furtive glance out at the empty landing before he shut and bolted the door.

Otto sat on his stool, rapidly counting loose wads of currency dumped from envelopes that lay to one side in a careless scatter, punching totals into his comptometer. He paid no attention when McIntyre drifted over, feigning curiosity. The street door stood unguarded, half a dozen paces distant.

It opened before McIntyre could take advantage of the situation. A second Mine Policeman came in and stamped his feet, twice, deliberately.

Otto looked up, startled.

The newcomer grinned innocently. "Gettin' to be whizzin' cold out there," he drawled, and bolted the door.

He was a younger man in a rough, sheepskin-lined coat. Bravado lit his eyes and untrimmed hair curled down from under a battered Stetson. He ambled over to the counter.

"Boy, howdy," he drawled wistfully. "Look at all that purty money."

Otto resumed his tally. "Move out of the light, please."

"Sorry," the man said with mocking delicacy. He swaggered past McIntyre, sizing him up. "How's the Tiger doing?"

"He's putting up a good scrap."

"Yeah?"

The man ambled to the wall and pushed his Stetson back to put one eye to a knothole. He liked what he saw, and pushed a holstered revolver back around behind his hip so he could lean comfortably against the wall. A roar went up outside, and he threw an imaginary punch.

The heavy-set man shook his head hopelessly. "It's fixed, you dummy."

"So it's fixed. It's still a good fight."

"We ain't getting paid to rubber-neck."

"Hell, Ledbetter, we ain't gettin' paid hardly at all."

"Get away from there."

The younger man turned slowly from the wall and gave Ledbetter an insolent grin. "All that shinin' up you been givin' the mine owners ain't got you Luther Grimes' job yet. And until it does, Buddy Earle takes his orders from Grimes and no one else."

"Since when did you take orders from anyone?"

"Ain't I the one went out and warmed up the damned car?" A cheer from the crowd outside turned Buddy Earle back to his knothole.

Ledbetter turned his frustration on Otto. "How much longer?"

"Vhen chob is done," Dantini's bookkeeper said firmly.

He banded a stack of currency, dropped it into a briefcase at his feet and started on another. The bell rang out in the yard. Buddy Earle stepped back from the wall, shadow boxing enthusiastically. McIntyre glanced at the street door, half a dozen quick strides away. Ledbetter stepped close, making his superior size obvious and intimidating.

"Yeah, it is getting cold," he said, and stamped his feet on the plank floor. He stamped deliberately, as Buddy Earle had done, but this time to make a distinct count of three.

Buddy Earle stopped shadow boxing. "Hey, I wanted to see the rest of the fight."

"Not ready," Otto said indignantly.

Ledbetter took a menacing step toward the bookkeeper. "Shove it in the bag. Count it later."

The noise of Ledbetter's boots had been a signal to men waiting in the cutting room below. Heavy feet could be heard climbing unseen stairs. McIntyre bolted for the street door.

"Son of a bitch!" Buddy Earle clawed for his revolver, forgetting he had pushed it around behind his hip.

Ledbetter spun too quickly, momentarily lost his balance.

McIntyre made it through the door, but a thin accumulation of frost ambushed him on the stairs outside. His feet went out from under him. He collided with the fender of a parked automobile. It was the red touring machine he had seen earlier. The motor radiated the warmth and smell of recent running. A glance told him the car was empty. As he scrambled up an unfamiliar voice inside the office caught his ear.

"Only three here," it said through a thick accent. "Should be four."

"The Railroad man vent outside," Otto answered.

"He's wise to the game," Ledbetter said. "We better get after—"

A shotgun blast cut him off. Yells from Otto and Buddy Earle were followed by two more shotgun blasts. The hum of the fight crowd died. The night was utterly silent. Then three deliberate pistol shots echoed into the stillness. McIntyre sprinted across Pendleton.

A bullet clipped past his head. He scrambled around a corner and put his back against a wall, breathing raggedly. Heavy feet were pounding after him. A glance down the side street told him headlong flight would be a fatal mistake. Light from the arterial at the far end would silhouette him for a pursuing marksman. He slid quickly along the wall until the shallow blackness of a doorway swallowed him. The door was locked. He flattened against it and worked the .25 Colt out of his watch pocket.

A faint shadow spread along the hard-packed dirt street, warning that someone had rounded the corner from Pendleton. An alien scent preceded McIntyre's lone pursuer. Then the glint of dim light on a gun barrel. Finally the stalker; squat, powerfully built, coarse featured. Sweat shone on pock-marked olive cheeks. Brilliantine made black hair glisten. He passed within feet of McIntyre's doorway, intent on the dark shapes of trash containers ahead and never glancing sideways. He stopped short when a warm engine caught back in the direction of the lumber yard. If he did not retreat before the car came, the headlights would silhouette him for anyone crouched in the dimness ahead. Before he could turn, McIntyre brought up the .25 Colt.

The flash of the little gun was no brighter than the strike of a match at the back of the man's head. The report was not much louder. A single convulsion jerked the man taut. Muscle tension evaporated. He collapsed straight downward until the limp masses of his body could no longer compress upon each other, then pitched forward on his face. His stillness was final.

Gears ground briefly on Pendleton. McIntyre hurdled the body and sprinted for the far end of the side street. Headlights swung down from Pendleton, flooding the street with illumination. McIntyre reached the end and ducked around the corner a heartbeat ahead of a shotgun charge. Glass shattered on the other side of the lighted arterial. He put his back to the nearest wall, full in the glow of a street lamp.

The reflection of the approaching lights grew bright in a window across the arterial. It was likely the men in the touring car could see McIntyre's reflection as well. The lights stopped. Two voices erupted, foreign and incomprehensible but almost certainly arguing the desire to exact vengeance for their dead comrade against the risk of confronting the armed man who had killed him. A police siren pierced the night and made their decision. A frantic grinding put the car in reverse. The headlights retreated from the window. Another inexpert gear change sent the touring car away along Pendleton.

Aftershock and accumulated perspiration left McIntyre shivering. The arterial where he stood was commercial, empty of traffic at that hour and flanked by dark frontages closed for the night. He thrust his hands into his pockets and set off along the sidewalk. His pace was quick, his eyes darting. He turned on Comstock and walked to Pendleton to return to the lumber yard by a circuitous route.

Tulley's Packard and the police van blocked the gate. The crowd inside sounded ugly. The door to the sales office opened. A uniformed officer brought out two well-dressed men. He propped both with their hands against the wall and patted them for weapons, then went back inside alone and shut the door. The pair saw a large camera being unloaded from what was apparently a newspaper car. They moved away quickly.

McIntyre still held the miniature Colt in his pocket. Palming the tiny pistol in his left hand, he tugged his glove on over it. He knocked on the door of the sales office and identified himself. Tulley was inside, and at a word from him, the officer let McIntyre in.

The room reeked of burned nitro powder. Ledbetter lay on his back with his arms and legs splayed. Blood soaked the front of his coat and leaked from a third vacant eye in the middle of his forehead. Otto was doubled into a fetal position at the base of the counter. Blood had run from his midsection and stained the floor, dribbling into the cracks between the planks and puddling against one leg of his overturned stool. His skin was black where the muzzle of a pistol had been put to his temple. For all his bravado, Buddy Earle had made good time to the landing door. He lay face down. The back of his coat had been shredded by a shotgun charge. His Stetson was gone and untrimmed hair had been blown outward in a precise circular pattern by a close range pistol shot. McIntyre moved from one man to the next, tightening his throat to keep the contents of his stomach down.

Tulley strode over and confronted him. "I figured you had more sense than to get yourself mixed up in this here fight promotion scheme."

"The killers got away in a red touring car. A Dodge Brothers, I think."

"Brace against the wall."

McIntyre complied carefully, so that the gun inside his glove made no noise. "I got the license number."

Tulley searched him quickly and found only his pocket knife. "Well, at least you ain't completely stupid. Get away from that wall."

"Do you already have the license number?" McIntyre asked.

"No, I'm a damn fool idiot. Car gets stole in my city, I don't bother asking for no license number. Dantini here said you was supposed to be on guard with these jaspers."

Dantini stood at the counter with his hands in the pockets of his Chesterfield coat, all but the thumbs, surveying a scatter of envelopes with names and bets scrawled on them. He turned slowly.

"I wouldn't mind hearing about that myself." His voice was soft, but his eyes were hot and hard.

McIntyre returned his stare. "I had the impression I was supposed to die with them."

Tulley let out a dissatisfied growl. "Where was you when the shooting started?"

"I got out as soon as Ledbetter signaled the killers."

"Signaled?"

McIntyre stamped a foot on the floor, three times. The sounds echoed below. Tulley strode over to look through an interior door that hung open back in the shadows. His gaze lowered down the stairs behind.

"What's down there?"

"Trash, mostly," Dantini said. "There's no light."

"Then somebody could've hid out before the fight and waited."

Dantini shrugged. "It was no secret where or when the fight would be. The only logical place to bring the money was here."

"For a sharp operator," Tulley said skeptically, "you was a pretty easy mark for a stick up gang."

"That's why I sent McIntyre up," Dantini said in a sulky voice. "I expected better of him than to run out and leave an unarmed book-keeper and a couple of muscle stiffs to face experienced hijackers alone."

"This was your party," McIntyre insisted.

"Sure it was. I set the whole thing up so I could sign my own death warrant."

"I didn't see you in the line of fire."

"The fight is no contest." Dantini took a hand out of his pocket and waved it over the envelopes and the few remaining bank notes. "I haven't money enough to pay back a fraction of these wagers. What do you think my life is going to be worth in this town?"

The landing door opened and another uniformed officer stepped in. Angry voices came with him.

"Crowd's getting mean, Chief. Grimes' men had to pistol whip a couple of rowdies. We can't hold them much longer."

"Tell Grimes I want to see him."

"Right away, Chief."

Burton Underhill pushed in before the officer could close the door. "Say, Chief," he said, then saw the bodies on the floor. Blood drained from his features. He didn't hear Tulley tell him to brace.

The uniformed officer hustled him over to the wall. Luther Grimes came in while the officer was searching Underhill. Grimes looked at the dead men and reached quickly for the comfort of his pipe and tobacco pouch.

"You wanted to see me, Chief?"

"We're going to crack the main gate," Tulley said. "I want four of your men to hold the inside, with you to supervise. The crowd leaves one at a time. We'll identify and search every man. Even if it takes all night."

Grimes nodded deadpan and began loading his pipe. The uniformed officer produced a revolver from inside Underhill's coat.

Tulley scowled at it. "Anyone carrying a gun joins Mr. Underhill here for a ride in Black Mariah. Anyone else leaves with his money in his pocket and no more bruises than he brought in. I'm hired to protect the folks in this city, not pistol-whip them. I'll stand for no more of that."

"Always glad to cooperate with the City Police."

Grimes lit his pipe and left. Tulley jerked his head. McIntyre followed him out into Pendleton Street. The Police Chief ordered the lumber yard gate unlocked and watched each man out, impervious to the angry eyes and muttered remarks directed at him.

"If you seen the car," he said to McIntyre, "you must've got a look at the killers. Maybe even heard what they said."

"They were foreigners. They didn't use much English."

"What kind of palaver did they use?"

"Do you know how some languages are broken into dialects?"

"I been in Mexico City not talking nothing but border Spanish and couldn't hardly make myself understood."

"My guess is the killers were Sicilian."

"You saying that because you got a mad on at Dantini?"

"This was no hit and run robbery," McIntyre said. "It was hired murder. Dantini has a record for killing people who come to know his secrets, if you care to check."

"I don't reckon I'd find him letting go of thousands in wager money to pay off the killers."

"They were black hand thugs. They'll return the money and Dantini will pay them off in spaghetti and sleeping quarters."

Tulley eyed him suspiciously. "Why would Dantini want to kill you?"

"All I know is the killers were signaled after Dantini sent me up to the office."

"You said it was Grimes' man done the signaling," Tulley reminded him.

"Yes. Ledbetter."

"The men he signaled shot him dead?"

"Grimes likely promised him money, and paid off in treachery."

"Grimes is facing a mine strike. He can't afford to lose men."

"Grimes needs to weed out any malcontents who might challenge his leadership of the Mine Police."

"How many in the gang that done the killing?"

"Three."

"Which way'd they head?"

McIntyre avoided looking at the side street where he had killed his pursuer. "The roads in this part of the country won't take them far.

They'll board a train within a hundred miles. I can telegraph ahead from the depot."

"You stay put."

At best it was a matter of time before one of the departing spectators took a shortcut and stumbled over the dead man. Minutes dragged by. McIntyre was able to fidget under cover of staying warm. At last Tulley was satisfied with the exit procedure. He jerked his head for McIntyre to climb into the Packard.

"I don't much appreciate the way things been shaking out these last couple of nights," the Chief said when he had the heavy sedan under way. "Folks hereabouts are liable to start thinking old Virgil Tulley ain't up to scratch no more. He needs the Railroad to catch the crooks and the Mine Police to hold the lid on his town. Even then he's got men dead and money missing."

McIntyre brushed imaginary dust off the glass-smooth hardwood trim. The hum of the tires was the loudest sound in the car.

Tulley said, "From now on, you're to walk soft in my town. You're to check in with me regular. Any more trouble, and you'll be in the same fix as that damned fool insurance investigator. There's more'n gun charges I can bring a man up on, if I've a mind to."

"I expect you'll want a formal statement."

Tulley stopped at the base of Comstock, across the footbridge from the depot. "What I'll want is the damned truth. You think hard on that tonight, and get yourself to the station come morning."

McIntyre climbed down and closed the door. He watched the Police Chief back the powerful sedan angrily to the corner and accelerate away in the direction of Pendleton Street and the second man McIntyre had killed in as many nights.

CHAPTER 11

A street lamp made highlights in the flawless yellow paint of Geneva Crowder's Austro Daimler. Upright lines and a monocle windshield gave the roadster an aristocratic air. A leather strap held the hood down over a potent competition engine. Rare and expensive even before the Great War, such a car was now a seldom seen indulgence of those wealthy enough to maintain it, willful enough to master it and indifferent to raising memories of casualties still fresh in the national conscience. Parked in front of economy lodgings for business travelers, it was as conspicuous as an engagement ring in a convent.

"Mr. McIntyre," Molly blurted when he let himself into the warmth of the lobby. "You're the first one back from the prize fight. Did you see the big robbery?"

"Who told you about that?"

"Iris, on the city switchboard. She said it's all over the police circuit."

"The police call boxes are routed through the public telephone exchange?"

Molly nodded, full of excitement. "Iris said four men got killed."

Four meant the man McIntyre shot had been found.

"Iris said all the wager money got stolen," Molly confided. "A lot of men are real mad at Mr. Dantini. The fight was stopped, and now he can't be giving back their bets."

"Do you know Dantini?"

She put her bony elbows on the desk, intertwined scrawny fingers and rested a sharp chin on them, staring away into space. "Ain't he just dream stuff? The first time I seen him, I knowed he was Italian. Before I even heard his name."

"You're not his lady friend, are you?"

Molly recoiled and crossed herself. "Me father would be hiding me for that. Anyway, they're both high born and pretty."

"Both?"

The girl drew herself up and shook her head. "I ain't telling it on him."

"Well, would you do me a favor, then?"

"Depends," she said in a kittenish voice that didn't have many chances to play hard to get.

"One of the men Iris told you about was shot in a street near the lumber yard."

"How would you be knowing that?" Fear took the color from her face.

"Will you ask Iris if she can get me his name? And anything else about him that goes through the exchange?"

"I—I don't know. It's a big place. Iris showed me inside once. She's only one of the operators."

"I'll bet they all talk to each other," McIntyre said with a sly wink. "I'll bet there isn't a secret they don't know."

Molly pulled her sweater tight against a chill no thickness of fabric could ward off. "Would you be coming to this town to kill them that killed Mr. Floyd?"

"No, Molly. That's not why I've come."

"For such a sin you'd never be lookin' on the face of God." Her eyes pleaded for him to repent before he found himself beyond redemption.

"May I have my key?"

Her hand trembled as she passed it to him. He climbed the stairs cautiously. The dimness of the upper hallway amplified the sliver of light that leaked out beneath the door to his room. He tightened his grip on the miniature Colt in his overcoat pocket and listened. No sound came from within. A vaguely exotic scent hung on the stagnant air. Standing to one side, he turned the key quietly in the lock and pivoted the door inward.

Geneva Crowder's voice drifted out, low and sulky. "I don't wait for men, McIntyre. They wait for me."

She sat on the bed with both pillows propped behind her. She had kicked off high button shoes and left them as they fell. A woolen skirt was hiked up so she could curl her long, athletic legs comfortably. She lowered the magazine she was reading and regarded McIntyre through the doorway.

"You can come in. It's safe. I never bite on the first date."

He stepped in and closed the door. The room was too small to conceal any physical danger. He remembered his manners and removed his cap.

"If I had known you were coming, Miss Crowder, I wouldn't have left."

"My name is Geneva."

"I'm sorry. Geneva."

"Who won the big fight?"

"It was stopped. There was an incident."

Her laugh was full of music and mockery. "You don't have to be polite. I grew up in this little Sodom."

"I would have guessed finishing school."

"Oh, I wasted a couple of years at a veddy propah Boston academy for young ladies. They taught us that delicacy and deportment were the qualities men prized most in a bride. They didn't keep any actual men around to practice on, so we beat the stuffing out of each other playing field hockey."

"You've healed nicely," McIntyre said.

"What happened at the fight?"

"There was a robbery." Quick, toneless words to dismiss the subject.

"You could take off that overcoat and sit down," she suggested. "After all, this is your room."

Geneva had thrown her own expensive coat over a wall peg. McIntyre removed it and draped it on the best of the room's hangers, handling it gingerly, as if he were guilty of touching intimate apparel. He hung his own coat with symmetrical precision. The room lacked a chair, so he sat stiffly at the foot of the bed.

"What brings you out on a cold night like this?"

Geneva leaned back against the pillows and laughed wildly. She threw her magazine at McIntyre, and laughed some more when he picked it up, straightened the pages and set it precisely square to the end of the bed.

"When are you going to catch those train robbers?" It was a mocking suggestion that a real man would have had results by now.

"Did your father tell you why I'm here?" he asked seriously.

"He seems to think you're going to send the IWW packing."

"That's the idea, anyway."

"All by yourself?"

"Not necessarily."

Geneva scooted across the bed next to him, pulling down the hem of her skirt modestly. "Railroad people were killed in that robbery, weren't they?"

"That's police business."

"What about all that money?"

"The insurance company sent an investigator."

"You were poking around the express car this afternoon."

A surprised look. No words.

"Well, you were, weren't you?"

"The Railroad sent me to deal with the labor radicals."

Geneva bolted to her feet. "Damn the Railroad!" she spat down at him. "I need you!"

The violence of her outburst stunned him. He stared up in confusion. She sat down close beside him, took his hands in hers. "I know about you," she cooed.

The lone steam radiator was barely able to keep the room at habitable temperature, but McIntyre's face flushed with heat.

"I phoned a man in Chicago," she said. "He told me everything."

"What man?"

"A friend of mine. He owns a club there. He knows all about you."

An unpleasant glint of recognition lit McIntyre's eyes. "Dinty Colbeck isn't anyone's friend."

"I didn't mention any names."

"Colbeck extorted information on valuable shipments from railroad employees foolish enough to do their gambling and whoring at the Steel Rail Club." McIntyre's flush deepened at his own frankness.

"What bothers you about that? The way he used the club? Or the gambling and whoring? Or just the fact that Dinty lives by his own rules?"

"Colbeck hasn't any rules."

"It's personal between you, isn't it?"

"He had to be stopped," McIntyre said. "I played a small role."

"You're the one who shot him," she realized.

McIntyre moved his shoulders uncomfortably.

"He never would tell me how it happened." She curled her legs under her, waiting raptly to hear the details.

"Colbeck never varied his method," McIntyre began reluctantly, "preying on human weakness and paying the police to look the other way. We brought in men from the western divisions—capable riflemen who weren't known in Chicago—and circulated word of a shipment too rich for Colbeck to trust to his thugs. Decoy box cars were shunted onto a siding and left overnight. Powerful arc lamps were set up so they could be switched on simultaneously. We caught Colbeck and seven more, frozen like animals in a poacher's light. I hit Colbeck with a .30/30, but he still got away."

"You hit him, all right," she said in a fascinated hush. "He has to screw like a Chinaman anymore. Lying on his side."

McIntyre removed his spectacles, began cleaning the lenses. "You know nothing about me," he warned.

"My father used to send me to head doctors."

He replaced his spectacles and stared at her.

"First in Denver, then in Chicago. They were worse off than I was. I think the last one slipped out at night to feed the stone lions in front of the museum."

"What sort of man is your father?"

"He's you, McIntyre."

He suppressed a startled laugh. "We couldn't be more opposite."

"He's you in a mirror," she insisted. "With everything reversed."

"How do you mean?"

"It's called rage, McIntyre. You're both filled up with rage. The only difference is that my father lets it out at everyone who crosses his path. You bottle it up and turn it in on yourself."

McIntyre shook his head.

"You follow all the rules, don't you? No smoking? No loitering? Keep off the grass?"

"That's what rules are for."

"A place for everything, and everything in its place?"

"Yes."

"That's rage, McIntyre. You've turned it inward, against yourself, where it builds and builds until it blows."

McIntyre's attempt at an indulgent smile came off badly.

"Does it bother you?" she asked. "My talking about you like this?"

"No. Not especially."

"Then if you take off that coat, maybe you won't sweat so much."

Grinning foolishly, he used his handkerchief to pat his face dry. He stood up, hung his suit coat carefully on the wall rack and sat down a decorous foot away from the industrialist's daughter.

She scooted next to him and worked his tie loose. Her boldness made him tense, but he couldn't muster the rudeness to protest.

"Tell me about your father's rage, Geneva."

"It's just what I told you. He blows it off at everyone who crosses his path. He blew some off at you, didn't he?"

"Yes," McIntyre recalled.

"What set him off?"

She discarded McIntyre's tie and began to unfasten the severely starched collar from his shirt. He was perspiring again.

"I asked him why he shipped currency when a bank transfer would have accomplished the same thing with no risk."

"What did he say?"

"He told me to mind my own business."

"I hear a lot of that myself." She threw his collar at a peg on the wall rack, like a game of ring toss, and laughed when she missed.

"Does he confide in you at all?"

"If you've read the Old Testament, you know what daughters are good for."

"He seems to be providing well for you."

McIntyre glanced at her diamond earrings, the diamond brooch that pinned her silk blouse. She dismissed them with an angry toss of her head.

"What was your father like?"

"He died when I was young."

"You must remember something about him."

"I remember his funeral."

McIntyre squeezed his eyes shut against the pain. Geneva put her face close to his. Her perfume filled his nostrils. Her soft breathing caressed his cheek. She pushed a stray lock of hair back from his forehead.

"You can talk to me, McIntyre. We're two of a kind."

He lifted his eyelids, gazing without focus, as if he were looking into the depths of the past. "My mother tried to explain it to me but I wasn't old enough to have a concept of death. She dressed me up and we went to church. It wasn't Sunday, and we sat up in front instead of our usual place. I asked my mother why my father wasn't with us. She started crying again, so I didn't ask any more. Afterward everyone filed past this long, shiny box. I was too short to see inside, so someone lifted me for a look. I saw my father lying on a bed of shiny white cloth. He was dressed in his best suit. I wanted him to open his eyes, or smile, or say something, but he didn't."

"Can you understand anyone wishing her father dead?" Geneva's voice was melancholy, tinged with guilt.

"I understand bullies," McIntyre said. "There were plenty of them where we had to move after my father died."

"That's what Dinty Colbeck was to you," she decided. "Someone like the boys who tormented you when you were young. When you shot him, you were shooting everyone who ever bullied you."

"My reaction to bullies was to run." McIntyre's words were unstable with a suggestion of panic-stricken flight down garbage-strewn alleys.

"Are you going to run now?"

He shook his head, a brief shiver. "My days of running are over. I've no place left to go."

"Does that mean you're going to break the IWW for my father?"

"There are other people in the world beside rich men and labor radicals. Decent people who shouldn't have to spend their lives hunkered down in the cross fire."

She searched his eyes. "You want to do the right thing, don't you?"

"Yes." Almost a whisper.

"But you don't know how. Your heart has been beaten so full of hate all you can do is lash out at the people you fear the most."

He offered no argument.

She sat up straight and a tiny laugh escaped her throat. "The Bolsheviks in this town were dead and buried the minute you stepped off the train. They're just not smart enough to know it yet."

"I'm sorry I couldn't have made a better impression."

"It takes one to know one, McIntyre."

"You're not like me, Geneva."

"We're two peas in a pod. Lost souls looking for Heaven. Only we pushed open the gates of Hell."

"What do you mean?"

"Could you find the train robbers?" She caressed the back of his neck. "If I wanted you to?"

"Three sets of investigators are already working on that."

"I'm asking you."

"If they don't have it figured out by the time I'm ready to leave, I'll tell them."

"You know?" The two words came out in a startled gasp.

"Just generally. Not all the details."

"Do you know where the money is?" Her eyes demanded the truth.

"I haven't actually checked to be sure."

"What are you waiting for?"

"I've been told to leave it alone. To concentrate on heading off the strike."

"Who told you that?"

"The Railroad. A man with the power to put me back in a lunatic asylum."

Her arm tightened around his neck and she buried her face close to his ear. "I know I deserve to die, McIntyre. I just don't want to be killed by my own father."

"What do you mean—you deserve to die?"

"I've thought about dying," she said in a voice suddenly small and vulnerable. "Riding fast in the Daimler, I've thought what it would be like to keep my foot down and go right over Devil's Drop. It's eight hundred feet to the bottom. I could float forever."

"What does that have to do with the express car robbery?"

"Find the money. Just find the money."

"What is it about the money?"

"Just find it, McIntyre."

She stood up and stepped back from him, relaxed and sure of herself. She unbuttoned her skirt and let it fall to the floor. A soft slip clung around her legs. Her hips moved in a subtle suggestion when she stepped out of the circle of cloth at her feet. She released the brooch and unbuttoned the heavy silk blouse.

McIntyre watched her without moving or speaking, almost without breathing.

"What's the matter?" she teased. "Don't you want to screw?"

He looked helplessly into his lap.

She let the blouse fall open. "Do you mean you can't? Or are you just afraid?"

"I like you, Geneva," he managed to choke out. "I don't want to compromise you."

She rolled her eyes toward the ceiling. "Sweet Jesus, what a time to draw a Presbyterian."

"I don't know if I can help you. I'm in trouble myself. I need to find a way to finish my own job and get out of town."

"I need a commitment from you, McIntyre."

She sat down beside him and began to unbutton his shirt. After each button she paused and rubbed his shoulders.

"Just relax. It's not as bad as they tell you in church."

"It's not that," McIntyre said. "I don't know how I'll react. I don't know how much control I—"

She cut him off with a high, wild laugh. "It's not about control, you idiot."

"I don't want to disappoint you."

"Don't worry. If it doesn't go right the first time, we can work on it until we get it."

"I don't even know what's supposed to come of my finding the money."

"Just find it, McIntyre." She kissed his neck. "Just be there when I need you."

She began to undo his trouser buttons. His breathing quickened, grew shallow. He lowered her blouse and held her bare shoulders while she worked. His fingertips explored the softness of her skin, slid silken straps down. His mouth moved down into forbidden territory. He caught his tongue in an act of trespass and moved his lips to her ear. A guilty whisper was the best he could manage.

"Geneva, you don't have to—"

"Just be there for me, McIntyre," she breathed with sudden, hoarse ferocity.

She put her mouth over his and pulled him down to the bed on top of her.

CHAPTER 12

Dynamite rumbled deep in the mountain and shook McIntyre awake. The pale glow of a dawn not yet fully realized filtered through the misty window. Perfume lingered on the cold air, but the bed beside him was empty. He sat up groggy and looked around the room. Scrawled on the mirror in lip rouge was a message:

See You In Hell

Rising quickly, McIntyre wiped the mirror clean and opened the window to vent the room. He went down the hall to the shower where he scrubbed his skin mercilessly under icy water, as if abrasive soap could scour away his sins.

Freshly laundered clothing hung outside his door when he returned. He dressed and went down to the lobby. Molly wasn't on duty. A drab Studebaker had replaced Geneva's Austro Daimler at the curb outside the hotel. Drizzle slanted from a low, gray sky. Walking to the restaurant where Hennessey had confronted him the previous morning, he made sure he was not followed.

The robbery and murders that cut short last night's prize fight dominated the morning newspaper. A photograph taken by the remorseless light of magnesium flash powder held McIntyre transfixed. A tarpaulin had been thrown hastily over a body. An exposed hand groped from

under the cover for some contact with life. The unpaved street held
nothing but wind-blown trash. The doorway from which McIntyre had
shot the man belonged to a rescue mission.

"The wages of sin."

McIntyre jerked his head up. The guilt in his eyes meant nothing to
the waitress who stood over him. She was accustomed to startling customers out of their newspapers.

"Seventy five cents my husband wanted to spend. And for what? To
stand and watch two men pummel each other. You can buy a fine meal
for seventy five cents."

"May I have an order of French toast and a glass of grapefruit juice?"

"Twenty five cents," she declared while she wrote. "That's what I told
him. If he was of a mind to leave a warm home and go catch his death of
cold, he could stand in back with the other men who haven't seen steady
work since the War ended."

She left McIntyre to his reading.

The stolen Dodge Brothers automobile had been found abandoned.
The two killers were still at large. The article took pains to remind read-
ers that this was only the latest in a series of robberies and murders in
the city. Police Chief Tulley had declined comment on growing criti-
cism of his department, or on allegations that widespread wagering had
taken place at the fight.

A related editorial did not directly accuse Dantini of organizing illegal betting, but instead pointed out that multiplying the average ticket
price by the estimated attendance then deducting the winner's and
loser's purses, the costs of advertising, rental, ring construction, security
and fighters' travel and board would leave an honest backer with a siz-
able loss on the venture. It was a hopeless sermon, but the editor
seemed to delight in skewering the local sporting gentlemen as common fools. He closed with a suggestion that they might reduce their
future losses if the unnamed but widely known promoter were invited
to conduct his activities elsewhere.

McIntyre's breakfast arrived. He ate with his customary care, marked the price in his pocket ledger and went to call for the hat damaged during his foray into shanty town.

The haberdasher smiled apologetically when he presented his invoice. "The dirt was ground in with considerable violence. A lesser quality article might not have been worth the expense."

McIntyre paid and wrote the amount. With his familiar hat, he put on a visible sense of ease. He folded the snap brim cap double and put it into his overcoat pocket. It made a bulge and part of it stuck out.

"Is there a library in town?"

"Yes, sir. Two blocks west and turn right. It's a light blue building. An old house, with white trim."

"Thank you."

"They were going to build a proper one," the haberdasher said. "Had the plans all drawn. Had a lot of big plans for this city, once. Then the War ended."

"Yes, it put a lot of soldiers out of work, too."

"Made anarchists and thugs out of them," the haberdasher declared. "They went off to make the world safe for democracy, and came back to prowl the streets threatening to do here what they did in Seattle."

"Have you been asked for protection money?"

"A contribution, they called it. I wouldn't pay. I know a racket when I see one."

"Did you report them to the police?"

"It's not against the law to ask for money."

"They made no threats?" McIntyre asked.

"Not in so many words."

"What did they say?"

"They talked about how a store owner might want friends in the right places when the strike came. It was plain enough what they meant."

"Has anyone paid?"

"Not yet. The whole city is waiting to see what happens."

McIntyre thanked the man and left.

The woman on duty at the library was an inquisitive soul. She peered at McIntyre without recognition.

"May I help you, sir?"

"I understand a Federal investigation of Aaron Crowder was written up recently in the Denver newspaper."

She had a well-read copy immediately at hand. "I don't know what's to become of us. The city brim-full of Bolsheviks and now the newspaper saying Mr. Crowder cheated the government in the war."

"When the mighty have fallen," McIntyre said, "the meek shall inherit the earth."

He selected a table where he could sit with his back to a wall and watch the door. After a quick glance to be sure the Librarian was occupied, he slipped his .38 automatic into the side pocket of his overcoat. The soft bulge of the snap brim cap smothered the outline of the weapon. He draped the coat over the chair next to him and pushed aside a display copy of the latest *Tom Swift* adventure so he would have room to spread the Denver newspaper and a week's worth of local editions.

The article on the depot robbery told him nothing he had not learned from Mortimer Jason's summary of Christopher Floyd's notes. Front page coverage of the express car robbery was long on sensation and short on fact. It hinted darkly that raiding a locked car without attracting attention required inside knowledge, if not outright connivance. The report on Floyd's death speculated that he was killed pursuing the bandits. It contained nothing to confirm or contradict Hennessey's claim that his sentry had seen a car bring Floyd's body to Hatcher Street. McIntyre put aside the local papers for the Denver edition.

Aaron Crowder's photograph appeared on the front page, over the opening paragraph of a feature article citing confidential sources close to a Federal investigation of war profiteering. Crowder had operated

several factories producing the pedestrian essentials of war, from soldiers' leggings to ration tins. His government contracts and sub-con-
tracts called for him to be paid his cost of manufacture plus five
percent. It was a perverse system, which dictated that the more he
could contrive to pay for his labor and materials, the more profit he
would realize. The article suggested he had gone beyond simple infla-
tion, enrolling phantom employees and buying at exorbitant prices
from suppliers he secretly controlled. The article, published ten days
prior to the express car robbery, hinted at a mystery witness and an
imminent indictment. The matter was notable in Denver because
Crowder sat on the board of directors of a bank there. A separate editorial called for his resignation.

McIntyre returned the newspapers and asked directions to the leading bank. At six stories, its headquarters was the city's tallest building.
He began his inquiries in a high-ceilinged street level branch and
presently found himself seated in front of an imposing desk in a top
floor executive office.

Webster P. Horn, Senior Vice President and Trust Officer, scowled at
McIntyre's business card. "This is the most singularly uninformative
presentment I have ever seen."

McIntyre brushed an imaginary speck of dirt from his sleeve and
offered no reply.

Webster P. Horn was a big man, going corpulent as his slicked-back
hair faded to gray and receded. His thickening neck bulged out over a
tight collar.

"You," he said, pointing the card at McIntyre, "have been asking
impertinent questions."

"I'm merely trying to ascertain the facts surrounding a recent loss
suffered by the Railroad."

"You specifically asked when the bank was notified of a cash shipment arranged by Aaron Crowder," Webster P. Horn said hoarsely,
"implying that information used by thieves came from this institution."

"I inquired because I believe I can eliminate the bank from any such consideration."

"Well, it so happens you are correct. The funds were already enroute when Mr. Crowder notified me that he would require a secure facility to store the currency."

"Store the currency?" McIntyre asked. "Do you mean just lock it up?"

"Yes." Webster P. Horn's patience was eroding rapidly.

"Didn't you advise Crowder to place it on deposit where it could earn interest?"

"When a businessman of Mr. Crowder's acumen and experience encounters a unique set of circumstances, such as the current labor difficulties, it is the policy of the bank to defer to his judgment and provide such assistance as we can."

"Meaning he turned you down without saying why?"

"I believe," Webster P. Horn said with icy indignation, "that I have satisfied any legitimate concerns in this matter. If you will kindly excuse me?"

A uniformed police officer waited in the outer office. A thick black mustache reinforced his stern visage.

"Is your name McIntyre?"

"Yes."

"Chief Tulley wants you."

"Has something happened?"

"Spread your arms."

"Excuse me?"

"Spread your arms. I'm to make sure you're not carrying a concealed weapon."

McIntyre complied. The officer began to pat him down. Webster P. Horn's private secretary was appalled. Such undignified behavior just didn't happen in her domain. She tapped her pencil impatiently on the desk. The officer gave her a brusque look. Her eyes went cold with disapproval. The officer finished his search more quickly than he had started.

McIntyre retrieved his topcoat from a rack and put it on. The officer noticed the bill of the cap sticking out of the pocket and didn't investigate the bulge there any further. He and McIntyre beat a hasty retreat.

"I'm sorry, Officer," McIntyre said as they got on an elevator. "I didn't catch your name."

"Cavanaugh." He pressed the lobby button firmly to let the machine know who was in charge. "You wasn't too bright, walking into a bank and asking a bunch of questions. They called up the station to see if you was on the level and the Chief sent me out to pick you up."

"I had no idea anyone was looking for me."

"The call went out an hour ago. The whole department has been turning the city on its ear trying to find you."

"Why?"

"You'll have to talk to the Chief about that."

The police Ford at the curb started on the first turn of the crank. Cavanaugh sat importantly behind the wheel. He drove with scrupulous regard for the law and glowered at any motorist who showed impatience. Parking behind the City Administration Building, he took McIntyre directly to the Police Chief's office.

Tulley looked up from a report he was filling out. "You search him?"

"Didn't find no gun, Chief."

Cavanaugh closed the door on his way out. McIntyre hung his coat and hat on the clothes tree in the corner. He went to a chair in front of the desk and paused politely, waiting for an invitation to be seated.

"You're the cool one," the Police Chief rumbled. "I got to give you that."

"Excuse me?"

"Maybe you figured old Virgil Tulley wouldn't never call Chicago? Wouldn't never check you up with the law there?"

"I can't imagine what the Chicago Police would have to say about me."

"Mostly how they hit a brick wall every time they tried to put you back in the crazy house."

Blood drained from McIntyre's face. He sat down unbidden rather than collapse. His breathing was shallow, his voice defensive.

"I was released by court order."

"The Chicago Police said you was more dangerous when you come out than you was when you went in."

"Two psychiatrists testified to my sanity."

"Chicago PD said they come within an eyelash of proving an ambush in the railroad yards against you about a year back."

"That was something the Chicago Police either couldn't or wouldn't handle. Someone had to stand up and take responsibility."

"There's no use pretending you ain't crazy, McIntyre. One killing has been proved on you, and I know there's been more. Maybe you can tell me how many?"

"I'm not sure." McIntyre's words were scarcely audible.

"So many you lost count?"

"It's time I lose. I'm never sure how much. I've no idea what I've done."

Tulley sighed heavily. "You're too sick to be walking around loose. I reckon you know that."

There was a knock at the door and the desk officer came in. He brought a set of legal-sized papers to Tulley's desk, passing McIntyre without looking at him.

"I never typed up nothing like this before, Chief, but I done like you said and called the Prosecutor's office and this is what they told me it ought to look like."

Tulley waited until the man was gone. "We'll hold you here until we get the transcripts from your proceedings in Chicago," he told McIntyre. "Then we'll have us a hearing."

McIntyre ran his tongue across dry lips. "You won't get anything from Chicago. The transcripts are sealed by court order. The Railroad won't let them out."

"We got doctors here, if need be."

"You can start a fight with the Railroad, but you can't win it," McIntyre warned.

"I ain't picking no fights," Tulley said. "Just doing my job."

"The Railroad sees your job as removing the Bolshevik threat."

"Is that the reason you snatched Hennessey's sweet pea out of shanty town and left me to clean up the mess."?

McIntyre got as far as, "The Railroad—" before Tulley's statement registered. "What mess?"

"Hennessey found out it was Luther Grimes sent you into shanty town. He made a try for Grimes this morning."

"Do you mean tried to kill him?"

"Grimes ain't so old and slow as he seems," Tulley said, "but his driver caught a head full of buckshot. Gent name of Rufus."

McIntyre winced.

Tulley relented with an uncomfortable shrug. "I ain't holding you to account. Even if you was right in the head, you mightn't have seen what you was starting."

"How do you plan to handle the situation?"

"Well, I got the Mine Police settled down, so's they don't go barging into shanty town and get someone else killed. I got Grimes to agree to spend his nights up at the mine offices, where there's a guard on him and plenty of light to see trouble coming. Leastwise until I can pull Hennessey in and set him to rights on how he behaves in my town. And now I got you in custody so's Hennessey can't add you to his list, nor vice versa."

"What about the rest of the people in the city? Are you just going to leave them to Hennessey's tender mercies?"

"Folks in this city got more to fear from their friends and relations than Hennessey," Tulley said. "Read any police day book and you'll see all the newspaper Bolsheviks and dime novel master crooks don't hold a candle to the damage done by them you'd call good folks until they lost hold of themselves."

"Hennessey is still a killer."

"Hennessey done what he done. He'll answer up to the law for it."

"Just deliver him to the eastbound train," McIntyre said. "I'll take him off your hands. You won't see either of us again."

"You figuring on putting a bullet in the back of his head, like you done that gent last night?"

McIntyre fidgeted under the Police Chief's scrutiny, but admitted nothing. "Have you identified the fellow yet?"

"He wasn't carrying nothing to say who he was nor where he come from. When we get the coroner's photo, we'll circulate it and find somebody who can give us a line."

"Send one to the New York Police," McIntyre suggested. "Ask if they can connect him to a man named Joe 'the Boss' Masseria. I'm told he's the one who provides Dantini with thugs."

"That don't explain the tramp you killed the night before."

McIntyre's throat tightened.

"Did you figure none of them hoboes we rousted would give a good description of you?"

McIntyre had no answer.

"You been here two nights, and killed two men."

McIntyre looked helplessly into his lap. "I didn't ask to be the way that I am. Any more than a blind man or a cripple asks to be what he is."

"Blind men and cripples got the moral sense to know what's right and what ain't."

"So do I," McIntyre said hotly. His voice fell to a haunted whisper. "In spite of everything."

"All you're doing is pretending you're normal folks and hoping nobody notices otherwise."

"I'm doing my best to manage my condition."

"You can't play act your way through life feeling sorry for yourself."

McIntyre's eyes fidgeted, trapped and desperate. "I don't want to go under the surgeon's knife. I don't want to spend the rest of my years as a vegetable."

"I got my responsibilities," Tulley insisted. "This—"

The telephone on the desk buzzed with the uneven ring of an inside call. The Chief lifted the earpiece and set it down immediately to silence the instrument.

"This here's my city, and I—"

The telephone interrupted again. Tulley snatched the earpiece up angrily.

"I said no calls. Ain't that plain enough for you?"

McIntyre risked a glance at his coat hanging in the corner, at the pocket that held his pistol.

"All right, put him through," Tulley said, and drew McIntyre's attention back to the telephone call. "Yes, Mr. Crowder...McIntyre?" The Chief glanced up. "He's right—What?...What?" A minute of stunned attentiveness. "Yes...Yes, I'll bring him...Yes, right away."

Tulley cradled the earpiece as if he were handling fine china. He returned McIntyre's questioning gaze with a disbelieving stare.

"Young Geneva Crowder has been took by kidnappers."

The news jolted McIntyre to his feet and left him unsure of what to do next. Tulley heaved himself out of his chair. He unlocked his closet, retrieved his Stetson and overcoat and locked up again.

"We're going up there. The both of us. Old Man Crowder wants to see you as well." Tulley clapped the Stetson on his shaggy head and eyed McIntyre while he wrestled the coat on. "I reckon you'd only lie if I asked why."

"I don't know why." McIntyre collected his own hat and coat.

The Police Chief yelled his destination at the man on the desk. The huge Packard waited in the rear yard like some great living beast, drizzle clinging to it like sweat and thin clouds of steam rising from the warm hood.

Tulley backed to the street, cut in the siren and opened the twelve-cylinder motor.

CHAPTER 13

Tulley cut the siren and moderated his speed as he drew into the city's exclusive residential neighborhood. Important people lived here. The need to keep trouble as quiet as possible infected everyone down to the crudest retainer.

A Mine Police guard held open the iron gate of the Crowder estate with nervous glances at the street. Geneva's Austro Daimler was coming home on the hook of a ponderous Kelly-Springfield tow truck. The truck filled the winding driveway between thick hedges and forced the Packard to follow at five miles per hour.

Tulley ground the transmission into its lowest gear. "Damn fool idiots. They should've left the car where they found it."

"Where was that?"

"How the hell would I know?"

The Austro Daimler rode backward on the hook. A smooth coat of drizzle glistened on the hood, indicating the engine had been cold for some time.

"Why tow it?" McIntyre asked. "It's in perfect condition."

"Old man Crowder probably don't want it messed up by some clumsy ox who don't know how to drive it. Damn fool cheapskate probably had it brought in so's the leather wouldn't get rained on. You wouldn't think he'd have to pinch pennies, living like he does."

Ornate and steeply gabled, the Crowder mansion loomed over an acre of manicured landscaping, imposing its presence on all who came. Streamers of sunlight filtered through slow moving clouds and shifting patterns of shadow infused the great house with a dark, disturbed life.

Tulley drew up in front, killed the engine and threw a warning look at McIntyre. "You're to keep shut unless you're spoke to. You're here because old man Crowder wants it that way. You got no part in this."

He clumped up onto the wide porch and thumbed the doorbell importantly. A brief diminuendo of musical notes mocked his authority. The maid let them into the entry hall. Her sorrow was a visible burden.

Tulley handed over his coat and Stetson with a reassuring smile. "Don't you worry none, Mum. We'll get her back, right enough."

She gave him a pitying look.

McIntyre surrendered his hat and overcoat. If the maid noticed the weight of his pistol in the pocket, she gave no sign. He followed Tulley to the door to Crowder's study. When a respectful knock went unanswered, they went in.

The Industrialist sat inert behind his massive desk. A high-backed leather chair kept his slack and stricken bulk upright. A stiff wing collar pinched the folds of his neck and forced him to hold his head erect. His face was as gray as the cold ashes in the fireplace.

"What have I done to God?"

The question was hollow rhetoric more than acknowledgement that someone had come. Tulley stood before the desk and spoke in a quiet, sympathetic rumble.

"Mr. Crowder, I want you to know I'm going to do whatever it takes to bring your little girl back."

"What have I done that He would deal me this way?"

Tulley drew a chair close to the desk and sat down. "I need you to tell me everything. Tell it any way that comes to you, but tell it all."

A flicker of resistance stiffened Crowder. It was the visceral reaction of a man not accustomed to taking orders, half remembered from times of strength. It passed, and he sagged back to inertia.

"My Geneva went for a drive before breakfast," he said, either not aware or not caring that McIntyre had drawn up a chair and was eyeing him closely. "She loves to drive. Loves that yellow car of hers. She'd tell me about it sometimes. How it felt to her. Running with her lights out. As fast as she could go, on the most treacherous road she could find, with only the glow of false dawn to guide her. When she didn't return, I had visions of a horrible accident. I sent the Mine Police out to search. They found her car where she had been overtaken and forced into a ditch. There was a note of ransom attached to the spark lever."

"A note?" Tulley demanded.

Crowder lifted a rough-edged brown sheet from the desk blotter. He handled it only by the corner, as if it carried contagion, and passed it across to the Police Chief with a hint of palsy. The contents were cut from a newspaper and pasted clumsily.

> get HUNDRED thousand
> noon
> walk east on linCoLN
> no police or never SEE girl again

McIntyre craned for a look. "Did you say that was on the spark control of your daughter's car?"

Crowder fixed baleful eyes on him.

"That car still had a coat of drizzle on it when it was towed in a few minutes ago," McIntyre said. "Shouldn't cheap newspaper ink have run?"

Tulley held the paper to the light. There was no sign of water spotting. He turned suspicious eyes on McIntyre.

"What are you trying to say? Talk plain."

"An Austro Daimler could run the wheels off anything in the county. The idea that Crowder's speed crazy daughter was chased down by road agents doesn't even qualify as a dream."

"She could've been surprised and blocked off."

"From her father's description, she was riding with Satan at her shoulder and a death wish in the jump seat. She would have kept her foot down and either scared your road agents out of the way or taken them to hell with her."

"That ain't what he said," Tulley retorted. "That's just your crazy way of thinking."

"Geneva's a troubled woman," McIntyre insisted. "That's not just my opinion. I heard it my first day in town, before I met her."

"That's damn fool gossip. Geneva's just young. Maybe a little high strung."

"Then her father has been paying psychiatrists for nothing."

Tulley warned McIntyre to silence with a sharp glance. "I reckon you got the money together, Mr. Crowder?"

"A hundred thousand dollars?" the Industrialist asked helplessly.

Disbelief brought the Police Chief to his feet. "You're a rich man. This is your little girl's life."

"I had that much, once, but the Railroad lost it." Crowder's eyes were a silent demand that McIntyre make good.

"Can't you borrow it?"

"Against what? My home is mortgaged. The Jade Elephant is mortgaged. My assets are pledged. All to support men who can think of nothing but striking against me."

"The express car money was insured," McIntyre reminded him. "Can you borrow against your claim?"

"Not until the insurance investigation is complete and the claim is validated."

Tulley shifted his bulk impatiently. "But this here's a special circumstance. There's got to be some way of getting the money to get your girl back."

"I called the Chairman of the Railroad to ask if his firm would guarantee a loan," Crowder said as a measure of his efforts. "He gave me McIntyre instead."

"What do you mean, he give you McIntyre?"

Crowder reached down beside his chair and lifted a satchel onto the desk. "McIntyre will carry this east on Lincoln Avenue. When he is contacted, you and your men will apprehend the fellow and make him tell where my Geneva is."

Tulley opened the satchel. He fished out a banded stack of banknotes and flipped through it.

"Singles with a twenty dollar top card."

He checked another, then another.

"They're all the same."

"Nearly six thousand dollars in total."

"That ain't but a fraction of the ransom."

"One dollar bills are identical in all but detail and denomination to twenty dollar bills." Force had returned to Crowder's voice. He had a plan. He was warming to the idea that it would work.

The Police Chief shook his head. "First concern in a kidnapping is the life of the victim. The procedure is to pay up and get the victim home safe, then catch the perpetrators. If you're not of a mind to believe me, you can phone up most any police department in the country and hear the same thing."

"Move quickly," Crowder instructed. "Don't allow the kidnappers' contact more than a cursory look in the satchel. He certainly won't be able to tell the amount of money by looking at the outside."

"It'd be better if we could find a way to pay up. We can always arrest these jaspers later."

Blood rose in Crowder's face. "The contact must be taken alive."

"That's a damn sight easier said than done. And even if we pull it off, we may just get us some messenger boy that don't know nothing."

Crowder surged to his feet. "You listen to me, Policeman. I've tolerated your stalling and tolerated your bungling and watched this city carried to the very gates of Hades while you stood by and did nothing. But I will not tolerate the loss of my daughter. You will do as I say, or I will have you before the City Council on charges of dereliction and incompetence."

"Now look here, Mr. Crowder, I ain't saying you ain't got a right to be upset, but—"

"Time is short. There is a telephone in the foyer. You may use it to alert your men."

Tulley rolled his hands into tense fists. He and Crowder glared at each other across the massive desk. No word came from Crowder. He was through arguing.

Tulley let out a grudging sigh. "All right, McIntyre. I reckon we got our marching orders."

"McIntyre stays," Crowder told the Chief. "I want to talk to him."

"That ain't such a good idea, Mr. Crowder. McIntyre ain't exactly—"

"Get out of this room and get about your work, Policeman. Or I will call the Mayor and have it done by your second in charge while you attempt to prepare what will certainly prove an impossible defense."

Tightly bridled anger chiseled hard lines into the Police Chief's face. He collected the satchel and lumbered out, closing the heavy door behind him.

Crowder fixed hot, savage eyes on McIntyre. "Where is my money? Where is the money those damned thieves took from the express car?"

McIntyre's need for logic and order was stronger than any fear he may have felt. "Why did you put that much currency at risk?"

"You know where it is. You told Geneva as much."

"Did you send her?"

"You do know where it is. You were not just lying to impress her. She would have seen through that very quickly."

"She seemed genuinely afraid of you."

"What kind of man are you? My Geneva's life is at stake. That money could buy her back."

"I know something has happened," McIntyre said. "I can see that much in your face. But I don't for a minute believe this kidnapping fairy tale."

"Why do you question me in my time of grief? Has madness consumed your soul?"

"Geneva told me about you."

Crowder drew himself up indignantly. "I am without sin. I am forgiven as Lot was forgiven when he took the pleasure of his daughters after his wife fell into the corruptions of Sodom and Gomorrah and was gone from him."

The revelation startled McIntyre to his feet. "You used her?"

"I am her father."

"No wonder she doesn't know the limits of right and wrong."

"Geneva's corruption was not of my making. I have hewed unto scripture in raising her. I have done my best to shield her from the loose morals of our time. But what chance did I have? In my youth, a woman's ankle could be seen by none but her lawful husband. Lewd dances like the *Foxtrot* would have meant banishment from decent society. Now such displays are the public norm, and tame in comparison with the depravity played out in darkness on the screens of moving picture houses."

"Plenty of girls have heard the band play *The Vamp* without going to hell." A shiver of disgust ran through McIntyre's words.

"The hand of the Lord will strike them down!" Crowder roared with sudden vehemence. "His wrath will lay low the wicked and sinful. Swift and terrible will be His vengeance."

"I imagine He'll have something in store for the two of us as well."

Crowder's eyes narrowed to shrewd slits. "You forget I know the chairman of your damned Railroad. I will tell him you refuse to return my money."

McIntyre removed his spectacles and began his ritual cleaning. "Go ahead. You've a telephone on your desk."

"Damn you, McIntyre. What is it? The ransom? All right, you won't have to carry it. One of Tulley's policemen can do that."

"I'll carry it," McIntyre said. "Because it will take me a step closer to the truth." He replaced his spectacles. "And when I learn the truth, everyone will learn it."

"You are insane, McIntyre. Condemned so by a court of competent jurisdiction. Tell me where my money is or I will have you thrown into the worst snake pit in Colorado."

McIntyre paled, but his eyes held steady under Crowder's threatening glare. He let silence speak for him.

"Why are you obstructing me? What can you hope to gain? To take my money for yourself? You know I would hunt you to the ends of the earth."

"The Chief of Police is in your foyer," McIntyre reminded him. "If you think I'm obstructing anything, you can come with me and tell him about it."

Tiny sputtering noises made their way between Crowder's tightly clenched teeth. "Get out!" were the first actual words he was able to articulate. He leveled a finger at the door. "Get out of my home and find your destiny."

The maid was waiting in the entry with McIntyre's coat and hat. His pistol still made weight in the coat pocket. The woman glanced uneasily at Tulley. The Police Chief stood with his back turned, using a telephone.

The maid's words to McIntyre were low and accusing. "She depended on you. Miss Geneva. She told me so."

"What happened to her?"

"She'll have no more disappointment from men, God rest her poor soul."

"Dead?" McIntyre paled.

"You have a hand in the deed."

"No," he insisted.

"You who let her down."

"What did she expect of me?" McIntyre asked urgently.

"Soon enough you'll be able to ask her yourself." The woman went to station herself at the door.

McIntyre used a mirror to check his appearance, fussing with his hat, his topcoat, his tie; all without satisfying himself. A tic had developed at the corner of one eye.

Tulley finished his telephone conversation. He nodded curtly for McIntyre to follow him. The maid opened the door for them. She gave McIntyre a final accusing look, unseen by Tulley, then closed the door as reverently as she might bring down the lid on a coffin.

The Police Chief checked his watch on the way to the Packard. "Fifteen minutes of noon. When I drop you off, walk slow and deliberate. You'll be covered, but don't look for nobody."

McIntyre said nothing. His face was taut and bloodless.

Tulley got the car underway. "You hearing me?"

"I'm to walk slowly and deliberately."

"I reckon you got call to be scared," Tulley conceded. "Don't know as I'd be none too steady myself, doing what you got to do. But you understand why it's got to be done?"

"I don't understand any of this. The kidnappers have miles of lonely road to transact their business. Why collect their ransom on a city street?"

"It's too late for questions. What's got to be done, you'll just have to do. There ain't no getting out of it."

The Packard cleared the gate and Tulley used the accelerator.

"It's okay to look scared," he said. "It's okay to look like you're trying to hide it. Either one will seem natural to anyone watching."

"I'm no actor. I've never been able to fool anyone but myself." The tic was gone from the corner of McIntyre's eye. Color was returning to his face.

"If there's shooting," Tulley went on, "take cover right away. It'll be up to me and my men to pin the gent down and take him alive."

"How badly does Crowder want to get rid of you?"

"That part of it don't matter. Leastwise not until we get young Geneva back. She's the one we got to worry about now."

"Is there anything special about Lincoln Avenue?" McIntyre asked.

"I been thinking on that one myself. Far as I know it's just another street."

"Was it named for Abraham Lincoln?"

"Most likely."

"If I remember my history correctly," McIntyre said, "Lincoln was shot in the back of the head while he was watching a second rate stage show."

"What's that got to do with anything?"

"I wonder what kind of show you and I are watching."

"This ain't the time for crazy talk."

"People do that," McIntyre insisted. "They give away their intentions with little slips they don't even notice. It's more common than you'd think."

Tulley drew a deep breath. "Look here, McIntyre, I know you ain't got much to look forward to, but if this goes right, I'll talk up for you at your hearing. I reckon Crowder will have something to say too, if you help him get his girl back. When he talks, folks hereabouts listen."

"So I gather."

McIntyre slipped his hand into his coat pocket and ran his fingertips over the cold, smooth steel of his automatic.

CHAPTER 14

The ransom note said only, 'walk east on Lincoln.' No starting point was given. Tulley followed a dirt road that curled along the western fringe of the city.

"What'd old man Crowder want?"

"The express car money."

"Damn skinflint." Tulley's knuckles were white as he gripped the steering wheel.

"Is he really down to his last six thousand dollars?"

"How the hell would I know? I'm only the damn Police Chief around here."

"You know this is the wrong move. You told Crowder as much."

"We got no choice." Tulley brought the Packard to a stop where Lincoln Avenue began. "Young Geneva's depending on us."

"You'd better watch your own back as well as mine," McIntyre warned.

"Just you do what the damn note says. Don't try no fancy shortcuts. You'll answer to me if things don't go like they're supposed to."

McIntyre climbed down from the Packard and shut the door with a soft, solid thud. The huge sedan moved away, silently gathering speed, and vanished around a curve. The last fragments of sunny sky were swallowed by clouds thickening into the uniform overcast prized by expert riflemen as ideal shooting light.

McIntyre took out his watch. The measured sweep of the second hand held him mesmerized. When the three hands stood precisely vertical, he replaced the watch and set off along Lincoln, solitary and exposed, the presence and weight of the satchel in his hand obvious to anyone watching him.

This was an older area, with deep roots in a simpler, more self-reliant time. Lincoln Avenue meandered without clear boundaries, an earthen track beaten hard by horses' hooves and iron-rimmed wagon wheels. Buggies stood with their shafts down, canvas curtains lowered and lashed against the coming winter. Small, sturdy houses had outbuildings set discreetly back in yards large enough to accommodate orchards. No movement was visible down the rows of bare trees. No faces could be seen in the windows McIntyre passed, no sign of life except for stray tendrils of chimney smoke left over from the fires that had broken the morning's chill. The smoke put a tang into air rotten with the soporific sweetness that lingered in the aftermath of fruit cultivation.

McIntyre walked with sureness of purpose, watching carefully as he drew into the city but seeing nothing beyond the gradual change in his surroundings. Yards grew smaller and houses crept closer to the street. Blocks shortened. Concrete appeared underfoot. Then bungalows were packed shoulder to shoulder on city lots. Picket fences held back dogs that set up a racket at his passing.

A harried young woman came his way with a heavily laden market basket over her arm and a squalling pre-schooler in tow. She didn't look promising as a kidnappers' contact, but she was the first person McIntyre had encountered.

"Good afternoon," he said as she drew near.

She nearly pulled the child off her feet skirting around him. McIntyre shrugged contritely, as if he had simply been too forward. He could not see the fearsome brilliance of his own eyes.

Lincoln Avenue grew busier as McIntyre's stride carried him into more urban blocks. People passed on the sidewalk, smiling defensively when he looked at them or averting their eyes and scurrying on their way. Cars were parked at the curb. Vehicles moved in the street. An open cab delivery van idled past in the opposite direction, wire mesh surrounding a cargo area full of cardboard cartons. The driver peered at house numbers. A touring car honked impatiently, then chugged around the slow moving van.

McIntyre entered a block of seedy tenement houses. Flights of stairs ran up from the sidewalks. Windows were everywhere, like malevolent eyes. Small basement windows spied from just above the sidewalk. Apartment windows looked down from every angle. Loft windows lurked under the eaves, with everything that happened beneath spread out for them to see. Any one could hide a lookout. Or a sniper.

People crowded the sidewalk. Women with the threadbare urgency of too many children and too little money, others with the slatternly stare of lost hope, a few with the glaze of cheap cough medicine already in their eyes. None showed more than fleeting interest in McIntyre. His nerves frayed visibly at the random screeching of youngsters racing to and fro in the urgency of some mindless game.

From the street behind him came the heavy clop of an iron shod dray animal. A startled glance, then relief as a milk wagon drew past, not moving much faster than McIntyre's deliberate pace. The momentary scare revealed that he had fallen into a tactical error. He was walking with his left shoulder toward the street, so that the nearer lane of traffic approached him from his rear. A gunman in a slow moving vehicle could come up unseen, with only a single file of parked cars and random pedestrians as temporary impediments in his line of fire.

McIntyre picked up his pace, making for the intersection where he could cross to the safer side of the street. The milk wagon pulled to the curb ahead. He passed it watching the burly driver climb down. The man went toward the back of the wagon without noticing him or bothering to tether the horse.

"Hey, you!"

A voice from the street. McIntyre swiveled his head.

"Yeah, you with bag."

The delivery van that had passed earlier going the opposite way had turned and was idling along, matching its speed to McIntyre's. The truck stood seven feet tall, so that the driver sat up at eye level with McIntyre. A heavy-set man, squat and swarthy, with a thick mustache and black curly hair greased flat to his scalp, he wore a white tradesman's duster with a couple buttons adrift at his stocky midsection.

"Come here, huh?" Thick lips spread in an ingratiating smile. "Help me find place, will you?"

He held out a scrap of paper with something that looked like a crudely penciled address. As much as his manner suggested he was just another hard-working immigrant hoping for a sympathetic soul to aid him in his struggle with a new land and a strange language, his thickly accented voice marked him unmistakably as one of the men who had waited under the lumber yard office the night of the prize fight, one of the killers who had pursued McIntyre in the Dodge.

McIntyre slipped his hand into the pocket that held his automatic. A precautionary glance revealed no one who might have been the second killer. Stepping off the curb, he squeezed between the bumpers of two parked cars to reach the running board of the delivery van.

"Do you have Geneva for me?" he asked the driver hopefully.

The man's thick-lipped smile twisted itself into a sneer. "Put bag on seat."

"Not until I know she's alive."

"Do what I tell. Put money on seat."

"Did you kill her?"

The driver's smile returned, mocking and malicious. "I kill you."

From inside his duster he drew an abbreviated shotgun, a double-barreled model called an Auto-Burglar. Lacking a shoulder stock, the weapon had to be grasped by the pistol grip and the barrels to aim and fire. It was a clumsy process at best, more so in the confines of the truck cab. McIntyre thrust his automatic into the cab and fired point blank into the driver's face.

The high velocity bullet shattered bone and blew out teeth. A convulsive jerk of the man's trigger finger sent a charge of buckshot through the windshield, spraying shards of glass. He stumbled out the far side of the delivery van, his lower jaw torn loose at one hinge. The exit wound was an eruption of flesh littered with white fragments. His mouth hung open in an impossibly crooked leer. Blood welled copiously, dribbling from his meaty lower lip to stain the white duster.

For all its ugliness, the wound was little more than an annoyance to him. The nerves in his face were shredded to the point that he could not feel pain. His eyes were wild with outrage. That his own victim would dare to shoot him violated his most sacred sense of honor and fair play. He would exact a terrible revenge.

He raised the shotgun, backing away to widen the pattern of buckshot so he would not miss. Behind the van the untethered draft horse shied in the traces of the milk wagon. There was no one in the seat to restrain the massive animal. It started forward at its habitual plodding gait, pulling the wagon into the street. The van driver backed into the moving horse. The impact sent him staggering sideways.

McIntyre settled into a balanced target shooting stance. He extended his arm, aligning his sights through the open cab of the delivery van. His movements were deliberate and precise. His eyes, empty of fear or remorse, regretted only the haste of his first shot. This time patience would prevail. As soon as the wounded man found his footing and became a stationary target, McIntyre took the slack out of the trigger and squeezed.

The bullet took the man just ahead of the right ear. A piece of skull with black, greasy hair still attached to it blew away from the far side of his head in a gruesome spray of fluid and tissue. A final spasm lifted his bushy mustache like fur on the back of a startled cat and discharged the second barrel of the shotgun dangerously toward the crowded sidewalk. Then he went slack, collapsing like a rag doll into an inert mass on the pavement.

Lincoln Avenue turned to bedlam. Traffic stopped. Bumpers locked. Fenders crumpled. Horns blared. Women dashed from doors and snatched befuddled children to cover.

A police Ford careened around a corner a block away. Uniformed men balanced on both running boards, clinging to the top bows to keep from being spilled. Stalled traffic forced the police car to a stop. Officers jumped to the pavement and vanished among vehicles and frightened horses, making for the delivery van on foot.

Tulley's Packard rounded a corner from the opposite direction, its siren howling. A rifle barked three times, rapid fire. The Packard's windshield shattered. The heavy sedan swerved, jumping a curb and clipping a lamp post. It slammed into a parked car and came to an abrupt stop. Steam boiled from a smashed radiator.

The rifle fire had originated among the cartons in the back of the delivery van, close enough to punish McIntyre's eardrums. Following immediately was the voice of the second lumber yard killer. The words were foreign and frantic, probably notice to the driver to flee.

"Subito!" he yelled for emphasis.

When that produced no result there was movement in the rear of the van. Empty cartons spilled into the street as a strapping young tough clambered out of the sniper's nest. Olive complected and thickly mustached, his plaid coat and snap brim cap gave him a gaudy eastern look. He held a heavy .351 Winchester. Fear and confusion twisted his features. He had heard the blast of his partner's shotgun. He didn't understand what could have gone wrong. He saw McIntyre and stopped so quickly that he momentarily lost his balance.

The inertia of his opponent's rifle permitted McIntyre to bring his pistol to bear first. His snap shot broke bone going through the man's forearm and ripped into his side. The rifle clattered on pavement.

The man backed toward the cover of parked cars, clawing under his coat with his good hand. There was a sharp pop as he jerked a revolver from his belt. Blood appeared on his trousers. He seemed unaware he had wounded himself.

McIntyre's second shot took the young tough in the chest. The bullet punched through and broke the windshield of a car behind with a quiet tinkle. The tough blew a wild shot into the pavement. He stumbled backward until he collided with the car then sat down hard, his back against the bumper.

Blood soaked into his coat from the side wound. There was only a little capillary discharge from his chest wound. His lungs were collapsing under the sudden pressure in his punctured thoracic cavity and the inrushing air allowed no fluid to escape. He was no longer a threat, and would probably need immediate medical attention just to survive.

He mouthed what looked like the Italian version of the word 'assassin' as McIntyre advanced on him. He brought the revolver up feebly.

McIntyre shot him from a range of five feet. The bullet took him in the forehead, jerking his head back. He lolled against the car, his snap brim cap knocked askew by the impact. Water ran freely from a bullet hole in the radiator behind him, washing the corresponding hole in his head clean and carrying diluted blood down his face.

McIntyre pocketed his automatic. He stepped in and scooped the revolver from the concrete where the young tough had dropped it. Death had released the fallen man's sphincter muscles and voided his waste cavities. The odor was immediate and foul. McIntyre stepped back quickly and swallowed hard to keep his stomach down.

The first patrolman to reach McIntyre was Cavanaugh, the officer who had found him in the bank. He tugged the revolver loose from McIntyre's grip.

"You wasn't supposed to have no gun."

McIntyre didn't seem to be aware of the policeman's presence. He wavered and looked as though he might keel over at any second.

Cavanaugh caught his arm and shook him. "You've killed the both of them."

"Yes," McIntyre said, as if he remembered the incident only vaguely.

"How will we find the Crowder girl?"

"See you in Hell." The message McIntyre had purged from the mirror in his hotel room was still vivid in his mind.

"Talk sense."

McIntyre just stared.

The policeman shook him roughly. "Why'd you do it?"

McIntyre blinked. "What?"

"Why'd you kill them?"

"She's gone." He shook his head hopelessly.

"Come on," Cavanaugh ordered. "Come with me. You're going to have to tell the Chief about this. He ain't going to be happy."

Before he could urge McIntyre to movement, voices boomed out.

"Tulley's hit!"

"The Chief's down!"

Feet pounded toward the steaming Packard.

A woman tugged at Cavanaugh's sleeve and screamed incomprehensibly at him. She had a small boy by the hand. Blood poured down the child's face. For all its terrible appearance, it was a superficial injury. The child had no difficulty either maintaining his feet or howling at the top of his lungs.

A simultaneous commotion arose nearby. The milk wagon driver had caught up with his horse and seized its head harness. The frightened animal backed away, shying against the wagon shafts. The side force was too much. A wheel snapped. The top-heavy wagon tipped over and took the horse down with it. Milk spread into a pond in the street, filled with bits of broken glass. Empty bulk transfer cans rolled at will. The animal struggled to rise in its restraints.

A tiny girl just out of diapers toddled down off the sidewalk. "Horsie! Horsie!" she squealed delightedly, and made for the panic stricken animal with no sense of peril. She reached out a small hand, moving to get any opportunity to pat the thrashing dray animal.

Cavanaugh glanced around for help in controlling the situation. There wasn't any. The available policemen had run to Tulley's assistance.

He released McIntyre. "You better go sit in the patrol car." He hurried to pull the child back from danger, calling over his shoulder as he did, "Just sit there and wait. Don't try to go nowhere."

A gathering crowd made way to let McIntyre pass. He wandered past the empty police Ford, not even seeming to notice it, and wandered up onto the sidewalk. His absent shuffle attracted no notice from people hurrying to see what the commotion was.

He turned a corner and kept on walking. The fingers of his left hand began to trouble him. They had clutched the ransom satchel with such possessive fury that he now had to pry them loose one at a time. He took the satchel in his right hand, holding it loosely so it would not irritate the web of skin between his thumb and forefinger, still throbbing from the sharp recoil of his automatic.

McIntyre walked without purpose or destination, blinking occasionally to clear the fog of tears from his eyes, not bothering with the steam of exertion that had begun to condense on the lenses of his spectacles.

A light drizzle began, shrouding him in cold mist.

CHAPTER 15

In the failing light of dusk McIntyre took advantage of sidewalks clogged with homebound crowds to return to his hotel. He slipped in quickly, one hand on the pistol in his pocket. No one was waiting for him in the small lobby. He sank gratefully into a chair and rested his feet until Molly finished registering a short-tempered fat man.

She watched the new lodger upstairs and out of sight before she dared to speak. "Mr. McIntyre," she said in a low, fearful voice, "the police were here. 'Twas you they were asking after."

"How long ago?"

"More than an hour, it's been."

"What did they say?"

"They said there'd been a killing. They said for me to call the minute you come in. They said I'd be arrested if I didn't. That's what they said."

McIntyre peered past the window drapes. Lights moved in the gloom on the street outside, blinding any attempt to penetrate the deepening shadows.

"Did they leave anyone to watch the hotel?"

"They've not men to be watching here. Geneva Crowder's been took by kidnappers. They're looking all over the city for her."

McIntyre rose from the chair and stepped quickly to the desk, keeping his back to the window. "You let Geneva into my room last night, didn't you?"

The girl blanched.

"You've done that before, haven't you, Molly? Let her into men's rooms?"

"Who says?"

"Nobody is left to say now, Molly. Geneva is dead."

"No!" A fervent whisper that expired an inch beyond her lips.

A stricken nod was all McIntyre had to offer.

"He did it, didn't he?"

"Who?"

"Her father. Her greedy, filthy father."

"What did she tell you about him?"

"Private things." Her eyes grew hot and angry. "Dirty things."

McIntyre measured the unlovely and uncultured girl. "Why did someone like Geneva pick you to tell those things to?"

Molly drew herself up indignantly. "She just did. That's all."

"Did you tell her things?" Sympathy softened the question.

Gaunt cheeks burned a sudden, furious crimson beneath the acne scars, and there was no more secret to be kept. Her eyes fell to hide her shame.

"Didn't matter so much with me. I've not so much to be lookin' forward to anyway. Ain't no fellows sparkin' around lookin' to make a bride of the likes of me. Didn't matter so much I had to start makin' meself useful after me mother died."

She was on the verge of tears, but the street door opened and reminded her she had a hotel to attend to. She handed a key to a loudly dressed salesman and ignored a sly wink. When he was gone up the stairs, she went on in a haunted voice.

"Geneva, she was so pretty, so full of life. She could've married good. She could've been a fine lady. But that father of hers, he made her hate men."

"She'd seduce them and you'd tell on them?"

"We never done it to no decent men," she insisted. "Only them with their filthy suggestions and their hands wandering where they got no right to be."

"How much did Geneva tell you about me?"

The girl eyed him nervously. "She said you was—she said they once were keeping you in a place for people that was—"

"Insane," McIntyre said to spare her.

"But you must have got better?" she asked hopefully.

He shook his head. "My condition will never be cured."

"But they let you out. They wouldn't be doing that if you'd bring harm to anyone."

"I'm not a mindless lunatic," McIntyre said with quiet passion. "But no one cares about that. Or even listens. I was released only because the men responsible for holding me betrayed their trust for money."

The girl shivered and pulled her baggy sweater tight around her bony frame. "Did Geneva know that?"

"Geneva came to me because she was frightened."

"She was scared bad," Molly remembered. "She wouldn't say it, but I knew just from the way she talked."

"What did she say?"

"It didn't make no sense to listen to. She was talking terrible fast. Something about she just tried to do right, but she made a bad mistake."

"What mistake, Molly?"

"She never would say. She said I'd just get hurt if I knowed. She—"

The switchboard buzzed. Molly sat down and put on her headpiece. She pushed a spring loaded plug into a lighted jack.

"Paragon Hotel…Oh, hi…Yes, I know. They were here asking for him…Uh-huh. He's here right now, bold as you please, standing at the desk."

McIntyre stiffened.

Molly covered the mouthpiece. "Don't worry. It's just Iris. On the switchboard at the telephone company."

He forced a smile.

The girl went back to the phone. "Did they say anything about Geneva? Mr. McIntyre says she's dead...No, his eyes was as steady as Father O'Neill's for the saying of it...Okay. Call me back when you can."

Molly pulled the connection and removed the headpiece. She caught McIntyre glancing out the window.

"What is it you'll be doing? Now that you've got the devil nipping at your own heels?"

"That depends, Molly. Do you feel strong enough to give me some help?"

"What help would that be?"

"How late does Iris work tonight?"

"Until midnight. That's the shift change."

"Are the police call boxes routed through a switchboard she has access to?"

"The police boxes?" Molly's eyes filled with dread.

"I need to have them switched out of service at eleven o'clock tonight."

"Mr. McIntyre you can't be doing that. Them is for emergencies."

"I need to get a raiding party into shanty town tonight. The chances are we'll be headed off by the police if the call boxes aren't switched out."

"Raiding party?" A startled laugh sounded a prelude to the disbelief in her voice. "Where would the likes of you be getting such as that?"

"Will you call Iris for me?"

"Is it Mr. Floyd you're trying to settle for?"

"There's nothing I can do about Christopher Floyd. But maybe I can finish what Geneva started with the express car robbery."

"Geneva?"

"She didn't kill anyone," McIntyre said. "She thought it would be a simple robbery. But she fell in with some people who were expert enough to know exactly what had to be done, and either callous or desperate enough to do it."

"No!" the girl breathed.

"Think about it," McIntyre ordered. "Geneva wasn't really frightened until after the robbery, was she?"

"Did she say so much to you herself? Look me straight and tell me she did."

"I've spent all afternoon walking and thinking. It's the only possibility that makes any sense."

"It's just you thinking low of her because of what the two of you done," the girl said in a harsh whisper that could not be heard by the traveler who had just come in.

McIntyre feigned interest in a newspaper while Molly registered the man. Traffic had thinned on the sidewalk outside, and on the street beyond. Lacking distractions, any police patrol that happened by was sure to glance through the window into the lighted lobby.

Molly finished with the newcomer. He disappeared up the stairs.

McIntyre put the paper down. "Will you ask Iris about the call boxes?"

"What if there was bad trouble and someone needed help?"

"All I need is fifteen minutes. Is the phone building anywhere near Hatcher Street?"

"Not so near, but not so far either. 'Tis down by the Railroad, where the main wires come in."

"Close enough. Tell Iris to switch the boxes back into service when she hears gunfire."

The girl paled. "You'll be killed, like Mr. Floyd."

"Where did Floyd go the night he was killed?"

She shifted uneasily. "How would the likes of me be knowing that?"

"He had to ask directions, Molly. He would have asked you. He had to find transportation. He would have asked you where to get it."

"Can't you just leave this place?" she pleaded.

"Where did he go, Molly?"

"Dutch Mill Road." Her voice was barely audible.

"Where is that?"

"It runs east of town."

"A dirt road? Parallel to the railroad?"

She nodded. "I don't what he'd be doing there, though. Nothing but old cabins and a few folks that's lived hereabouts all their lives. Before the city was built, some of them."

"He was asking about a car on Dutch Mill Road, Molly. You know that, don't you?"

"Who says?"

"Christopher Floyd was your friend. You would have felt guilty when he was killed. You would have wondered if you had sent him to his death without meaning to, or knowing that you were. You know people who live on Dutch Mill Road. You would have gone to see them. To find out what happened to your friend."

Molly shuffled her feet and wouldn't meet his gaze. "There's an old Indian lady. She come to the school once to tell us about Cree customs. She don't get around so good no more, so some of the girls will shop for her sometimes."

"You know whose car was on Dutch Mill Road the day of the robbery, don't you, Molly?"

She bit her lip and a tear formed in the corner of one eye. "Better the haints had killed Mr. Floyd. There's nothing to be done for it."

"Who drove Floyd that night?"

"Mr. O'Haney. Him with the jitney, if you know who I mean."

McIntyre checked his watch. "I'm going up to get my bag. If O'Haney comes before I'm down, tell him to wait for me."

"No, Mr. McIntyre! For the love of God, No!"

"This has to be cleared up, Molly."

McIntyre waited until the Comstock jitney unloaded its passengers, then he stepped quickly from the hotel carrying his suitcase and the satchel that held Geneva Crowder's ransom. He got in back, where his face would be hidden in the shadows of the canvas top.

O'Haney turned in the seat and looked at his passenger. "You're wanted by the police. Ain't a cab driver in the city that don't know it."

"We'll be taking the same ride you took Christopher Floyd on just before he was killed," McIntyre informed him.

"Oh, we will, will we?"

"You were either too frightened or too savvy to come forward after Floyd was killed, and no one can blame you for that. But he will haunt you forever if you don't make some effort to square things for him."

"What would you know about it?"

"Drop me across from the depot and wait," McIntyre instructed. "I'll be only a few minutes."

Heavy traffic slowed their progress on Comstock. They passed a policeman directing cars at an intersection. O'Haney made no effort to attract his attention.

The depot was deserted but for the night telegrapher. The youth sat bolt upright when McIntyre carried his luggage in.

"H—hello, sir."

"I imagine the police have been here looking for me."

The youth tried to swallow his Adam's apple.

"I'll clear things up later tonight," McIntyre assured him.

"Mr. Knowlton said if you came I was to tell you Mr. Jason called. And that he wants to talk to you right away."

"Do you know who Jason is?" McIntyre asked.

"Yes, sir. He's—well, no, not exactly. But he's real important, the way Mr. Knowlton talked."

"I'm going up to Knowlton's office to call him. Do you suppose you could hold off calling Knowlton for a few minutes?"

"Yes, sir." A guilty flush heated the youth's face.

McIntyre went upstairs and locked himself into Knowlton's office. He opened his suitcase on the desk, retrieved a gun cleaning kit, field stripped his automatic and brushed on a light coat of nitro powder solvent. He let it soak in while he placed his call.

The hour was later in Chicago and the operator located Mortimer Jason at his home telephone number. Jason's normally composed purr was frayed and hoarse.

"Will you kindly tell me, Mr. McIntyre, what in the name of God is going on there?"

"Whatever it is, it's been done in the name of greed rather than God."

Soft music and a tinkle of feminine laughter came over the wire. The whoosh of a faraway pocket door muffled the background noise.

Jason's whisper returned, dry and dire. "Aaron Crowder's daughter has been kidnapped."

"According to Crowder," McIntyre said.

"Word has reached the Chairman that you bungled a ransom delivery. That you killed the kidnappers. That you executed them in cold blood, cutting off any hope of ever finding the girl."

"According to other information Geneva Crowder is dead. And probably was when the so-called kidnapping was reported. If her father wasn't personally responsible, he certainly knew the circumstances."

"Can you support that allegation?" It wasn't clear from Jason's uneasy tone whether he was worried that McIntyre might be an embarrassment because he could not substantiate what he was saying, or that he might upset the established order because he could.

"It stands up to logical examination."

"Logic will not be sufficient in this case. Aaron Crowder is a pillar of his community. Can you establish his complicity by the presentation of a detailed narrative supported by sound physical and parol evidence?"

"No."

Jason made his purr caustic. "Aaron Crowder also accuses you of taking indecent liberties with the girl."

Embarrassment and anger reddened McIntyre's face. "You're not getting the whole story."

"Are you aware that there is a police call out for you?"

"That's not important."

"Mr. McIntyre, I want you to listen to me, and listen carefully. You are relieved of your assignment. You are to return to Chicago by the first available transportation. The Chairman is worried that the Railroad may be compromised if you fall into the hands of the local authorities. I have instructed the Section Superintendent to render any assistance possible. Even if it means his own arrest. Do I make myself clear?"

"If I'm still alive tomorrow morning, I'll catch the first available train," McIntyre promised.

Jason made his purr conciliatory. "Mr. McIntyre, do not do anything desperate. Your relief from this assignment has been ordered to serve the best interests of the Railroad. It does not mean that you will be sent back to the asylum."

"I left a will in my desk at home. I think the neighbors will take my cat in, but if they don't I'll trust you to find her a good home."

"Are you contemplating suicide?"

"Maybe the Chairman's lecture on good and evil is beginning to sink in."

"Do not take the Chairman's remarks more literally than they were intended. You are an instrument of economic expediency. Not of social engineering."

"I'll call you tomorrow with the best news I can manage."

McIntyre hung up. He wiped his pistol and set to work oiling the moving parts. The phone rang, and kept on ringing. It happened too quickly for Jason to have gotten a ringback through the switchboard. McIntyre picked it up, just listening.

"Mr. McIntyre?" It was a woman's voice, young and hushed and secretive.

"Yes."

"Mr. McIntyre, this is Iris. At the switchboard."

"Yes, Iris." Eagerness made his words husky. "Did Molly talk to you?"

"She said you wanted me to switch out the police call boxes." Her voice was sure there had been a mistake.

"At eleven o'clock, Iris. Can you manage that?"

"What if there's an emergency?"

"Can you do it, Iris?"

"We talked about it, Mr. McIntyre. All the operators did. When the supervisor was out of the room." There was a long pause, followed by timid words. "Geneva Crowder really is dead, isn't she?"

"Did you know her, Iris?"

"She didn't talk to people like me. Only important, social people."

"Did you admire her?"

"We all did, I guess. All of us here. She could do the things she wanted. She wasn't afraid."

"Are you afraid, Iris?"

"It's been really scary ever since the labor trouble started. Our shift ends in the middle of the night. We have to walk home in the dark. We don't dare go alone."

"Switch the call boxes out at eleven, Iris. Keep them switched out until you hear sustained gunfire."

"From shanty town?"

"Perhaps we'll make it that far. More likely we'll be stopped in Hatcher Street. There will be enough shooting that you won't miss it."

"Molly is afraid you'll get killed."

"So am I, Iris."

"How come you're doing it?"

"Maybe to finish what Geneva started," McIntyre began, fumbling for words. "Maybe to make up for any part I may have had in her death. Maybe because this could be the only chance I'll ever have to stand up and count for something, instead of hunkering down and pretending I'm someone I'm not. My only chance to contribute something to society in return for all the grief I've caused. Don't ask me to explain it to you, Iris. I'm not sure I can explain it to myself."

Iris knew none of the context, but she could not have missed the throb of emotion in McIntyre's voice. "I hope you kill them all," she blurted, and rang off.

McIntyre's hands trembled as he reassembled and reloaded his pistol. He left his suitcase and the satchel of ransom money behind a file cabinet. There was no ambush waiting when he unlocked the door and stepped quickly out of Knowlton's office. Quiet, careful steps took him down the stairs. No trouble lurked in the waiting room. He winked at the telegrapher's worried expression.

"Tell Knowlton I'll see him later at the police station," he said, and left the depot.

O'Haney was still waiting across the foot bridge at the base of Comstock Street. Liquor had loosened his tongue without warming his blood. He was shivering and cursing the pride that had kept him there, cursing McIntyre for finding it.

"Dutch Mill Road and my duty you say it is. The devil will be wanting his due from you some fine black night."

"This fine black night." McIntyre climbed up beside the jitney driver.

"I'll ride you where I rode that Floyd fellow, him being a likeable sort and me being sorry for the harm that come to him, but I'll be having no part in any of your shenanigans."

"Fair enough," McIntyre said.

The Ford chugged along parallel to the tracks, past warehouses shut up for the night, past darkened factories and parked trucks, across the creek and past the smelter and the electric generating plant then out of the city.

The darkness of the forest closed around them, full of small, mysterious noises.

CHAPTER 16

Minuscule flakes of snow drifted in the headlight beams as the jitney chugged back into the city. A deepening chill had chased all but a few cars from Comstock and left only the odd pedestrian still visible under the street lamps. The vague glow of security lights marked the mine workings far up the mountain.

McIntyre stirred inside his overcoat and broke a moody silence. "Go on up to the mine office."

"Which one?" O'Haney asked.

"How many are there?"

"I don't know. I never counted." O'Haney turned down a side street.

"Where are you going?"

"Maybe you can get through a cold night with nary a stop, but there's some of us is human and can't. It pays a man in my business to know where the clean facilities are."

O'Haney brought the Ford to a wheezing idle in front of a modest hotel. He climbed down and went inside. McIntyre gave him a minute's lead then went in after him. The narrow lobby stood empty. McIntyre followed a discreet arrow back toward the men's room. The stalls were open and empty. O'Haney was nowhere in sight. McIntyre relieved himself and stepped out to wait in the shadows of a staircase.

O'Haney came down with the neck of a flat liquor bottle sticking out of his coat pocket. The bottle was fresh, its seal unbroken. Burton

Underhill came down with him, buttoning an overcoat. McIntyre trailed them silently out the door. The Insurance Investigator strode to the idling Ford and peered inside.

McIntyre stepped close and spoke quietly. "Go back up to your room and go to bed, Mr. Underhill."

The startled Insurance Investigator spun around, nearly losing his balance. He straightened to confront McIntyre with the full effect of his height and bulk.

"You proved the express car job on Luther Grimes," he said indignantly.

"You have been misinformed, Mr. Underhill."

"You went down Dutch Mill Road. You knocked on doors. You found witnesses."

"Not to anything done by Luther Grimes."

"You told O'Haney to take you up to the mines."

"I didn't tell O'Haney why."

"Either you're going to pinch Grimes, or Grimes is going to help you make the pinch."

"That is a dangerously poor guess, Mr. Underhill. Go back into your hotel and go to bed."

The Insurance Investigator leaned close enough to make a poor choice of cologne obvious. "O'Haney knows what doors you knocked," he said smugly. "I can knock the same doors and find out what was said to you."

"If I fail tonight, you should do just that tomorrow."

"I'm not sitting on my backside while you grab the credit. A piece of this arrest will give my career the boost it's been needing for a long time."

"I have no authority to arrest anyone. Nor do you."

"You're not going up to the mines to admire the view."

"I'm on my way to try something that may prove fatal even if it works. And I'm not sure how I'm going to make it work."

"You're in trouble with the law," Underhill reminded him.

"Another good reason to stay away from me."

"Either I go along, or I tell that so-and-so police chief what you're up to."

"Tulley was ambushed and shot this afternoon."

"Tulley walked out of the hospital an hour later," the Insurance Investigator said. "To hear him tell it, the whole thing didn't do more than make him hungry."

The soft clatter of the idling Ford was the only sound. Snowflakes drifting in the aura from curtained hotel windows had grown larger. Several settled on McIntyre's face, where they clung like the icy chill of truth.

"Do you mind riding in the front seat, Mr. Underhill? I'd rather not have you behind me."

"We'll both ride in back," the Insurance Investigator said generously. The springs of the Ford groaned in protest when he climbed up and plopped himself into the seat. He made a production of sliding over to make room.

McIntyre climbed in beside him. "Try the Jade Elephant first," he told the driver.

O'Haney made a U-turn back toward Comstock. "I drop you two off. I don't go no farther than the mine gate."

"Wait for us there," Underhill instructed.

"Drop us off and go visit the widow," McIntyre said.

"How do we get back?" Underhill asked.

"I'm not sure we will."

Hunched in his overcoat next to the corpulent Insurance Investigator, McIntyre was a small and forlorn figure. He declined a cigar. Underhill lit one for himself.

"Just for the record, McIntyre, who did pull the express car job?"

"Christopher Floyd probably thought it was that simple, too. He probably thought he could expose the bandits and that would end everything."

"What did that Floyd character know that none of the rest of us did?" Underhill asked.

"We're all working from the same information."

"I'm not stupid," Underhill said. "Neither are the Sheriff's people. We knocked doors on Dutch Mill Road and came up dry. You and Floyd went down there and scored right off the bat. Floyd knew something and he passed it on to you."

"The only thing I learned from Christopher Floyd was how easy it is to die in this city."

"I don't scare." Underhill patted the bulge under his arm.

"You might want to sit this one out anyway."

The Insurance Investigator sat back and laughed. "No chance," he said, savoring his cigar and his triumph. "You've got this case made. And you're taking Burton Underhill along for the ride."

The ride was slow and rough, up a rutted truck path. Snow began to dust the ground. A blur of light in the swirl of windblown flakes resolved gradually into a hooded electric globe illuminating a sturdy rail gate. O'Haney brought the Ford to a stop there. A man stepped out of a small guard shack, turning the collar of a sheepskin-lined coat up to the brim of his Stetson. He carried a heavy bolt action rifle. Dirty boots crunched frozen ground as he came to the running board.

"Turn it around, gents," he said in a rough-edged drawl. "No visitors allowed."

"My name is McIntyre. I'm looking for Luther Grimes."

The man put a boot on the running board and peered into the jitney. The arrival of well-dressed strangers on a snowy night was enough to make him leery.

"What do you want with Grimes?"

McIntyre glanced at telephone wires leading from the shack up through the blowing snow toward vague bits of light that suggested someone might be in the mine office above. "Aaron Crowder told me to check in with him. Would you call him, please?"

"You stay put." The guard went into the shack. He came out a minute later, opened the gate a couple of feet. "Walk on up. No cars."

McIntyre climbed down from the jitney and found precarious footing on rough ground. "It's not too late to go back, Mr. Underhill."

The Insurance Investigator brought his bulk down from the car and surveyed the barren slope around them with disdain. "Let's don't keep the man waiting."

McIntyre spoke quietly to O'Haney. "You were drunk tonight. You don't remember anything. Stick to that story, no matter how serious the charges are, or how many witnesses they come up with."

O'Haney's bluster vanished. His face was bloodless. He tried to put the Ford in reverse, and failed. With the realization that he was panic stricken came a look of shame.

"That Floyd fellow was all right," he said solemnly, "even considering what it was he done for work and who it was he done it for. I hope you kill them all."

He turned the Ford with as much dignity as he could muster and started back down toward the city. McIntyre turned his collar against the wind. He and Underhill watched the red pin prick of the Ford's single tail light recede into the falling snow.

The climb was steep, slippery and cold. A naked electric bulb burned at the entrance to a dark shaft, spreading the shadows of a huge flywheel over a chain of ore cars waiting for the morning shift. More light leaked out around the door of a low building. A lean, hawk-nosed man answered McIntyre's knock, working a plug of tobacco and peering out to be sure the night behind the two men was empty. He kept one hand on the butt of a holstered revolver while he let them in, then fastened the door against the chill.

Tarpaper lining the walls provided scant insulation. Streamers of icy air found their way in beneath the roof and imparted a gentle sway to a light bulb dangling at the end of an electrical cord. Under the light a time-keeper's table had been cleared to make room for two hands of cards. One belonged to the hawk-nosed man, the other to the little man named Walt, who had betrayed McIntyre to John Hennessey two nights before. Walt had retreated to a remote corner, where he fed wood to an iron stove that supplied the only heat.

Luther Grimes sat at a roll top desk, reading by the light of a goose-neck lamp. A half empty bottle of rye stood beside a porcelain mug. An army Colt automatic lay close at hand. He marked his place in a thick tactical history of the Great War, not something an unschooled man would attempt.

Leaning back in his squeaky wooden swivel chair, Grimes unhooked a pair of spectacles and considered the newcomers skeptically.

"Old Man Crowder sent you two?"

Candor filled one of McIntyre's rare smiles. "He told me to include you in anything I was planning."

"What have you got in mind?"

"Assuming there was a chance to raid shanty town in about an hour, how big a force could you raise?"

The shack fell silent. Satisfaction lit Underhill's small eyes and formed a smile around his cigar. The hawk-nosed man hit a fire bucket with his plug of tobacco. Little Walt stopped prodding the stove, listening but not daring to look.

Grimes had seen too many surprises to be put off balance. "Is this coming from Old Man Crowder?"

"From me," McIntyre said.

Grimes lifted his pipe from a pewter ashtray. "If I wanted to put myself out of a soft job, I couldn't think of a faster way to go about it."

"Mr. Grimes, would you kindly look around yourself and tell me what you see?"

Grimes maintained eye contact with McIntyre while he scooped tobacco from an oilskin pouch. "What am I supposed to see?"

"Your soft job is finished. John Hennessey has run you to ground. Aaron Crowder won't pay you to hide out in a tar paper shack on the side of a God forsaken mountain waiting for some scruffy tramp to kill you."

Grimes tamped tobacco into the bowl of his pipe with a stained finger, clamped the stem between yellow teeth, struck a match and drew smoke; all slowly and deliberately, poker faced, buying himself some thinking time.

"I suppose the city police will be playing canasta while we're shooting our way into shanty town?"

"We'll be finished before Tulley can react."

"You sound mighty sure for a man in as much trouble as you stepped into this afternoon." It was Grimes' turn to taunt, but he didn't seem to relish it.

"That couldn't be helped," McIntyre insisted. "This time surprise will be on our side."

Grimes shook his head, pity in his weary eyes. "There are only two ways into shanty town. If we went directly, by the foot path, Hennessey's people would see us coming. If we circled through town and came up Hatcher from the south, like you did the other night, the first beat cop to spot us would call it in. Tulley would be on us before we got close."

"Tulley's call boxes are going out of service at eleven o'clock."

McIntyre's eyes remained steady under Grimes' scrutiny. The silence between them was thin and taut, broken only by the sputter of damp wood in the stove. Walt brought a coffee pot over and filled Grimes' cup. Underhill smiled broadly to indicate he wouldn't mind some himself. He wasn't offered any.

Grimes shot a glance at him. "What do you think about all this?"

The Insurance Investigator's face was still flushed from the climb and the chill. "It sounds pretty dicey to me." He turned uneasy eyes on McIntyre. "There'll be questions if Hennessey gets killed."

"I don't mind questions," McIntyre said, "as long as I'm alive to answer them."

"Why not give this to the city cops? They can take Hennessey alive. That way we can sweat the location of the express car bundle out of him. He'll deal. They all do when they're facing the gallows."

Grimes let out a derisive snort. "Hennessey is a rabble rousing raga-muffin. He couldn't rob an express car if they left one open on an abandoned siding."

Underhill puffed out his chest. "We proved it on him. Me and McIntyre. We got witnesses. Ain't we, McIntyre?"

"Mr. Grimes is a authority on robbing trains," McIntyre said. "His word is good enough for me."

Underhill snatched the cigar from his mouth. "Well, then, what the devil are we doing here?"

Grimes' laugh was coarse and mocking. "McIntyre is no railroad detective. He's a strike breaker."

McIntyre ignored a startled look from the Insurance Investigator. "Mr. Grimes, this morning your driver was shot dead. Tomorrow it could be you."

The older man sagged back in his chair and smiled faintly. "Thirty years ago I'd've ridden into shanty town alone for the raw thrill of it."

"Hennessey isn't bluffing. Either we kill him or he kills us. He won't have it any other way."

Grimes glanced at his book of tactics. "A smart man bides his time until the odds are in his favor."

"A smart leader takes advantage of the opportunities that come his way."

"This ain't much of an opportunity."

"How many do you think you'll get?"

Grimes poured a jolt of rye into his coffee and drank. It didn't agree with him. He put the pipe into his mouth to draw comforting smoke. The pipe had died, along with the last of his arguments. The truth was in front of him. There was no place to hide.

Underhill saw the decision coming. He dropped his cigar on the floor and ground it underfoot.

"Count me out."

"You'll ride the lead car," Grimes told the Insurance Investigator. He pointed the stem of his pipe at the hawk-nosed man. "Get on the phone. Call the bunkhouse. Then call the mine gates. Tell them this one is for Rufus."

Grim light filled the man's eyes. He lifted the earpiece of a wall phone and used the crank.

"Walt," Grimes said, "you cover the saloons in town. Tell any of our people you find the same thing."

"Right, Mr. Grimes."

"But keep it quiet."

"Right."

"Then you get down to Hatcher Street. Get as close to shanty town as you can. Take a light with you and stay hidden. Keep a sharp watch. When you see us coming, flash two long if there's trouble, three short if it's all clear. Got it?"

"Two long for trouble, three short for all clear." The little man scuttled to retrieve his coat.

McIntyre went to warm himself by the stove.

Underhill sidled over. "What the hell are you doing?" he asked in a panicky whisper. "You said we were going to pinch the express car gang."

"No, you said that," McIntyre reminded him.

"You didn't say anything about this."

"I gave you all the argument I could afford to."

"Meaning you didn't want me shopping your plans all over town if I did decide to take it on the arches?"

"It might have been embarrassing."

"This could be fatal. You took Hennessey's sweetie out of shanty town two nights ago. That'll keep him spooked for at least a week. He'll be waiting for you to try again."

"He won't be disappointed."

"It's true, isn't it? All those stories from Chicago. You really are crazy."

McIntyre said nothing.

Luther Grimes rose stiffly and unlocked a chain securing a row of heavy Krag-Jorgensen military rifles into a wall rack. From one end of the rack he lifted a Lewis machine gun, an infantry assault model with a shoulder stock and a bipod supporting the shrouded barrel. The time-keeper's table creaked when he set down the ponderous weapon.

Underhill watched him in disbelief. "You used to ride with the Wild Bunch. Do you want to wind up like Butch Cassidy?"

"I wouldn't mind that at all."

"Cassidy got shot dead down in Bolivia."

"Cassidy owns a machine shop in Spokane. I had a drink with him a few months ago. On my way here."

Underhill stared, dumbstruck.

The first of Grimes' men clumped in. They were roughly dressed; keyed up, cursing and curious. Grimes told them to draw rifles and oil them for action.

McIntyre remained aloof, trying to close out the coarse language and crude behavior pressing in around him. Tension in the small muscles of his face indicated he was having little success.

Grimes sat at the desk, brushing oil onto the moving parts of his .45. "You two city slickers planned all this, of course. I thought I was doing my civic duty, helping you arrest Hennessey for the express car robbery. Why, I had no idea what was really on your minds until you pulled the guns you carry under those fancy coats and shot poor Hennessey dead right in front of me."

Underhill's eyes grew frantic.

"I'll do the shooting," McIntyre assured him. "I can't afford to have this bungled."

Grimes winked at the Insurance Investigator. "That gun is his equal-izer. It makes up for not being as big as other people. For not having friends to count on when he gets himself in trouble. For everything that's ever gone wrong in his life. All we have to do is point him in the right direction. He'll kill Hennessey and leave us in the clear."

Grimes' men continued to file in. Rifles were issued, lubricated and loaded. One man stayed in a corner, away from the stove, taping together three-stick dynamite bombs. McIntyre grew increasingly edgy and withdrawn. He spoke to no one and avoided eye contact, shifting aimlessly to stay out of the way. Control had passed to Luther Grimes. All McIntyre could do was wait to learn the outcome of what he had set in motion.

Grimes' instructions were succinct. Everything simple enough to remember and execute under fire, if need be. Three vehicles waited when the men filed outside. The hawk nosed man held open the rear door of the Maxwell touring car and motioned for Underhill to climb inside.

"Maybe I'll see you in Hell," the Insurance Investigator said bitterly to McIntyre.

"I'm sorry. I already have a date."

McIntyre was placed in the rear of Luther Grimes' Winton, between two huskies. Grimes sat in the front passenger seat, holding a .351 Winchester across his lap. The remaining men climbed onto the flat bed of a mine truck. The Lewis gun was set to fire forward to the right of the cab, just above fender level, with sandbags placed to protect it and drums of ammunition close at hand. In case of ambush, it would fire two to three round bursts along the right side of the vehicles ahead, to provide cover for the men in the cars to crawl out of the killing zone.

The Maxwell led the way down the hill. The pop and sputter of compression braking issued from its tired engine. The Winton followed with an almost ghostly silence. Behind it came the grumble of the heavy truck.

It was nearing eleven when the vehicles passed through the mine gate and spread out to convoy interval.

CHAPTER 17

The emotions preceding combat are eternal and unchanging. The last minutes before it begins bring a profound and lonely quiet. Men are drawn inward by what may be their final thoughts. Adrenaline sharpens the senses until every doubt and fear is magnified to grotesque proportion. The mind becomes an instrument of torture. Long forgotten times of beauty and tranquility rise up and beckon, eloquent arguments against risking the irreplaceable gift of life. Resolve begins to falter and souls cry out for the inevitable to come before it ebbs away entirely.

The convoy crept down Comstock at the heavy truck's agonizing maximum speed of fifteen miles an hour. Snow fell in earnest. Big dry flakes floated down through the glow of the street lamps, laying a blanket of white over the industrial patina of a city gone still and silent for the night. No other vehicles were abroad. Sparse tracks showed that few had passed in either direction since the snow had started to accumulate.

They passed a police foot patrol. The officer peered at the Lewis gun sandbagged on the flat bed of the truck and the riflemen huddled around it. Common sense prevailed over courage and he set off for the nearest call box.

The convoy turned to parallel the railroad. Its pace fell to no more than a brisk walk. Strong wind whistled through gaps between dark buildings that flanked the tracks, whipping powdery snow into a swirling mass and cutting visibility. The canvas top of the Winton billowed. McIntyre sank deeper into his coat.

The thug on his right found a half-smoked cigar in the pocket of a dirty coat and stuck it between thick lips. The flare of a match swooped and dove in the cup of his hands, refusing to maintain contact with the tip of the cigar. The match burned down to his fingers and he dropped it.

McIntyre wasted no time stepping on it. "That's a sack of dynamite bombs between your feet, if you've forgotten."

"If'n I don't get this dadgum stogie going, we ain't gonna have no way to start the dadgum fuses. If'n we need to. Which, from the look on Luther's puss, we're gonna."

On the next try McIntyre used his hat to the cut the wind. The cigar tip flamed briefly then glowed red. Malodorous smoke filled the rear of the Winton.

A scant hundred feet ahead the Maxwell could be seen only by its headlights and single tail lamp, a phantom turning onto Hatcher Street. Blowing snow covered its tracks before the Winton could reach them. If danger had passed that way a minute earlier, it would be obscured by the time the convoy arrived.

Snow stuck to the frozen glass of the Winton's windshield, obscuring everything outside the restricted arc of the single wiper. Grimes put his head out of the car. Using the wide brim of his campaign hat to shield his eyes, he scanned the margin of the street ahead.

Pinpricks of light made a pattern, then repeated it.

"Three short," Grimes announced over his shoulder. "All clear."

Relief congealed as a collective sigh. McIntyre used the distraction to release the center button of his overcoat, clearing the way to his automatic. The only response to his expectations was the quiet burble of the Winton's engine and the steady grumbling of the truck behind. The buildings and fenced yards that flanked Hatcher Street hung back half

seen in the periphery of the head lamps. All was stillness under a deepening blanket of white.

Trouble came quietly.

A heavy truck rolled into the lights of the Maxwell. No noise came
from its engine, no driver sat in its open cab. Gravity moved it and
momentum steered it. An empty juggernaut, it creaked across the rutted street and rammed a building with a soft, splintering crunch of
wood. Hatcher was narrow where it came to a stop, hemmed in by dark
frontages. The truck bed was long enough to block passage completely,
forcing the Maxwell to stop.

McIntyre sucked in cold air to fire his lungs.

"Ambush!" he screamed, and a bullet shattered the windshield.

The heavy touring car slid to a crooked stop in the snow, leaving its
lights shining on a fence. Boards warped by the hard climate let slivers
of illumination penetrate. Shadows could be seen running behind.
Guns flashed on the rooftops. Bullets popped through the Winton's top
with an explosive rip of taut canvas and punched into the floorboards
and upholstery.

The thug to McIntyre's right wrenched open the door and grabbed
his sack of bombs. McIntyre followed him out in a low dive, landing
hard in the snow. Both men wriggled backward beneath the high-slung
chassis of the Winton. The truck had come to a stop fifty feet back. Its
headlights shone full on the Winton, making clear targets of the men
unfortunate enough to be trapped there.

"Kill those lights!" McIntyre shrieked. "Use the machine gun."

No one seemed to hear him.

The five men in the Maxwell had piled out to exchange gunfire with
shadows that appeared in the vicinity of the dark truck. Gun flashes
multiplied around the Winton. The heavy touring car sank two inches
when a bullet from the nearest building blew out a rear tire.

McIntyre clawed the automatic out from under his coat. The man beside him worked a bomb out of the sack. He put the tip of his cigar to the fuse.

"Fire in the hole!"

He flipped the bomb toward the nearest building. It was a panicky backhand throw with a low trajectory and not much distance. To make matters worse, it hit a rain barrel and ricocheted back toward the Winton.

"Sweet Jesus!"

McIntyre and the thug covered their heads. The Winton heaved under the impact of the explosion. It settled back with a tortured squeak from the suspension. Debris fell all around. The Lewis gun began its slow, barking cough. Bullets snapped low overhead in bursts of two and three, unsure of their targets in the swirl of blowing snow.

Luther Grimes fell from the running board and struggled to maintain a sitting position. Red droplets colored the snow around him. He braced himself against the front fender and got his Winchester into action, directing his fire against anyone who threatened his men around the Maxwell, ignoring any danger to himself from nearby buildings.

The door of the nearest hung open in the aftermath of the dynamite bomb. Flames danced inside. A silhouette lurched into the opening, swinging a long-barreled shoulder weapon to bear on Grimes. McIntyre dispatched the man with a single, instinctive shot.

His own speed and accuracy startled him. He still shook from cold and fear, but his voice filled with sudden confidence.

"Clear out the building!" he yelled at the man beside him. "Blow us a way out of here!"

The thug put his cigar to the tip of a second fuse. This time he scrambled out from under the car and threw from a kneeling position. The dynamite bomb arced up into the falling snow and went cleanly through the open doorway on the way down. The blast was an instant of contained fury. The walls of the building bulged. Boards peeled away. Glass flew in bullet-like shards. When the smoke and the fall of debris cleared, the structure still stood, but none of its corners remained square.

McIntyre wormed out from under the car. "Let's go!" he yelled and crawled through the snow under the suppressive fire of the Lewis gun, making for the ruined doorway.

"No, Wait!" the man who had thrown the bomb yelled after him. "Help me with Luther! He's—" The man's voice dissolved into a choked cry.

McIntyre scrambled to the doorway before he looked back. The man was on his knees in the snow, bent double and clutching his stomach, sobbing painfully. The driver of the Winton was still at the wheel. He had been hit early. His wound had immobilized him. He sat twitching, waiting helplessly for a fatal shot. The other man in the back seat had gotten clear of the car, but no farther. He lay face down in the street. Snow had already begun to cover him.

Luther Grimes sat with his back against the running board, watching McIntyre. His campaign hat hung down over one ear, held only by its chin strap. Snow salted his hair and clung to his mustache, whitening his coat, beginning to cleanse and bury him even while he still had movement. He held the Winchester upside down across his lap, struggling to work a fresh magazine into the well. The truck lights showed bitterness and savagery in his face. McIntyre had betrayed him. However badly wounded he was, he did not intend to die leaving treachery unpunished. McIntyre scuttled through the doorway.

Half a dozen small fires burned inside the ruined building, spreading flickering light over splintered supports and fallen shelving. Tins of every size and description littered the floor. The nearest labels identified paint and flammable industrial solvents. Something erupted in a brilliant flash and sent flames roaring up one corner of the building. The flames silhouetted a man, moving erratically among the wreckage. He held a shovel in front of him, thrusting it at shadows to ward off attack.

"Don't come near me!" a shaken voice mumbled desperately. "Get away! Get away!"

The man gave a sudden jerk and stopped mumbling. The shovel fell from his hands. He melted soundlessly down into the poisonous smoke that boiled up from the burning floor. The following echo of a rifle shot meant Luther Grimes had reloaded.

McIntyre crawled on his stomach to the back of the building, coughing and choking as he went. The fires around him spread outward until they merged into one another. Another tin exploded. The flash lit the interior of the building. A rifle bullet cracked low over McIntyre's head.

He scrambled through a hole half blown and half burned in the back wall and rolled in the snow behind the building to extinguish any flames that had caught his coat. Still coughing, he gained his feet. Running shadows passed him without challenge. In the smoke-shrouded flicker of firelight, he looked little different from the men who had come up from shanty town and lain in ambush for him. His coat was covered with snow, his face smudged, his hat as battered as any.

"C'mon," a voice urged. "Grimes and that Railroad skunk are done for. 'Tis the machine gun we're after gettin' now."

McIntyre joined the flow of moving men, making the best of treacherous footing. His only hope lay in remaining one of them, drawing no attention to himself, depending on darkness and blowing snow and eye-stinging smoke to keep his identity masked. It was a risky proposition. At any moment flames could boil from a smoldering building and light his face. The miners would fall on him with murderous fury.

The man just ahead fell screaming, his hip shattered by one of the high velocity .30-40 bullets ripping through the buildings at random, fired from unseen Krag Jorgensens in Hatcher Street.

His comrades passed him heedlessly and carried McIntyre into a dark side street where men coagulated into a milling group. Jostling shadows were everywhere. Disembodied whispers drifted, eager and profane under an enforced hush. McIntyre leaned against a fence, panting. He could see between the boards.

Shrouded in wind-whipped snow, Hatcher Street had the violent, unpredictable quality of the Northern Aurora. While vehicle lights made steady illumination, buildings burned on both sides and spread flickering patterns of light and shadow. Periodically an industrial incendiary reached its flash point and sent a geyser of flame into the night. Tiny, transient sparks of gunfire seemed almost insignificant.

Mine Police survivors at the Maxwell were pinned under the car by gunfire from the dark truck blocking the street ahead of them and from buildings to either side. The surrounding force outnumbered them greatly. Only persistent fire from the Lewis gun sandbagged on the bed of the Mine Police truck prevented the besiegers from massing for an assault. Between the two positions Luther Grimes' Winton idled patiently. Men lay still in the snow around it. Surrounded themselves, the Mine Police defending their own truck could go to no one's aid.

The fight climaxed with brutal suddenness.

A sputtering glow took on life beneath the Maxwell and arced through the swirling snow like a Fourth of July sparkler. It hit the ground and skittered past the front tire of the dark truck, coming to rest beneath the vehicle. Dynamite lifted several tons of metal a foot in the air. The blast broke the spine of the truck. It fell back, crumpled.

Stunned survivors staggered away from the cover it had offered. They were easy targets in the lights of the Maxwell. The Lewis gun went into cyclic fire, spitting bullets as fast as it could. Tongues of fire licked out from its muzzle. The barrel jacket glowed a dull red. Bolt action rifles and revolvers played a minor accompaniment.

The Lewis gun chugged to an abrupt halt. One of the Mine Police released the empty ammunition drum and lifted a full one to align it with the mechanism.

John Hennessey's bass penetrated the noise of fighting. "Now! Now! Get them! Get them!"

McIntyre found himself swept forward in a surging mass of men. Physical labor and hard outdoor life had left them far stronger than he was. To maintain his balance he had to match his momentum to theirs. He became part of a headlong assault against the Mine Police truck.

The miners who had guns fired them wildly. Others swung picks and shovels and anything else they had brought to the fight. They clambered up onto the bed of the truck. The assistant gunner dispatched two with his revolver before he was swarmed under. The gunner tried to bring the muzzle of the machine gun to bear. John Hennessey rose from the crowd and put him out of action with a point blank pistol shot. Hennessey had to extend himself to reach for the Lewis gun.

McIntyre, no more than five paces behind him, brought his automatic up and put a bullet squarely between Hennessey's shoulder blades. Hennessey had hold of the Lewis gun when he was hit. He was too determined to let go. McIntyre fired again as soon as his sights came back into alignment. Hennessey crumpled into the melee around the truck, dragging the machine gun with him. McIntyre's two quick shots passed unnoticed in the fracas. Gunfire tapered away into the cursing and cries of close fighting.

A police siren penetrated the night, joined by a fire gong. Approaching lights appeared as a vague presence beyond the curtain of white that filled the air. Miners less committed to the struggle edged back from the margin of the fight and slipped away toward shanty town. McIntyre went the other way, moving along Hatcher toward the oncoming lights. He hugged the buildings, using their shadows for concealment. Police and fire vehicles passed him in slow motion, feeling their way toward the unseen killing ground ahead. Their lights dissipated in the blowing snow, casting a protective phalanx of spectral shapes before them.

McIntyre pushed on and took the first lighted cross street. Illuminated windows suggested the commotion had roused a few citizens, but the only other person abroad was a show-shrouded police patrolman hurrying along the opposite sidewalk toward Hatcher.

Adrenaline kept McIntyre moving at a fast walk despite pain in one ankle and the dampness of blood dribbling down his torso. He did not stop until he reached the City Administration Building. A hasty search established that the police department had been emptied to meet the emergency.

McIntyre collapsed into the chair at the switchboard. The telephone had been ringing since he came in. He picked up the earpiece to silence the irritation. Before he could hang up a woman's agitated voice came across the line, distorted by the residual ringing of recent gunfire in his ears. She was terrified. There were German spies in her basement. They had stolen pieces of her underwear. They were going to murder her.

"I'm afraid it's worse than German spies, Madam. It's Bolsheviks. The Red menace has come. Lock your doors and don't go out under any circumstances."

McIntyre hung up before she could respond. The telephone rang almost immediately and kept on ringing. He ignored it while he unloaded and dismantled his automatic on the desk. He found a cleaning kit in a drawer. Waiting for the powder solvent to soak in, he went back to the telephone. The callers were an assortment of citizens venting their terror in everything from a loud yell to a stuttered whisper. Human contact gave him something to focus on beside the fear and compulsion that haunted his eyes. In a voice as grave as he could manage, McIntyre told each that the Bolshevik menace was abroad. He advised them to remain in their homes until the authorities brought the situation under control.

He cleaned, reassembled and reloaded the pistol. Then only his personal appearance remained. An increasingly sore ankle made his trip to the men's room painful. He stripped off his overcoat. It was singed and sooty, mottled by grime soaked in when snow had melted into the fabric. His hat was missing, gone for good this time. His shoes were sodden and filthy. One was ripped at the uppers. He peeled off his suit coat. Blood had soaked into his shirt and dried there. The originating wound seemed to have stopped draining.

Washing was less than successful. Darkness beneath the dirt and smudges proved to be bruises he had been too keyed up to feel when they had happened but which, once seen and identified, began to throb. Washing also reopened several cuts. He pried out a shard of glass that had lodged along the bone of his jaw.

Compulsion festered and he fought the urge to wash to skin that was already clean, to dab at trivial bits of capillary bleeding. Nervous glances out into the police station betrayed his fear that someone might come in and catch him unaware. He put on his suit coat and overcoat, making the best of his battered appearance.

Shaky legs took him back to the switchboard. He sat down and set his automatic precisely square to the edge of the table. The telephone kept ringing. He yanked plugs from their jacks until it fell silent. He removed his spectacles and began the endless routine of polishing the lenses.

Tulley came in the rear door. He could be heard stamping snow off his boots before he could be seen. He came forward unbuttoning his overcoat, saw McIntyre and stopped short.

"Went right on over the edge this time, didn't you?"

"Not as far as Christopher Floyd." McIntyre stood up to make the automatic in his hand obvious. "Raise your hands. Turn around."

"This won't help you none. There's men dead because of you. There'll be no denying you was the cause of it all."

"I'd rather do this without killing you, Tulley, but it wouldn't take much to push me over that edge you were talking about."

The brilliance of McIntyre's eyes made the threat vivid and immediate. Tulley lifted his hands shoulder high and turned reluctantly.

"Forty years a lawman and I ain't never seen the like. Eleven miners dead and thirty hurt that we know about. Probably more nursing wounds down in shanty town, scared they'll be arrested, or worse, if they come out. Mine police took three dead and fifteen hurt. Fourteen and that insurance investigator. He said you cooked up the whole thing. Said Grimes will back his story. And if I was you, I wouldn't count on Grimes dying. Even with eight bullets in him."

McIntyre came out from behind the desk. "You enjoy putting people against the wall. Let's see how you like it."

Lumbering, resentful movements put the Police Chief in position. McIntyre held the automatic to the back of Tulley's head, reached under the Chief's overcoat and extracted a police revolver from a belt holster.

"We'll wait in your office. Move slowly and carefully."

Tulley came off the wall. "Look here, McIntyre," he said in a conciliatory rumble, "I know this ain't really your fault. I know you ain't right in the head. If you turn yourself in now, I'll see to it you get help."

"You've had the devil's own luck until now," McIntyre said. "I wouldn't tempt Providence any farther."

CHAPTER 18

Tulley shuffled back along the hall, his deliberately slow pace taunting McIntyre to step within his grasp. "I reckon it was you killed Hennessey. Leastwise, it looked like your style. Shot in the back. Two holes you could cover with a dollar."

"Push the door to your office all the way open. Walk directly to your closet. Stand facing the closet door."

Tulley edged into his office, watching McIntyre warily over his shoulder. "Old Man Crowder called the Governor. Told him what happened tonight. Asked for the National Guard."

"How did he make out?"

"The first company is being mustered now. They'll be brought in by special train. Ought to be here by sun-up."

A transient smile was all the satisfaction McIntyre allowed himself. He waited at the door until the Police Chief was in position, then stepped into the office and stood with the desk between himself and Tulley, leaving the door open so he could hear anyone coming into the station.

"Take out your keys. Put the closet key in the lock and step back."

The Police Chief tensed at the order. McIntyre's eyes warned him that hesitation could fatal. He fished a ring of keys from his trousers and pushed one into the lock. Sweat glistened on his forehead when he stepped back. McIntyre swung out the cylinder of Tulley's revolver,

ejected the shells into a desk ashtray and snapped it closed. He put the
weapon on the desk and stepped back.

"Holster your gun and button your overcoat so you can't get to it."

Tulley reached nervously for the revolver, as if he expected to be shot
as soon as he touched it. When he wasn't, he put the weapon away on
his hip and buttoned his overcoat.

McIntyre moved his eyes to indicate the corner. "Sit on the floor. One
shoulder against one wall and one against the other. Legs straight out."

Tulley was past sixty. He had received a gunshot wound that afternoon. He winced more than once as he eased himself down. Convinced
that rising would be a slow, painful process for him, McIntyre eased
around the desk and opened the closet. A police uniform hung there,
along with a rain slicker and a cleaner's bag. Two pieces of luggage
crowded the floor. McIntyre wrestled out a weather-beaten valise, then
heaved it up onto the desk.

Its considerable weight was a shadow of what he encountered when
he did the same with the accompanying suitcase. He set the suitcase on
its side and unbuckled two leather straps. Pressure of the contents
popped the lid up an inch. McIntyre swung it open. It had been loaded
in great haste, banded sheaves of currency pushed in every which way.

Air leaked out of Tulley in a dejected sigh. "How'd you figure it out?"

"Christopher Floyd."

"What about him?"

"He brought his evidence in the depot robbery to you, but he went
after the express car bandits on his own."

"Meaning he knowed I was mixed up in the express car push?"

McIntyre flipped up two clasps on the valise and pried open the alli-
gator mouth. It was stuffed with more banded currency. He fished out
an automatic pistol, a .22 Colt Woodsman made long and unwieldy by a
silencing tube screwed onto the muzzle. The ten round magazine held
two unfired cartridges. He cycled a third out of the chamber.

"Ten minus three leaves seven. Six used in the express car plus the one you used to kill Floyd."

"How'd he get wise?"

"Your car was seen making speed up Dutch Mill Road just after the robbery."

"I had that rigged up to look like police business."

"You fooled the Sheriff's men and the insurance investigator, but Floyd saw through the game and came back to search your office. I guess you caught him in the act."

The memory made Tulley squirm. "I got back early from supper and sent the desk man out to get a bite to eat while I covered for him. The switchboard was quiet, so I come on back to the office to get some papers to work on. Hard to say which of us was more surprised. Floyd with the bags open on the desk, or me standing flat-footed in the doorway."

A skeptical frown creased McIntyre's forehead. "You beat a powerfully built man half your age from an even start?"

"It wasn't so much me beating Floyd as him beating hisself."

"You'll have to explain that."

"If he'd've balanced hisself up and used his fists, he could've put an old-timer like me down in jig time. Instead he turned to grab the .22 off the desk. Even doing it wrong, he was still quick as a snake. I was lucky to get an arm bar on him. I kicked his feet out from under him and tried to twist the gun out of his hand. I don't know yet how it got turned around on him."

"But you were left with a dead Railroad detective and a desk officer who might come back at any minute."

"Not that all that thinking come to me right off," Tulley said. "I stood there awhile, just staring at Floyd like a damn fool rookie, thinking maybe he'd get up or something. I don't rightly know how long it took me to come to my senses and see what kind of pickle I was in."

"What did you do when it did dawn on you?"

"Wasn't nothing I could do but stow the body under a blanket in the Packard and wait my chance to get rid of it."

"How did you pick Hatcher Street?"

"The switchboard was ringing when I come back in to lock up the bags and see to what little blood there was. Just happened to be the Hatcher Street rounds officer, on a routine check in. I give him a cock and bull story about a sabotage call and sent him to the electric generating plant to get him out of the way. I phonied a call on the log sheet, and when the desk man come back I went down and left Floyd in Hatcher."

"Why not dump him out in the forest? He might never have been found."

"There'd be questions aplenty when he turned up missing. I had to make sure he was found in my jurisdiction, so I could control the investigation."

"Were you afraid he'd left something behind? Something that might lead investigators to you?"

"Looks like I weren't far wrong, what with you showing up tonight."

McIntyre dismissed the idea with an impatient shake of his head. "I'll tell you how you got yourselves caught when the others get here. When are they due?"

"Huh?"

"The others involved in the express car robbery. You emptied the station so you could split the money with them tonight."

Tulley growled in his throat.

"Did you tell me about Floyd to keep me distracted until one of them could stick a gun in my back? Did you think it wouldn't matter because I was as good as dead?"

"How did you figure we was splitting tonight? I didn't know that myself until old man Crowder told me I weren't long for"— Tulley's jaw sagged and he stared at McIntyre—"you set up that shooting in Hatcher Street to force my hand. You knowed I couldn't count on staying Chief after a dust-up like that. I'd have to split with the others just to get the money out of the station, in case I got fired."

"I thought up Hatcher Street believing you were in the hospital," McIntyre said. "My original plan had only two objectives. First, to stir up enough trouble to bring in the National Guard and spoil any chance of the Bolsheviks using a mine strike to take over the city. Second, to empty the police station long enough to find the money and make a run for it before I could be thrown into the local vegetable bin."

"Why'd you change your mind?"

"To prove I could."

"That don't make no sense."

"Maybe not to you."

Tulley eyed him nervously. "You feeling alright?"

"I feel like I'm about to explode," McIntyre confessed. "Every fiber is screaming at me to run. To clean myself up. To put things back in order. To forget any of this happened."

Tulley moistened his lips. "You can still make it."

"No."

"Take some money. Hell, take the Packard."

"How far would I get?"

"Plenty far—if there wasn't nobody looking for you."

"After Hatcher Street?"

"I could report you was killed in the fracas."

"I can't." Sweat on McIntyre's face suggested otherwise.

"Wouldn't take much doing," Tulley encouraged. "We got one body we can't identify. I could phony up some paperwork saying how we had to bury you here because you was tore up too bad to ship."

"I can't run away from myself. If I let my compulsions control my life, then I'm just what you and everyone else thinks I am—a hopeless lunatic."

"You are what you are. You can't change it. You just got to live with it."

"I'm not a monster," McIntyre insisted. "I've thought this situation out very carefully. I can salvage something worthwhile."

"You ain't foolin' nobody but yourself," Tulley said. "Men got killed in Hatcher Street."

"A few thugs had overdue accounts settled."

"I seen some that wasn't more'n kids."

"Do you think I marched them to Hatcher Street at gunpoint and forced them to shoot it out?"

"Boys get to a certain age, they'll do most anything if someone like Hennessey tells them it'll prove they're men."

"If they could be talked into tonight's business, they could be talked into anything. They were a danger to every citizen in this town."

"They didn't know no better, and they hadn't no more say in the way they was than you got in the way you are."

"Why are you making excuses for them, Tulley?"

"Why was you so damned set on killing them? And don't give me no bull about innocent citizens. You don't give a damn for nobody but yourself."

"Did you used to be one of them? Before you pinned on a badge?"

"What did you used to be, McIntyre? What fills a man so crazy full of hate that he—?"

A door opened and closed out in the station. Boots stamped themselves free of snow. A man's voice uttered an uncertain, "Hello!"

McIntyre stepped back against the wall and spoke softly. "Call him in here."

"Wrong gent," Tulley said. "That ain't one of—"

"Call him. Unless you want to take the blame by yourself. And a bullet to go with it."

Tulley relented with an angry glare. "In my office."

G. Robert Knowlton strode in smiling broadly. A capacious briefcase swung lightly in his hand. He saw Tulley sitting on the floor and stopped short.

McIntyre touched the muzzle of his automatic to the back of the Superintendent's head. "I hope the night telegrapher mentioned that I expected to meet you here."

He tugged the briefcase from Knowlton's grasp and put it on the desk. In Knowlton's coat pocket he found a compact Colt revolver. He pivoted the cylinder out. The six digits stamped behind the crane were familiar.

"Christopher Floyd's. Did you find it when you went to collect his luggage?"

"Yes." The single word was all Knowlton could choke out. A vein throbbed at his temple. His eyes shifted swiftly, full of adrenaline and terror. He looked to Tulley for help.

"Don't try nothing," the Police Chief warned. "McIntyre ain't right in the head. He thinks he's some kind of dark angel, sent here to punish anyone that don't see things the same crazy way he does."

McIntyre closed the revolver and slipped it into his overcoat pocket. "My original idea was just for you to give me a ride out of town. Things are more complicated now. I want you to sit against the wall with Tulley. Put your hands in your pockets and sit with your legs straight out."

Knowlton moved mechanically, as if his body were detached from the emotions seething behind his flushed features. He turned his back to the wall to sit down and got his first look at McIntyre.

"God Almighty! I've been in some fights, but your face—what happened?"

Tulley laughed grimly. "McIntyre here was the big winner. The losers is laid out in the ice house."

"All that shooting?"

"I should have invited you," McIntyre said. "Based on that sniping down the tracks, you need all the practice you can get."

"I wasn't trying to hit you," the Superintendent said quickly. "Just frighten you."

The sound of the outer door startled McIntyre. "Sit down. Hands in your pockets."

Knowlton complied reluctantly. Quick steps brought Evelyn White through the open office door, still shaking fresh snow from her umbrella. She stopped short at the sight of the two men seated on the floor. A fetching smile vanished.

McIntyre stepped close behind her and tugged her purse from under her arm. She whirled in surprise.

"You!"

A smile flickered on McIntyre's battered face, something between apology and an introvert's embarrassment. He opened her handbag on the desk and withdrew a small frame Smith and Wesson Hand Ejector. Without taking his eyes from the woman, he swung the cylinder out, punched the cartridges down into the bag and put the revolver back.

"Go around the desk please, Evelyn. You can sit in Tulley's chair."

She stood her ground, measuring him with her luminous green eyes. "I wonder if you really would shoot me?"

Tulley laughed, a short, sarcastic rumble. "That charm stuff of yours ain't gonna work on him, Evelyn. He ain't right in the head."

McIntyre acknowledged with a small nod. "To spare you any embarrassment, the .22 isn't loaded."

She moved around the desk with unhurried grace, set her umbrella on the floor to dry and put a small travel case beside it. "What happened to your face?" she asked as she perched on Tulley's swivel chair. "That eye looks awful. It must hurt."

A dark bruise had spread from the outer corner and worked its way under one lens of his spectacles to swell the eye almost closed. Compulsion sent his fingers to explore it.

Evelyn winced in sympathy with him. "Can you see through it?"

"Well enough to defend myself," he said in a barely audible voice, putting a finger to his lips and showing her the muzzle of his automatic for emphasis.

The outer door had already opened and closed. Quiet steps brought the newcomer back along the hall. Frank Dantini sauntered into the office with a smile on his lips. He had a satchel in one hand. The other was in the pocket of his snow-covered Chesterfield overcoat. A blanket of white on his pearl gray fedora suggested he had waited outside, watching until everyone was inside before he came himself.

"Hello, people," he said in a breezy voice meant to put the room at ease.

It was a planned front, and it made him a fraction of a second late sizing up the situation. He froze at the touch of McIntyre's pistol on the back of his neck. Dropping the satchel, he raised his hands to clasp them behind his head. It was too much cooperation. McIntyre snatched off the Sicilian's hat.

Inside he found a pocket with a folding stiletto. The handle was exquisite scrimshaw. A delicately engraved blade sprung out at the touch of a button. McIntyre stuck the blade into the crack between a chair seat and the leg, raised his foot and stamped down hard enough to snap it off.

Dantini shot a baleful glance at Tulley. "Now you see why I wanted him knocked off."

"Along with me," Tulley said bitterly. "Them was your killers on Lincoln Avenue."

"That was orders, not a double-cross."

"I must be getting on in the years. It's getting so I can't tell the difference no more."

McIntyre set Dantini's hat back on his head. "What was your plan?" He found a hammerless .38 revolver in Dantini's coat pocket. "Kill Tulley and grab the money for yourself?" He dumped the cartridges on the floor, kicked them under the desk and tossed the revolver into the open closet. "Then kill the others so they couldn't talk?"

"If I was planning a double-cross," Dantini said with a reassuring smile at his partners, "I didn't have to wait until today."

"Sit in the other corner," McIntyre ordered. "Exactly as you see Tulley sitting."

Dantini sat down easily, with an acrobat's limber movements. In spite of the awkward position, he looked like he could rise with little effort.

McIntyre kept his pistol trained on Dantini while he put the Sicilian's satchel beside Knowlton's briefcase on the desk. "If I've missed any hideouts, you're welcome to try for them any time."

"No need to be hostile," Dantini said. "There's plenty for all. Evelyn can count out five piles as easily as four."

"Six piles, please, Evelyn," McIntyre said.

"Six?" She glanced at the others.

Dantini's voice chilled. "I don't know if we're ready to give you a double share."

McIntyre ignored grumbles of agreement from the other two. "One pile is to be one hundred twelve thousand dollars, Evelyn. Count that one first. Count it out loud so I can verify. And count it as if your life depends on it, because it damn well does."

Evelyn heard the riptide of desperation under McIntyre's words. She cleared a space on the desk and began counting currency from the suitcase. Her voice was the only sound in the room, aside from the occasional clank of the steam radiator.

McIntyre kept his pistol on the three men. "One thing I have to know, Dantini. How did Geneva Crowder die?"

The Sicilian appraised him critically. "That's a hell of a shiner you got there. If you don't get some ice on it, you're going to be sorry. I know. I've had a few of—"

"How did she die?"

"I guess you killed her."

McIntyre stiffened. "If there's one person here I don't need, Dantini, it's you."

The Sicilian showed white teeth in a helpless smile. "I can't change the way things happened."

"Tell me," McIntyre demanded.

"The old man wanted his money back. You told her you knew where it was, didn't you?"

"What of it?"

"He didn't believe you didn't give her the actual location. He tried to choke it out of her. I guess he squeezed a little too hard."

Evelyn stopped counting. "His own daughter?" she asked in a horrified hush and stared unbelieving at Dantini.

"His daughter. His lover. His whore. Who knows what she was in that Bible-crazy mind of his? When she threw it in his face that she'd laid the Railroad's investigator, he lost control."

A startled laugh escaped from Evelyn. She stared at McIntyre.

He flushed and kept his eyes on Dantini. "Is that what he told you when he called you to fake the kidnapping?"

"I put it together from what he was saying, and from the bruises on her throat."

"What did he say?"

"It was more like raving. Everything from Eve in the Garden to Jezebel and prophets of Yahweh to Salome and the head of John the Baptist. Screaming until his voice cracked, then hissing out words like a snake. I don't mind telling you, it was pretty spooky. I'm not an easy scare, if I say so myself, but I never took my hand off my gun the whole time I was there."

"Your men disposed of the body?"

"You killed them before they told me where, if that's where this is going."

"See you in hell," McIntyre repeated ironically.

"What?"

"Nothing. Forget it."

"Put her behind you," Dantini advised. "She was lost long before you came to this town."

Tulley fixed accusing eyes on McIntyre. "You knowed she was dead. You knowed it through that whole ransom business, and you never said nothing."

"As I recall, you weren't listening to anyone but Crowder."

"You kept shut so you could kill Dantini's two thugs. You put my men and people in my town at risk for your own crazy revenge."

"What's your plan here, Tulley? Are you going to needle me until I pop my cork and blow your brains out?"

"What's your plan, McIntyre? How come you're dealing yourself in all of a sudden?"

"It's the best chance I have to stay alive. Maybe the only chance."

"That's going to need a mite of explaining," Tulley said.

"There's a lot more money in those two bags than Crowder declared on the express manifest. He wants it back. As you know, he can't go to the law to get it. And he knows that I know where it is."

"That's another reason you sponsored that shootout," Tulley realized. "Taking the Mine Police out of action pulls Crowder's fangs."

"For a while," McIntyre said. "Probably not long."

Knowlton was more interested in the money. "What is the purpose of separating the one hundred twelve thousand dollars?"

"That's the amount that was manifested on the express car," McIntyre reminded him.

"So?"

"So that's the amount we have to give back."

A murmur of protest went around the room.

"That's the way it has to be," McIntyre said.

Tulley said, "Five shares, five votes."

Knowlton said, "After all, you are a late comer."

"A late comer with a gun," McIntyre pointed out.

Dantini's smile was the barest hint of white under the sinister black satin of his mustache. "You can't hold us at gunpoint forever. Sooner or later, you'll need our cooperation for whatever you've got in mind."

"Wake up," McIntyre snapped. "You've been caught twice in less than a week, and that includes my time to commute here from Chicago. If we don't turn in the hundred twelve thousand and close the file on this case, you'll be caught again."

"You know how you caught us," Dantini said. "You ought to be able to cover our tracks."

"You weren't caught because Floyd and I were smart. You were caught because you made glaring mistakes. Mistakes that will be spotted by any competent investigator."

McIntyre shifted his pistol to his left hand and flexed the stiff fingers of his right.

"Either we sort it out here and now," he said, "or I kill you all and make a run for it."

Chapter 19

McIntyre took advantage of the uneasy silence to close the office door. "Evelyn, you'd better hurry the count along. This is a police station. We won't have it to ourselves much longer."

She resumed the task, but at her own unruffled pace.

Tulley spoke up with a hard, hostile rumble of police authority. "You can't just turn in a hundred twelve thousand dollars and expect everything to be hunky dory. There'll be questions aplenty."

"That's why I'll need to know every detail of the robbery."

Dantini's laugh had an edge to it. "How do we know you're not just pretending to go along with us until we give you enough to send us all to the gallows?"

"I can do that now."

"Like hell."

Tulley said, "There's four of us to swear you showed up with that there money looking to frame us."

Knowlton added, "You've been acting suspiciously since you arrived from Chicago. Not telling anyone where you were going or what you were doing. Making trouble in shanty town."

Evelyn smiled innocently. "And you were very angry with me when I rejected your romantic advances."

Dantini said, "Stalemate."

McIntyre dragged a chair back from the desk. Physical and emotional strain were visible in the movements that sat him in a corner where he could watch his four prisoners. He met Dantini's daring grin with a look of weary impatience.

"This all started when Aaron Crowder contacted you to buy some counterfeit war bonds, didn't it?"

The Sicilian's eyes grew dark and dangerous.

Tulley looked from Dantini to McIntyre. "What would Old Man Crowder want with counterfeit war bonds?"

"He needed them to cover the robbery and murder of the former owner of your Packard," McIntyre said.

"You saying that dude give real bonds? That Crowder killed him and give over counterfeit he bought off Dantini as false evidence?"

"And probably took a tax write off on the supposed fraud. The Police Chief wound up driving the victim's expensive car, so there weren't many questions asked."

Tulley's face reddened. "That true?" he asked Dantini.

"All I know is the old goat wanted queer bonds. What he did with them is between you and him."

"That sale give you a nice hold on Crowder when St. Louis got too hot and you needed a place to cool off," Tulley said. "I always wondered how you got the old man's help getting your damn phony business license past the City Council."

The corner of McIntyre's good eye twitched. "And in the process you got to know his daughter."

"You weren't exactly slow in that department yourself," Dantini reminded him.

"How did you get to know Evelyn?"

"She had lonely written all over her for any man to read."

McIntyre studied the woman. "Is Dantini lying, or was he really not aware that you aimed yourself at him?"

"I beg your pardon?" She stopped counting, indignant and waiting for an apology.

"The robbery was your idea," he said irritably. "Your husband had been section superintendent. He had the combination to the express car safe. You found it among his possessions after he was killed. It was your ticket to a better life. But you needed professional help with the finer points of felony."

Perfect stillness imparted an alabaster beauty to her face. Not denying, just waiting.

"What I don't understand," McIntyre said, "is how a well-bred woman like you happened on a gaudy crook like Dantini. How did you meet him? How did you know he could help you?"

"Oh, he was quite forward about his past. At least with women. Some found it exciting."

"And you overheard the powder room gossip and moved in?"

Evelyn ignored the question and went back to building stacks of currency. Dantini winked at her, but spoke to McIntyre.

"How did you know about Evelyn? Geneva didn't tell you. She didn't know."

"That's the attitude that put you on your backside looking into a .38. Thinking someone must have tattled on you. Never giving the opposition credit for any intelligence."

"Geneva told you something," Dantini insisted.

"She told me she was afraid for her life. She wanted me to find the express car money."

"You put it together from that?" The disbelief in Dantini's voice was close to laughter.

McIntyre's shoulders moved in a modest shrug. "Aaron Crowder was under investigation for war profiteering. The logical place to store those profits was the Denver bank where he was a director and could use his influence to keep them hidden. When the scandal threatened to force him out, he had to move the money quickly. And he had to move it as currency so it couldn't be traced. He cooked up a story about bringing his cash reserves here to fight a strike, declared his legitimate cash holdings of one hundred twelve thousand dollars on the express car manifest, but actually shipped a much larger amount."

"He thought he was really putting one over," Dantini recalled with a fond smile. "He bragged to Geneva that he would move the money in plain sight, with Railroad protection."

"So you had Evelyn in one bed pestering you to organize an express car robbery, and Geneva in another ready to tell you which car her father would move his fortune in."

Dantini put his head back and let out a laugh. "I couldn't believe it was happening. Geneva didn't even want a share. She just wanted to ruin the old man. It was too good to be true."

"Did Geneva know you were planning murder?"

"The actual job wasn't going to be any cakewalk," Dantini said. "We had to take the money from two men on a moving train with no one the wiser, get it off without being seen then make our getaway across some of the roughest terrain in the country. And it had to look like none of us had departed from our normal routines."

"Did she know?"

"She's dead, man. Let it go."

"Did she?"

"Geneva didn't trouble herself with details. She couldn't even remember how much money the old man said he was moving."

A skeptical frown brought a twinge of pain to McIntyre's bruised eye. "If you didn't know the amount and denominations, how could you calculate the weight and cube? How did you know you could handle it?"

"We didn't. Not for sure."

"You had to. You were risking everything on one shot at getting the money off the train."

"Two shots," Dantini corrected. "Knowlton and Tulley would be in control of the express car when the train pulled in. It was a dicier proposition, but we did have a back-up plan for them to pick up any cash Evelyn couldn't manage."

"Evelyn had seduced Knowlton early on?"

Dantini threw a contemptuous glance at the Superintendent. "I told you to line up another twist. When a young bull like you isn't chasing, it's obvious he's getting his horns trimmed down somewhere."

"It seems to me we're the victims of too many of your lady friends," Knowlton shot back, "not too few of mine."

Nerves and exhaustion had left McIntyre with no patience for squabbles. "What about you, Tulley? You're bitter, I know, and you wanted money to retire on, but I get the feeling it took more than that to force you off the straight and narrow."

"I was the investigating officer when Evelyn's husband had his accident. Gent my age gets to looking at a classy widow, he's liable to forget his eyes work better than some of his other equipment. I got myself in an embarrassing pickle. Come this here express car job, I got Dantini promising me a soft retirement if I go along, and Evelyn saying she'll tell it all over town how old Virgil Tulley ain't up to scratch no more if I don't."

"All right, Evelyn has her happy little group together. Let's go on with the robbery."

No one spoke. A siren howled in the night. McIntyre glanced at a clock on the wall. Dawn would not be long in coming.

"Knowlton, you said you were never notified of the shipment. How did you confirm what Geneva told Dantini?"

"Normally the express car carried only a messenger. When a guard was scheduled on the same day Miss Crowder said her father would ship the money, we knew her information was accurate."

"Okay, Tulley," McIntyre said, "you picked up Evelyn and went to Dantini's. He had a shipping crate in which he had recently received a load of spittoons. The crate was empty. The spittoons themselves were loaded into a collection of suitcases. Dantini also provided the automatic with the silencer. Correct?"

The Police Chief stared, flabbergasted. "Floyd must have mailed in some kind of report. He never made no phone call. I checked the switchboard. Knowlton checked with the telegrapher, and Floyd didn't send nothing after the robbery."

"I didn't need anything from Floyd. There was only one way to get someone inside the express car. You drove a couple of stops down the line, short-nailed Evelyn into the crate and shipped her aboard at the last minute. You probably loaded her yourselves to make she was right side up. No overworked freight clerk would turn down help from a couple of huskies like you and Dantini. Speak up anytime you feel like adding a few details."

"You ain't missed nothing yet."

"You drove fast enough to beat the train to the next station—not difficult with a powerful car and police lights if you needed them. Dantini gave the station master a fairy tale about his sister running off to get married to explain why he wanted to check so many suitcases aboard the car. After that it was Evelyn's show, until you met her at the tunnel."

Her count reached one hundred twelve thousand. "What do you want me to do with it?"

"Empty the valise," McIntyre instructed. "Put the hundred twelve thousand and the .22 inside. Divide the rest of the money into five equal piles. Don't try to count it. Just sort it by denomination. Try to make the speed you had to make in the express car."

Her smile chided him for his abruptness. "We rehearsed that for more than a week."

"You pushed out of the crate as soon as the train cleared the last station and knocked on the connecting door. You knew both men in the express section by name, of course. You probably know all the Railroad people in these parts. They would have been surprised to find you in the baggage section, but not particularly alarmed. Until you dropped the hammer on them."

The memory left her voice timid and faint. "I have a daughter. Nobility is not a luxury I can afford."

"You loaded the spittoons into the crate, nailed it back up, opened the safe and got one or more heavy bags of currency out onto the forward platform of the express car in the twenty-five or so minutes it took the train to reach the tunnel, all without help?"

"If my courage didn't fail me, I was sure my strength would."

"How did you get off the train?"

"Frank was just inside the mouth of the tunnel, where he couldn't be seen by anyone whose eyes weren't accustomed to the dark. I had balanced the bags on the bottom step so that they would fall as soon as I released them. He began a sprint just as the express car drew in and picked me off. We both went down with quite a jolt, but none of my bruises were visible."

"Risky," McIntyre said, with a glance at the Sicilian, "even for an ex-circus acrobat."

"We rehearsed it from the running board of Knowlton's car," Dantini said. "The idea is that the sprinter reaches his maximum speed as the car passes and the person on the car pushes off to minimize the velocity differential. In a circus ring, you can pick off a bareback rider passing at a gallop. Over rough ground in a dark tunnel, it wasn't quite as smooth."

"All right," McIntyre said. "You and Evelyn carried the money up to Dutch Mill Road, where Tulley was waiting with the Packard. What then?"

"Tulley made speed back to town. Evelyn changed clothes while I cut the bank bags open and shoved the money into the suitcase and the valise."

McIntyre nodded. "Evelyn, Tulley dropped you at the depot to establish your alibi?"

"Yes."

"What exactly did you do?"

"I passed the gun to Robert then met Anne on the platform. I made sure I talked to people who would remember me."

McIntyre looked at Knowlton. "Your job was to make sure the two men in the express car were dead?"

"If either had survived the shooting, the game was up."

"Had they?"

"Mercifully, no. It was bad enough, just having to look at them. Until I broke into the car and saw two men I knew dead, this whole thing never seemed quite real. When Evelyn first mentioned it, I thought she was teasing me. We would banter about it, and I would daydream what a fine way it would be to escape a life of begging for table scraps because I hadn't been born to the right family. Even when she brought Dantini and the Police Chief in, it sounded like a pipe dream. The rehearsals were like a game. The call from Dantini relaying Miss Crowder's information seemed faraway, like it was happening to someone else. The next thing I was really aware of was Evelyn pressing the pistol into my hand. The train was pulling in. I—" Knowlton broke off, pale and sweating. He looked as if the memory might consume him.

McIntyre spoke sharply. "You shouldn't have pretended to find the door locked."

"Pretended?"

"I expect that was what first caught Floyd's attention. No thief bothers to lock doors behind himself."

Tulley muttered, "Damn fool stunt."

"It *was* locked," Knowlton protested. "I don't think there was anything sinister in it. Evelyn probably just didn't get the bolt all the way back to the stop in her hurry to reach the platform, and the motion of the train worked it closed."

Tulley scowled at McIntyre. "You mean to tell me we was caught by a fluke?"

"Your own bad acting probably had more to do with it than the locked door. Of course, Dantini's plan forced your hand to some degree."

"Meaning what?" the Sicilian wanted to know.

"You've been on the receiving end of police raids. How do they usually begin?"

Dantini shrugged. "The cops yell a lot and push everyone around to show them who is boss."

"Police investigations work the same way," McIntyre said. "They show up as confused as everyone else and spend half an hour asserting their authority before they get down to business. Floyd had seen enough of them to know the routine. When he watched Tulley show up and get things organized in thirty seconds, he would have smelled a rat. When Tulley pretended to eliminate the crate of spittoons in full view of everyone on the platform, Floyd knew exactly how the robbery had been worked."

Tulley was dubious. "How come he didn't say nothing to the County Sheriff's men when they showed up?"

"It would have been his word against an established law enforcement officer. He needed corroboration. He went down Dutch Mill Road to check his reconstruction with witnesses who would have seen your Packard making speed up from the tunnel. Then he watched the police station until you left and slipped in to search your office. What safer place to hide the money than the Police Chief's coat closet?"

Tulley muttered something under his breath and subsided into his corner. McIntyre slipped a hand inside his coat. Dampness permeated his shirt, a small patch. His wound had begun to seep again.

"Knowlton, there is a trainload of National Guard due in this morning. When does it arrive?"

The Superintendent checked the clock. "In fifty-five minutes."

"Evelyn and her daughter have to be on that train when it returns to Denver."

"Yes. Of course. I'll see to it personally."

Evelyn paused her work to smile indulgently. "Thank you, but I'm not quite ready yet. I still have some—"

"Didn't you hear Dantini?" McIntyre snapped. "Crowder choked the life out of his own daughter trying to get his hands on that money. What do you think he'll do to Anne?"

Their eyes locked, as angry as two cats on a fence. McIntyre had truth behind his argument, Evelyn only a beautiful woman's ingrained rebellion against being bossed and hurried. She back to sorting the money, pointedly ignoring him while her hands moved swiftly and precisely. Freed of the tyranny of arithmetic, she made rapid progress.

McIntyre stood and ordered the three men on the floor to stand. Dantini and Knowlton were up quickly; taut and uncertain.

Tulley came awkwardly to his feet. "What do you figure the County Sheriff is going to do? He's got jurisdiction over this here robbery."

"He's going to read your report and close the case."

"My report?"

"Floyd was murdered in your jurisdiction. You're an experienced police officer. The Sheriff won't have any trouble believing you and your men trapped his killers in Lincoln Avenue. Or that they were desperate enough to shoot it out." An ironic smile curved McIntyre's lips. "Or that they turned out to be the express car bandits."

"Them thugs of Dantini's?"

"They're perfect. They're foreign and they're dead. Unfortunately, we'll never know exactly how they robbed the express car and killed Floyd. But you recovered the money, the automatic that was used to kill Floyd and the express car crew, and Floyd's revolver."

"You don't know politics hereabouts," Tulley said. "Aaron Crowder helped the Sheriff get elected."

"Which is half the reason I'm taking the money and the guns back with me to turn over to the Railroad."

"And the other half?"

"Once the money is returned, Crowder has no call on either the Railroad or the insurance company to do his investigating for him. He'll be on his own. It won't stop him, but it will slow him down."

"And when he does catch on?"

"We'll be gone before he can retaliate. You've all set up reasons to leave town. Tulley, you're about to be fired. Evelyn lost her home to foreclosure. Knowlton has submitted his resignation because he's afraid his career has been compromised. Dantini arranged a prize fight that left half the men in town ready to kill him over wagers he can't pay back."

"Maybe that'll work for this end of the line," Tulley rumbled, "but the Railroad ain't likely to just file your report away. It'll be gone over by some savvy gents, looking to see if maybe you didn't miss something."

"You don't know Railroad politics," McIntyre said. "I work for the Treasurer. Investigations are done by the Controller's office. The Treasurer and the Controller are constantly at war, each trying to expand his turf at the other's expense."

"Seems to me that'll make things worse," Tulley said. "This here Controller's going to give your report an extra hard going over."

"The Controller will never see the report. The Treasurer will give him an abstract, carefully edited to emphasize that one of his own employees with no formal investigative training resolved the express car situation in his spare time while the Audits and Investigations staff were busy making fools of themselves and the Railroad."

"Suppose'n this here Treasurer gent reads your report and smells a rat hisself?"

"Mortimer Jason is shrewd, civilized and utterly ruthless. He cares no more about Colorado than he does about the dark side of the moon. When he reads my report, he will be looking only for ways to further his own ambitions. Is the money ready, Evelyn?"

"In five equal piles." She smiled around the room. challenging anyone to ask for a recount of the substantial stacks of currency.

McIntyre pushed a newspaper into the valise on top of the money to be returned and began loading currency from the nearest pile on top of that. Even holding three dangerous men at bay, he made sure the banded sheaves of money lay flat and square.

"You and Dantini and I will get out immediately," he told the woman. "Knowlton, can you stick out your two weeks notice?"

"Yes. Of course. I'd planned on that."

"I'll put a few choice remarks about your performance in my report, so no one will argue with your resignation. Tulley, how long can you hang on as Chief of Police?"

"Old Man Crowder'll use tonight's fracas to try to get me fired right away, but it's the Mayor that's got to take action. I know a few things Hizoner wouldn't want noised around. I reckon I can cut some kind of deal with him. Maybe two weeks grace to get things cleaned up if I promise to resign and keep my trap shut."

"Send him a letter when you do. Disappear before they know you're gone. Crowder will be waiting to pounce the second you turn in your badge."

"You're damn concerned over my welfare all of a sudden."

"You know the details of what we're doing. It could be too bad for the rest of us if Crowder takes you alive."

McIntyre finished loading the valise, snapped it closed. Its weight threatened to pull it free from his grip when he stepped back from the desk. He set it on the chair.

"Pack your shares," he told the others. "Hurry it up."

Dantini moved sullenly. "I still don't like giving the hundred twelve thousand back. That kind of money is worth taking a chance for."

McIntyre put his automatic away under his coat and slipped his hand into the pocket where he had dropped Floyd's Colt. "If you thought Aaron Crowder's last sermon was spooky, wait until you hear the next one."

"That's another thing," Dantini said. "Those were my people you're throwing to the wolves. That sort of puts me on the spot with Crowder."

"That's why you're leaving right away. That and the fact that I don't want to give you a chance to get word to any other New York thugs you've got hidden out in town."

Dantini laughed. "It was just those three. Crowder had me bring them in to knock off Hennessey for him."

Tulley glared at the Sicilian while he loaded his own share into the suitcase. "I reckon that's how you got your permit for that damned prize fight. Crowder rigged it up with the Council to pay you off for killing Hennessey without spending none of his own money."

"I never planned to go through with it. Hennessey was everyone's meal ticket. Mine, Luther's, even yours, Tulley. As long as he lived, we worked. Until McIntyre blew in, he was the safest John in this burg."

"You're no worse off," McIntyre told the Sicilian. "Crowder couldn't have let you live anyway. You could testify that he murdered his daughter."

Knowlton finished filling his briefcase. "Well, I have enough for a clean start. I'm just glad to have it over."

"If any of you think this is over," McIntyre said, "you are even madder than I am." Pale and filthy and spent, he looked every inch a lunatic.

Tulley closed his suitcase and locked it in the closet. Evelyn closed and locked the traveling case that held her share. She shook the remaining dampness from her umbrella and closed it. The weight of the traveling case was only a minor annoyance. Coming around the desk she was a picture of serenity and grace.

Dantini opened the door gallantly to let her out. If he planned to slam it afterward to isolate McIntyre, he was too late.

Two uniformed policemen blocked the opening.

CHAPTER 20

The two officers stood shoulder to shoulder in snow spotted overcoats and helmets. One was Cavanaugh, the man McIntyre had eluded in Lincoln Avenue. He dangled a night stick from a wrist strap, letting it swing ominously. The other was the desk man who had typed McIntyre's commitment papers. He fingered the butt of a holstered revolver.

"Wasn't nobody out front, Chief," the desk man said, peering uncertainly at the assortment of people in the office. "We heard voices back here."

McIntyre's hand tightened on the Colt concealed in his pocket. Tulley took out his empty service revolver, opened the cylinder and inserted shells from the ashtray on his desk.

"Won't be no more trouble tonight, Miz White," he said in a reassuring rumble. "You go on home now. Get your little girl ready to catch that train."

"Thank you, Chief," Evelyn said softly.

The officers made way for her to pass, closing ranks again to seal the doorway. Whatever suspicions they might harbor, Evelyn's uncontested departure established that they had heard none of what had been said in the office.

Tulley put the loaded revolver away on his hip. "Cavanaugh, you ain't never objected to using that stick of yours."

Cavanaugh caught the baton to stop it swinging. "Nobody never proved nothing wrong on me, Chief. Not one of them complaints ever amounted to nothing."

"Well, this here is Mr. Frank Dantini," Tulley said with a disgusted glance at the Sicilian. "He won't be doing no complaining."

Cavanaugh and Dantini sized each other up. Cavanaugh was the bigger of the two, pale and dour. His eyes were eloquent in their distrust of anyone with a darker complexion and a ready smile. He said nothing in response to Dantini's amiable, "Hello."

"Mr. Frank Dantini runs a saloon never mind this is a dry town," Tulley said. "He keeps sporting women upstairs never mind that's illegal too. He promotes prize fights where there's gambling and folks get killed. Put plain, Mr. Frank Dantini is a public nuisance."

Cavanaugh scowled. "What do you want me to do, Chief?"

"There's a bus going east. Pulls out a touch before sunup. If you was to leave right away, do you reckon you could have Mr. Frank Dantini on it?"

"Ford's still warm from driving here."

"You're to drive him direct to the bus station, with nothing but that satchel he's holding. He don't stop off to pick up no lingerie nor mementos nor nothing."

"Right, Chief."

"Mr. Frank Dantini here—he's plumb full of tricks. He'll spin you a yarn about more money than dumb cops like you and me ever heard of. Then he'll let on how you could earn yourself a big piece of it just for doing this and that little favor for him."

"Won't get him nothing from me."

"It'll get him the butt end of your stick in them shiny teeth. And don't you be bashful how hard you put it there. You hear me?"

Cavanaugh's smile was grim and righteous.

Tulley wanted more. "You follow the bus at least ten miles out of town to make sure he don't con that damn fool driver into letting him off within walking distance."

Cavanaugh nodded obediently and slapped the stick into his palm. "Okay, Mr. Frank Dantini. Let's you and me go for a ride."

He stepped aside to let Dantini precede him. The look Dantini shot at Tulley dripped with vendetta. He stalked out of the office without a word. Cavanaugh fell in close behind. A door opened and closed out in the station.

The other officer nodded to indicate McIntyre. "You want this one in interrogation, Chief? Or should I put him in a holding cell for now?"

"Mr. McIntyre's got him a train to catch." Tulley spat out the words as if they tasted bitter.

The officer's mouth fell open. "There's men in the hospital ready to swear testimony against him. If he wasn't crazy, he'd hang. We'll have evidence to put him in the pest house for good."

"We ain't collecting such evidence," Tulley said.

The Police Chief's brazen repudiation of duty caught the officer flat-footed. He swallowed an entire career of obedience in one gulp.

"That ain't right."

"I don't recollect saying it was," Tulley said irritably.

"I don't know as I can go along with that. I swore an oath to the law."

"I'm still chief here," Tulley bristled. "Until I'm replaced, you'll do as I say, or you'll turn in your badge."

"And you're saying for me to take a crazy killer to the train station and turn him loose?"

"This here's my responsibility. I'll take him myself."

Concern took the edge off the officer's defiance. "Are you sure you're up to it, Chief? You was hit by a bullet just yesterday."

Tulley gave McIntyre's unimpressive stature a disparaging glance. "Mr. Knowlton, you fought some in college, didn't you?"

"Light heavyweight."

"You reckon we can get Mr. McIntyre to the depot between the two of us?"

"My car is just outside. I'll be glad to drive, and to lend any other assistance necessary."

"How much time we got before that special train brings them National Guards in?"

"If we leave right away, we should arrive in time to meet it."

Tulley clapped a paternal hand on the officer's shoulder and walked him out into the police station. "You're a good man, Nielan. There ain't nobody in the Department that don't respect you, and I ain't never heard a bad word said against you in all the time you wore that uniform. It'd be a real loss if you was to up and leave, and I know there's others besides me that'd take it real hard."

Knowlton spoke up sympathetically. "Chief Tulley is doing the only thing possible in the circumstances."

"I didn't mean nothing by it, Chief," Nielan muttered with an uneasy glance at McIntyre. "I know there's politics and all, only—"

Tulley patted his shoulder. "Don't you give it another thought. You just man the switchboard, and we'll forget anything was ever said. If you need me, I'll be down to the depot."

The freight clerk shoveled snow from the platform, a solitary figure in the depot lights. The storm had abated. Visible through the remaining drift of flakes was the distant glow of an approaching train, drawing slowly into the yards.

Knowlton brought his Oakland to a stop and let the engine cough out. He gripped the steering wheel and blew the air from his lungs.

"God, how glad I'll be to finally put this behind me."

"You're not going to spook, are you?" McIntyre asked.

"I see the express car crew in my sleep. I wake up covered in sweat."

"Wait until they start asking you why."

Tulley spoke in a soft, reflective rumble. "The why of it seemed pretty clear when we was planning it all out. Forty years I'd put my life on the line keeping the peace so's other folks could get on with their business. Got so's they took me for granted. Nobody much cared what happened to Virgil Tulley when he got too old to work, or even knowed he was alive. Just seemed I ought to have a turn at the trough too. Seemed like it was only fair."

"Save it for your nightmares," McIntyre said wearily. "You don't owe heroes like Knowlton and me any explanations."

"I ain't trying to make out like it was right. Just saying how it was."

Knowlton pushed his door open, but stopped short of climbing out. "How long before they pass? The dreams…the dead men."

"Pass to where?" McIntyre asked. "They're in your memory. There's no place to go from there."

"I'm not a weak man," Knowlton said.

"Weak is the only flavor men come in."

"I'll manage," the Superintendent insisted.

"How about you, Tulley?"

"I don't need no mollycoddle. I seen other old goats put out to pasture. I don't reckon I'll be no different. I'll start out telling your damned lies to the Sheriff and it won't be long I'll be rockin' on a porch somewheres, showing newspaper clippings to any passing kid fool enough to listen to how me and the Chicago Railroad dick broke the express car gang. Pretty soon you'll be seven foot tall with a punch like a steam hammer, all duded out in tailor-cut clothes, sporting a pearl handled pistol on each hip."

They climbed down from the car and slogged through a foot of fresh snow. As they climbed to the platform the locomotive drew in, exhaling steam and radiating heat, wearing melted snow like a coat of sweat. The firebox glowed dull red in the early morning dark. Lights in the windows of two coaches showed them crammed with soldiers.

McIntyre went into the depot and retrieved his suitcase and the satchel containing Geneva Crowder's ransom from Knowlton's office. When he came back out skittish horses were clumping down a ramp

from a cattle car, nickering in protest and blowing plumes of steam
from their nostrils. Soldiers formed hasty ranks on the roadbed, stack-
ing heavy Springfield rifles and sorting out a confusion of gear. Tulley
conferred with several officers.

Evelyn White arrived with a sleepy daughter in tow. Knowlton and
O'Haney transferred their luggage from the jitney to the first of the
coaches that made up the special train. Evelyn paid O'Haney and took
her daughter aboard.

The jitney driver saw McIntyre, but would not meet his eye. He
slogged back to the Ford and chugged off to deal with his life.

McIntyre boarded the coach. He glanced at the overhead luggage
rack, but his strength was spent. The aisle where he stood ran between
two rows of seats set in facing pairs, each pair meant to hold six, three
abreast on either side. He pushed his bags between the nearest pair and
sat down, sagging back against the cushions. The stagnant warmth left
over from too many bodies crowded too long in too little space brought
perspiration to his battered face. A haze of tobacco smoke made him
blink painfully.

Evelyn came and sat down beside him. "I brought some tincture for
that eye."

From her handbag she withdrew a small brown bottle and a cotton
tipped swab. He removed his spectacles. She soaked the swab, smiled
apologetically and began to dab at the broken and discolored skin.

"I'm sorry," she said when he winced, "but if we don't get something
into those cuts they could infect."

"I was rude at the police station," McIntyre said. "I hope you'll accept
my apology."

"You were right, of course. In every shameful detail."

"I'm in no position to pass judgment. You had your reasons for what
you did."

She glanced toward the end of the coach, where her daughter knelt
on a seat rubbing condensation from a window so she could watch the

activity outside. "You know my reasons, but I don't know yours. Why are you letting us go?"

McIntyre shrugged. "Put it down to greed."

"No, I've known men who lived for money. You're not at all like them."

"I guess you've known a lot of men," McIntyre said, adding quickly, "not that it's any of my business."

"I was born far too pretty," she said humbly. "I learned how to get my way before I knew what I really wanted. I found myself with a husband who was practically a stranger after the physical attraction faded, and a daughter we both treasured. He was a better man than I probably deserved. He put up with more from me than you could possibly imagine. When I lost him, I had to face the fact that my time was past. That Anne's turn was coming, and it was up to me to see her safely on her way. My own guilt and shame are a small price to pay, but I have to know that we are free to start fresh." She caught a dribble of tincture with a delicate swipe of her little finger. "I must be sure you won't turn on us later."

"My plan depends on you and your daughter going as far from here as you can get and spending as much of Aaron Crowder's money as possible."

"Are you doing this because Aaron Crowder killed his daughter?"

McIntyre said nothing.

"I know you felt something for Geneva. I could hear it in the way you asked Frank about her."

More silence.

She appraised McIntyre's eye critically. She wasn't particularly satisfied with her work, but there was nothing more she could do. Capping the bottle, she put it away in her handbag.

She settled close beside him and spoke softly. "I understand it's difficult for you to talk about things that really matter to you, but I have to know. I have to be sure. Really, I do."

McIntyre replaced his spectacles. "She must have hated him fiercely," he began in a tentative whisper. "All those years enduring his abuse, being sent to quack psychiatrists because she wouldn't submit tamely."

"Frank said all she talked about was finding some way to hurt him."

"Did you know her?"

"I met her once. Socially. There was a reception when she came back from Boston. From finishing school."

"What did you talk about?"

"We exchanged only a few words. It was a very large affair."

"Can you remember what she said? I'd like to know as much as I can about her."

"She said she hoped someday she could find the happiness I had found. I remember because it was so startling."

"Why startling?"

Evelyn smiled at his naiveté. "She was arguably the most beautiful woman in Colorado, the daughter of one of the state's wealthiest men, eighteen years old with her whole life ahead of her. I was the wife of a minor Railroad official. There was no earthly reason for her to know I was alive, let alone want to model her life after mine."

"No reason but her father," McIntyre said bitterly.

"I would never have guessed that from her manner, though she was quite different from what I expected."

"How so?"

"I had been warned that she had a sharp tongue and few inhibitions. Women of my station were invited to her reception only to remind us how far down the pecking order we were. I had steeled myself for a snub, or worse. She turned out to be warm and a bit quiet, almost like she was confiding in an older sister."

"Or looking for one."

Evelyn gave her head a quick shake. "Geneva was no clinging vine. Everything about her radiated confidence. If she was looking for anything, it was a direction she could follow once she took control of her own life."

"Freedom," McIntyre said, with sudden inspiration. "That's what she wanted. The only way to escape from her father was to destroy him."

"Destroy him?"

"The Denver papers mentioned a secret witness against Aaron Crowder. It must have been Geneva. She went to the Government and told what she knew to get him thrown in prison. When it looked like her father might beat the rap by moving the money, she went to Dantini to get him to steal it and bankrupt the old man."

"Are you trying to destroy Aaron Crowder the same way?"

"Yes," McIntyre said grimly.

"Do you think you can?" Sympathy tempered her skepticism.

"Crowder has already done most of the work himself. He never realized that John Hennessey, the man he wanted assassinated, was his greatest ally. As long as Hennessey was alive and screaming for the blood of the middle class, it was easy to paint the miners as the Red menace, to isolate them from everyone else. With Hennessey gone, the barriers will start to come down. The miners will learn as others have before them that numbers and votes count for more than bombast and violence.

"But worse than losing ground to the miners will be losing the money. He has nothing to show for a life of scheming and cheating except the knowledge that the fruits of his crimes are being frittered away by people he either can't find or can't accuse without exposing himself to Federal investigators. He'll spend the rest of his years hunting those people, haunted by the thought that his treasure is dwindling with each passing day."

"Why didn't you take all the money yourself?"

"Crowder might chase one man down fairly easily. Five of us will spread wider and spend faster."

She put a cautioning hand on his sleeve. "Aaron Crowder won't be the only one chasing you. Frank Dantini may have been smiling tonight, but he was seething inside. He hates to lose. He will want revenge."

"Dantini is no threat to anyone but himself."

"You don't know Frank. He's a member of the Black Hand."

"Sicilian criminal society is a feudal system, like a European princi-pality or a large corporation. Men of Dantini's position are allowed only so much in the way of prestige and wealth. When he shows up boasting about his satchel full of money, the Mafia will demand that he turn it over as tribute. When he refuses, they'll cut his throat and take it."

Evelyn's horror passed quickly and left no remorse. "What will the Railroad think about what you are doing?"

"The Railroad cares only about results. They don't want to hear the sordid details. My value to them lies in their ability to blame anything that comes to light on the fact that I've been adjudged a lunatic."

"Are you mad?" Delicate words that suggested she wanted only to understand, not to judge.

"Not in the simple-minded sense of someone who spends every wak-ing moment behaving erratically."

"In what sense, then?"

"What I have—what I'm hiding—is an exaggerated need for order. A compulsive obsession. Every once in a great while it pushes me too far."

"Like tonight?"

"No. Tonight I was coldly rational. I knew what I was doing every step of the way."

"And when you aren't rational?"

He shivered.

"I'm sorry," she said. "I know it must be difficult for you."

"Locked up in an asylum I had a lot of time to think, to come to terms with the fact that I wasn't perfect, and never would be. If I had come face to face with a psychotic a year earlier, I would have demanded he be shut away where he could do no harm. Suddenly I was looking at one in the mirror, and it occurred to me that as long as I was shut away, any evil I had done would be nothing but evil. Only if I could go on with life could I turn my past mistakes into lessons and try to manage my compulsions and make something useful out of whatever time I had left."

"You wanted freedom."

"Yes."

"Like Geneva."

"Yes."

"I think I understand now. You weren't just a quiet man infatuated with an unreachable beauty. The two of you were kindred spirits."

"Geneva saw it at a glance."

"I'm so sorry." She took his hand to offer what comfort she could. "What will you do with your share of the money?"

"Send some to the families of the express car crew. Enough that the kids will get a decent start in life. The rest, I don't know. I've never had any money to speak of. I'm not sure what to do with it."

A violent hiss of steam issued from the locomotive. The coach gave a shuddering lurch as the train began to move. Anne waved out the cloudy windows, coming back along the aisle. The night telegrapher was visible on the platform, waving back. When she reached the seat that held McIntyre and her mother, she sat opposite them, pouting.

"Hello, Mr. McIntyre. What happened to your face?"

"A little accident." He smiled nervously.

"Don't stare, Honey," Evelyn said. "It's not polite."

"Where are we going, Mom?" A hard question, full of the unfairness of being snatched from a familiar life.

"We'll find a place you'll like, Honey."

Anne looked at McIntyre and her mother, sitting close beside each other. "Is Mr. McIntyre going with us?"

Evelyn smiled at her romantic notions. "No, Honey. He's not."

"How come you're holding hands?"

"Mr. McIntyre's love was lost to him, as I lost your father. I want him to know his life still has value. His courage and intelligence are needed."

He glanced out the window at the receding lights of the city, at curls of smoke rising from the smoldering ashes of the fires that had burned there. "We chase our dreams, Anne. Until we come to a gate that blocks our way. The toll to pass is never cheap. We have to come to terms with who we really are. We have to sort out the one thing we cherish most and give up all the rest to go on. Your mother and I have paid our separate tolls. Now we have to go our separate ways."

Made in the USA
Las Vegas, NV
01 May 2021